IN HER EYES

To Meredith ~
Thank you for supporting
my dreams! Enjoy the story!

Lynn Sutton

Books make great friends ☺

LYNN SUTTON

IN HER EYES

A THRILLER

ISBN: 978-1-4834-3885-6 (sc)
ISBN: 978-1-4834-3884-9 (e)

Library of Congress Control Number: 2015915935

Lulu Publishing Services rev. date: 09/29/2015

For my husband.
Without your constant love and support, this
story would still be lingering in my head.

PROLOGUE

~ ~ ~

The day had been long and the evening longer. The treacherous heat from the day had barely subsided. Walking the short distance it took for him to get to his car generated a visible trail of perspiration down his back. The double beep sounded as he unlocked his sleek black Maxima. The steam from the internal heat of the vehicle stole his breath. Only during the Texas summer heat did he question his decision to buy a dark-colored vehicle.

He tossed his briefcase across the front seat and finally settled in for the drive home. The drive to his house had become a monotonous routine. Pollen from the blooms of the Bradford pear trees coated his windshield and stunk up his car. He temporarily turned on the washer and wipers to create a clear view of the road.

Leaving the parking lot, he entered the busy freeway. He pressed the gas pedal to accelerate to the speed of the passersby on the highway. The sounds of aggressive traffic flowing by filled the empty silence in his car, but his mind barely registered it because thoughts of the day's accomplishments replayed in his mind. Determination for ultimate success had him already planning tomorrow's task list.

Today had been one of the biggest meetings of his career, and he had spent numerous hours in order to be prepared. Now he was eager. Impatient. The time he'd spent on this project was about to pay off. No longer would every minute of every day be spent working to make the American million. He had finally made the right connections, made deals with aggressive investors—one in particular. After tomorrow, his company would almost run by itself, and then the projected five-year sell plan would be fruitful. He could settle some ongoing cash-flow problems, pay off huge debts, and finally take the vacation he had so exhaustingly earned.

In twenty-four hours he would have it all.

He reached for his cell phone, hit speed dial, and even though he was exhausted, his words were laced with the day's triumph. "I'm on my way home."

"She's sleeping, so be quiet when you come in." His wife's voice, pleasant but void of emotion, was followed by the clicking sound of the receiver. He snapped his phone shut and tossed it aside. The day-in and day-out routines had taken a toll on his marriage. There was no chemistry anymore, but they stayed together because they made a good team. His choice to marry this particular woman was another example of his acute decision-making skills. She had been acceptable and tolerable with the union because it was the perfect match for her too. She was an intelligent partner. Devoted. Supportive. He was driven in his professionalism, and she handled that responsibility with the utmost integrity. They complemented each other quite well.

A *ping* sound indicated the fuel was low in his car. With a heavy sigh, he eased off the accelerator as he exited the freeway, pulled in to the nearest gas station, and began to go through the mundane motions of filling the tank.

As he stood in the shadows of the rundown parking lot, his stomach growled. He could see his reflection in his side mirror and realized he even looked hungry. He bent his arm and checked his watch; it was nearing ten o'clock. Not remembering when he ate last, he walked into the scarcely occupied convenience store and paid little to no attention to the clerk standing behind the counter reading a magazine. He reached into the cooler and grabbed the first bottle of juice he saw, and then he turned and chose two protein bars. Since he hadn't made it home in time for dinner, this would be the better way not to disturb a sleeping household, as requested by his wife.

He placed his purchases on the counter and reached into this wallet for his debit card. He swiped his card and completed the transaction in silence. The clerk mumbled an inaudible thank-you and turned his attention back to his magazine.

When he exited the store, he glanced up as a dark-colored Escalade slowed in front of him. The windows were so tinted, he couldn't see inside. A niggle of caution tingled on the back of his neck when the rear window of the driver's side slowly began to roll down.

A flash of metal caught his eye. He hadn't had time to fully register the imminent warning when a black, gloved hand emerged, aiming a silver handgun toward him. Fear swept over him as the danger became clear in his mind.

The sounds of the shots were deafening as they burned and ripped into his body. Fire erupted in his chest. Blood spurted onto the concrete as he was knocked backward and fell to the ground motionlessly.

CHAPTER 1

~ ~ ~

At 1:17 a.m., the sound of his cell phone pulled Tyler McCormack from a deep slumber. He had the air conditioner cranked, and he was spread eagle in the middle of the bed with only a sheet for cover, so when he reached for the device, the cold metal was a slight shock. He figured it was either the police department or his attorney and only friend, Alexander Blakely. They were the only two that would have reasons to dare call him this late—and since he was currently on sabbatical, chances were good it was the latter.

Tyler had been sleeping for less than an hour. He had spent the evening closing a case file on a cheating husband whose wife had paid him to expose him. Technology was a modern-day luxury that he didn't quite trust, so he practiced the old-fashioned routines of logging paper files. By the time he had systematically printed off each photo and a dozen reports and logged his closed case files, it was nearing midnight.

He had nineteen days left of his ordered vacation from the Austin Police Department. Moonlighting—albeit a no-no—had been a perfect distraction. Sitting idle and thinking about life was not his idea of resting. But he was tired.

The LED lights on his phone illuminated the dark, and the ringtone blasted through the silent room. He glanced at the caller ID and groaned. It wouldn't be the first time Alexander called with one of his famous middle-of-the-night excursions and was in need of assistance. His friend was not a fan of taxis or Uber. He preferred to keep his entertainment discreet. The last time he called this late, Tyler had had to drive into downtown Austin and pick up his boss, who had obviously been partying a little too much. His friend's idea of a good time included paid women and an illegal white powdery substance. The problem (or reprieve, depending on how you looked at it) was that he often lost the location of his car, hence the numerous late-night phone calls.

Without regard to his unfriendly tone, he asked, "What?"

"I got a hot one for you," Alexander answered as he ignored the rude greeting.

"What the hell? You call me in the middle of the damn night, and I'm supposed to jump up and come running to get you out of some kind of trouble again? No, Alex; this is not what I'm hired to do. I'm tired, and I'm going back to sleep. People on sabbatical don't go running out all hours of the night. They sleep."

"Shut up." The attorney's voice bit into the phone. "Wake the hell up. It's a good one. Besides, you wouldn't know what *sabbatical* meant if it bit you in the ass."

Tyler breathed a sigh of disturbance, sat up, and swung his legs over the side of the bed. His sleeping Labrador retriever raised her head, moaned, and went back to sleep.

Apparently, from the sound of his friend's voice, it was work related, and since Tyler agreed to the occasional retainer, sleep was over for the moment. At least it kept him busy; the three-month extended leave enforced on him by his chief of police was not a welcomed vacation.

For as long as he had known Alexander, normal business hours were a rarity, so over time, he had conditioned himself to be instantly awake and alert when duty called.

"I'm up."

He listened for several seconds, snapped his phone shut, and left the bed.

Less than thirty minutes later, Tyler sat across from Alexander at an all-night breakfast café. A semi-clean table wasn't going to make much difference in the quality of reviews for the greasy spoon. With all the restaurants available in the Austin area, his friend swore this was the best food in town.

The tables and chairs had a film of grime on them. Three ceiling fans hummed and fluttered in the center of the restaurant and stirred a heavy smell of grease mixed with aromas of bacon and eggs in the air. The windows had a film that indicated they hadn't been cleaned in months—if ever. He simply could not bring himself to order anything more than coffee, and even then, he remained concerned about the cleanliness of the cup.

"A little traditional, down-home cooking isn't going to kill you," was always Alexander's response when a healthier option was suggested.

He shook his head and watched his friend order the breakfast special that was guaranteed to clog at least two arteries in one meal. If it weren't the extracurricular social habit that was going to kill his friend, it would be his less-than-nutritional choices.

"You want anything, sugar?" the middle-aged waitress asked Tyler with a tired tone.

"Just coffee, thanks."

As the waitress turned, she began to holler out the order in lingo that only the cooks would understand. Tyler waited until she was out of view before taking a few napkins from the metal container and wiping up remnants from the meal previously eaten at the table before they'd sat down. He had a hard time resting his arms on the table, so he put them at his sides.

"Relax," Alex chided. "Might stain your shirt a little, but I promise that the food is worth the cleaning bill."

Tyler swore they probably had this same discussion every time. "I'm surprised there's not a surgeon general's warning at the main entrance."

Both men waited to begin their discussion until the waitress had brought their drink order. As Tyler sipped his coffee, Alexander reached for the creamer and sugar container and generously dumped the contents into his cup, making the rich black color take on a lighter brown hue.

"Best coffee in town," he said. "Its places like this that remind a man to enjoy the little things in life, because you won't live forever. You know, put yourself out there and make things happen. Live a little."

Tyler's face froze, expressionless, not missing the double entendre.

His friend pushed on. "Go ahead and get all pissed off. It won't stop me. You need to hear this. You were one of the best damn lawyers around. I don't know why you continue to toss that talent away down at the police station or by doing my damn legwork. You were born to be a lawyer. Go be a lawyer. Better yet, come be a lawyer with me."

"Again, thanks, but no thanks. I'm happy doing what I do." One of these days, he might even believe himself.

For several minutes, they sipped their coffee in silence. Tyler knew his friend meant well, but that had been in another life. Another time. Instead, he sat and watched the neon sign blink on and off through the window beside them. Neither chose to continue the path of the conversation, yet each remained mindful and unbending of the repetitive argument.

Finally becoming impatient, Alexander tried again. "Tyler—"

"Don't. I'm not in the mood. If this is what you woke me up for, then screw you."

"You're wasting your talents."

Tyler clenched his jaw and refrained from telling his friend to go to hell.

"There are other ways. Still are."

"It was my choice. Still is."

"Anyone that knows you can tell that you are wasting a God-given talent to argue with the best of us in the sanctity of America's judicial courthouses. Not to mention the ridiculous pay cut. You're not even making a fourth of what you were bringing in. You're crazy to give that up."

That cracked his temper. Tyler growled through gritted teeth, "I'm not a head case."

Showing no concern regarding Tyler's growing temper, Alexander countered, "I never thought you were. It wasn't me that put you on shrink leave. I'm the one trying to tell your ass to get back to the job. The job you were meant to do. There's no law that says you have to be a defense attorney. Go prosecute criminals this time. Being a detective is not your natural niche, so why you've decided to deal with that bullshit is beyond me."

"Why am I here in the middle of the night discussing my career choices and financial status?"

Alexander let out a sigh of temporary defeat. He shook his head and drank his coffee.

The men had history that dated back many years, when Tyler had been an attorney in West Texas. Although Tyler had remained strictly a criminal defense attorney, his colleague dabbled in all areas: criminal, family, probate, and even corporate. They had become allies over a few common cases that required a change of venue or co-counsel, and a friendship had naturally grown. While Alex had enjoyed the social doors that being an attorney opened—as well as the money that fed his habits—Tyler remained more driven because of the status and prestige. In spite of their differences, they had always worked well together.

When Tyler walked away from the legal profession and went off the grid for six months, it was Alexander who had tracked him down and informed him that his father was in the hospital undergoing heart surgery. He returned to Texas so he could care for his father, and, well, he never left.

At one time, he'd considered becoming a teacher or opening up a pet store—anything but legal work. Alex had coaxed him back into it by asking him to check this out, and then that. Next thing he knew, he found himself ranked as a detective at the Austin Police Department. It was not a normal career change, but it worked for him. Curiosity drove him. Not to mention, he had a knack for digging, and finding, the truth.

The only beef he had with Alexander was that he never stopped nagging about entering into a partnership and practicing law again.

Hence, the habitual conflict that reared its head as routinely as monthly bills. After the silence stretched, neither wanting to be the first to concede their stance, Tyler finally broke and changed the subject. "What's so hot that it couldn't wait until morning?"

"Didn't you watch the news?" When Tyler shrugged he teased, "Twitter? Newspaper?"

"Nope. It's full of stuff I'm trying to avoid."

After an exaggerated roll of the eyes, Alexander leaned forward in his seat and lowered his voice. "Damian Jones was murdered."

"The guy that just won an award for a cutting-edge technology thing?"

"Yep. That 'thing' is a future Fortune 500 company called Identity Smart, which developed an app that monitors identity-theft threats right from a smart phone, iPad, or computer. It eliminates the need to pay some company to do it."

"Huh. How'd it happen?"

"Drive-by shooting outside a gas station on the corner of Caesar Chavez, close to I-35."

"APD will handle that. I still don't get why I'm here."

Before he answered, the waitress approached and placed a large, oval platter that was covered with two eggs over easy, skillet potatoes, sausage, two waffles, and to make it healthy, whole-wheat toast. Alexander grinned up at the waitress, winked his approval, and reached for the saltshaker.

Tyler swore he felt his own arteries begin to clog just by sitting there watching.

After shoveling in about three bites, Alexander answered around a mouth full, "Money. That's why. Jones was a client, but he took his corporate matters to a mile-high law firm since his company was about to cash in big. We kept in touch though, over personal legal matters."

Tyler drew a strained breath. "You think it's more than a drive-by?"

"Murder-for-hire." Alexander's voice dropped to a hushed tone as he slid a file across the table.

Flipping it open, Tyler quickly scanned the basic case parameters. He watched in awe as his old friend folded a piece of toast and sopped up the remaining juices from the meal, took a large bite, and then belched—thankfully, he kept his mouth closed.

"This is a complex situation. I want it handled delicately. The wife contacted me this evening regarding the probate, albeit a little quick on the draw, if you ask me. Damian was a good friend and client, but I never got to know her that well. If there's a hint they're coming after her on this, I want a head start. Just a gut feeling."

Well, hell. A gut feeling for Alexander usually meant trouble. He couldn't really ignore the spark of interest the case generated. Simple background checks and a little surveillance here and there had kept him occupied. Nothing very intriguing. It's not like he was missed at work, but he missed having a reason to get up each day. Half the force hated him, and the other half didn't trust him. All in all, he kept to himself and usually functioned alone. Occasionally he was forced to work with a partner, and he would see that through the best he could.

He actually thought things were starting to smooth over until about a month ago, when he had unknowingly walked upon a man trying to rape his date. Now he had more time on his hands than usual, thanks to a good-for-nothing, hippie-dressing shrink who planned to "heal his psyche." So what if he nearly beat the dude into a coma? The guy shouldn't have forced himself on a young woman. He found it rather ironic that the department didn't think too positively about him using "excessive force" to save the girl and punished him with extended time off. Now he was back to square one. *Seriously?*

He had been instructed to take classes on anger management. Instead, he had truly considered walking away from it all. Again. Maybe he had just had enough. The system was flawed, and he was getting weary trying to fight it. It didn't matter how many people he either arrested or exposed doing dirty deeds; it never seemed to erase the guilt of the numerous criminals he'd freed in the courtroom—not to mention the incessant looks of condemnation. No matter how many classes were forced on him, nothing would change that. Why should he put forth the effort?

But dammit, his buddy knew what buttons to push. If he felt there was a good reason for him to go sniffing around the ex-wife, then there was probably something to be found. And they both knew damn good and well that he wouldn't turn it down.

With no further discussion, Tyler sipped his coffee and waited for Alexander to finish his meal in comfortable silence.

And cursed his own curiosity.

~ ~ ~

Tyler wore a dark pair of jeans, a crisp, new blue Polo shirt, and tan loafers. If needed, he could always pretend to be an interested photographer just shooting the scenes of downtown Austin. Once he had an opening, he would waltz into the web-design company and fumble his way through the basic initial consultation with the owner, Mrs. Jones. It was better than the truth: that he was checking her out to see if she could possibly be linked to the hired thug that shot her husband at the convenience store. Yeah, that probably wouldn't get him very far.

One thing he didn't think through was that it was the middle of June, and he was sitting in between two concrete buildings working up an inconceivable sweat. He was pretty sure he wouldn't nail the impromptu meeting soaking wet and smelling rank.

Besides, he was getting thirsty. The nearest store that would sell him a bottle of water was half a block to the east. From reading the initial work up on his subject, he guessed she would be the type to show up for work even before she attended her husband's funeral. He shook his head at that thought. Money-hungry people did stuff like that. He didn't want to risk missing the subject in question, so he decided to literally sweat it out in this unrelenting heat and forgo the bottle of water for the time being. He reached up and wiped his brow and then put his telephoto lens to his eye to keep watch.

As passersby approached him, he would change the angle of his leans and snap a few photos. He had already gained an interesting collection of a stray dog marking his spot on random buildings, a mother fussing with her two unruly children, and an older couple that seriously needed to get a room. Sheesh, his brain did not need that visual.

Looking back toward the small business building, he figured he could get the gist of the recent widow's daily routine, snap a few photos of the people she interacted with and maybe a few shots of her employees. Then he would tail her to the funeral to make sure she didn't make any interesting stops along the way.

Noticing the no-nonsense businesswoman approaching the building, Tyler said, "Bingo."

Zooming in for a better look, he realized she wore dark sunglasses, her hair was neatly pinned up off her neck, and she wore a tailored, cut dark suit—in the middle of the oven-scorching heat. Her legs were incredibly tanned and looked well-toned in conservative black heels. She basically presented herself as uptight and snooty. Tyler shook his head, and it reminded him of at least one thing he didn't miss about being a lawyer: those damn suits he had to wear every day. There's no way she was comfortable.

But there was something about her that struck a sense of familiarity.

Once the woman had entered the office building, Tyler casually walked down the street, stopping every so often to snap a photo of this and that. Within minutes, he had positioned himself on a bench inconspicuously right across the street. He had a perfect view through the large windows in front of the building.

He adjusted his lens for a closer assessment and sat patiently until she came back. He snapped several photos of her walking through the office—once while she talked on her cell phone. Another as she had her head bent, looking at something on a desk.

It was a few moments before he could get a clear shot of her face. When he did, his heart stopped. He yanked his head from the camera in shock. Shaking his head, he did a double take behind the camera and snapped several more photos.

He quickly checked the screen of his camera for review. He clicked a few buttons to zoom in on her face. It was like being sucker punched right in the gut.

No doubt about it, Tyler McCormack could not deny what he was looking at, or rather … *who* he was looking at.

He was staring at face of the one woman who had stolen his heart and never gave it back.

CHAPTER 2

~ ~ ~

"It's good to see you again."

It still baffled him. It was … *staggering.* Mallory Jones, still petite, still blonde, sat before him determinedly and poised. Though
she carried the appearance of a grieving widow, the truth of it was,
she was beautiful. Her expression looked as if she was fighting an
immense depth of shock. Yeah, he could relate to that.

"Yes, and you." She answered in a crisp tone. "Last I had heard,
you were practicing law in West Texas."

And there it was—the elephant that joined them in a quaint
coffee shop. The look on her face couldn't quite hide the fact that
she was well aware of the ominous judgments and rumors that
were forever linked with his professional reputation. It was quite the
opposite for him, however, as he didn't know a damn thing about
her anymore.

"I moved here a few years ago. It was time for a change." He took
a small sip of his coffee.

She nodded but didn't respond. He was grateful she didn't try
to gloss over the whole thing. He had learned the hard way that a
past was hard to bury, and moreover, today's digital society had a
long memory.

Tyler cleared his throat. "I'm very sorry for your loss." He wished
he could have said more, but he had learned by experience in his
line of work that often, the less said, the better.

He did his best to contain his composure and professionalism.

The moment he recognized her, he knew he was about to have to change tactics completely. His instructions were to follow her and do a little recon, but he had to get closer. He had to talk to her. Facts on paper were one thing—the woman sitting across from him, staring intently at him, was another matter entirely. It was a game changer.

She was more beautiful than he remembered. It intrigued him and very much disturbed him. To say he was momentarily flummoxed when his brain registered the face through the lens was an understatement.

He was scoring a full ten on the Richter scale for rudeness, having invaded the funeral proceedings for Damian Jones and all. But in his defense, the last thing he expected to be doing during his extended leave was to be targeting his long-ago sweetheart, Mallory Tucker now Mallory Jones, widow of the deceased and possible prime suspect in a police investigation.

There was little hope that he was succeeding in hiding his astonishment. He had taken a moment to gather his wits before approaching her, but the moment she turned around at the sound of her name, he could have sworn his heart stopped beating for the second time that day. Seeing her through the lens of the camera did not equate to his physical reaction of seeing her in person.

You're three feet away from the one that got away.

When he read the initial fact sheet, which currently lay inches away from his arm, he had only glanced at the names, scanned the facts, and headed out to grab a few more hours of sleep. Not once did he check the photos. Nor did he do any prior computer research. It couldn't have been that difficult to find the grieving widow at a funeral if she hadn't chosen to stop by her workplace, right? He didn't want to delve that far into that answer; it might require reconsideration of his basic abilities as an investigator.

In the short time that Tyler had been a detective for the force and side-jobbed for Alexander, he had exposed several cheating husbands, found a few missing people who hadn't really wanted to be found, busted countless identity thieves, and solved three murders. Needless to say, he was dumbfounded at his critical error. He would like to blame it on sleep deprivation, but excuses only got a person so far and didn't solve a damn thing. This was a FUBAR he should have not let happen.

He was slowly rebuilding a name for himself in the state's capital city, despite his past. At this point in his life, the last thing he needed was to entangle himself with an old girlfriend who just might be connected to her husband's death, whether knowingly or not. Definitely an understatement.

In an effort to clear his throat, an inappropriate chuckle escaped him. Who was he kidding? He was making so many mistakes just by sitting there having this conversation. It would be a toss-up of who would have his head on a platter first, the APD or Alexander. In for a penny and all that …

Doing his best to regain his composure, he posed a question to inquire as to how much she knew or didn't know. "Have the police indicated anything other than a possible random shooting?"

"No, that's the angle they are still thinking."

He knew otherwise, and it was no surprise that they hadn't given her any other information, since she was now targeted as the main suspect. As a matter of fact, it was beginning to look like an average case of murder-for-hire to the police department. He had been texted that little bit of information right before he approached her at the funeral. That meant qualifying evidence had turned up rather quickly. And if he wasn't hell bent on strolling down memory lane and acted like a professional, he wouldn't rule out the possibility she very well could be guilty.

He hoped like hell he wasn't lying to himself, but his instincts told him there was no possible way this woman was capable of murder.

His mind raced over the conversation Alexander and he had had as they left the restaurant. A few hours after receiving the initial call from Mallory, Alexander had an appointment with a defendant at the police station. As he was standing in the hall, he overheard the two police officers assigned to the case. There had been an anonymous tip called in that had given the cops cause for further investigation.

So here they sat. What could she possibly know about killing someone? Tyler found himself immediately hoping the answer was nada, zip, nothing.

"Is there anything that could make you think his death was anything other than wrong place, wrong time?"

"His first wife is crazy. I have court-filed documentation from her psychiatrists and other counselors over the years to prove it. She exhibits symptoms associated with antisocial personality disorder, but not enough to warrant the full diagnosis. I beg to differ on that, but that's my opinion. I have numerous banker boxes full of other court records to support my theory as well. But none of that really matters, right? The police declared it a drive-by."

She spoke of that knowledge without reservation. The sorrow in her eyes was briefly overtaken by anger. She took a moment to collect herself, but she made no qualms about her feelings toward the ex-wife.

Tyler began to jot down notes on the yellow legal pad that rested on top of the case file. He nodded his head in response to urge her to continue.

"Tell me more about Kendall, if you don't mind."

Mallory expelled a deep breath and gathered her thoughts. "Kendall is very good at what she does. Her intelligence keeps her out of jail and one step ahead of everyone else. She is very be-lievable when necessary. I've personally witnessed her Academy Award-winning performances more than once."

Tyler's silence continued for another moment, not just so he could gather his thoughts but also to take in his impression of the new Mallory that sat across from him. Long gone was the partying, carefree, vibrant teenager who almost always wore tight jeans, thin-strapped tank tops, and boots. Damn, she had been hot. His muscles still tightened just picturing her in those jeans.

The woman he was with now sat across from him wearing the traditional black suit with a charcoal-gray silk blouse. Her hair was darker now but still blonde. Her shape was curvier—the way a woman's should be—and probably only a size larger than it had been when they were young. She looked like a woman who took an interest in her health. But the blue eyes staring at him told a different story. Her eyes had always reminded him of a country song; she had the bluest eyes in Texas. As beautiful as they were, her makeup could not hide the dark circles under them. Her cheeks were gaunt, and she sat stiff as a board.

He couldn't help the urge to shelter her from all that plagued her.

"Let me ask you a question, Mr. McCormack."

Her question brought Tyler back into the moment. She remained controlled and professional, which really irked him. He couldn't blame her; it had been years since they'd spoken, and, well, the timing and circumstances were less than desirable.

He offered his encouragement anyway. "Mallory, we've dated, known each other, for nearly twenty years; there's no need for formality."

"I beg to differ. I don't know you at all anymore. You approached me at my husband's graveside and demanded an immediate meeting. You gave no consideration to the fact that I should currently be attending my husband's wake and comforting our grieving young daughter. Since you deemed this meeting as imminent, that could only mean you're investigating my possible involvement with Damian's death." Her right eyebrow rose, which he knew from past experience indicated a silent challenge.

But he knew *her*. He waited for the question that he knew was forming in her mind—it took less than a few seconds.

"If I'm a suspect, then Kendall planted that seed. So what I want to know is who the hell hired you if you're not here representing the police?"

"You're quick; I'll give you that." Tyler leaned back in his chair and tapped his pen twice on the table, taking a quick moment to decide how to approach her inquiry. He found himself talking before he even registered a decision. Lowering his voice, he said, "Blakely called me. Told me the PD is looking at you for murder-for-hire."

He just blew it. What the hell was the matter with him? The reason as to why that came out of his mouth was not something he wanted to dwell on.

"Blakely. Alexander Blakely? But he's the probate attorney."

In an effort to redeem himself, he tapped into his distinct ability to read nonverbal communication. Tyler scrutinized Mallory's reaction. Her stunned response, instinctive dropping of her jaw, and widening of her eyes led to a split moment of panic. As if sensing his scrutiny, she automatically tried to recover by straightening her shoulders and lifting her chin. She had always carried herself confidently—almost brave and unmoving, like a tiger backed into a corner. And that bugged the hell out of him. In this situation, it was a proverbial double-edged sword. Was this reaction guilt or shock?

"It doesn't matter. If he doesn't want my case, fine, I will find another attorney. Like I said, if I'm a suspect, then it's by the manipulations and plotting of Kendall Kramer—Jenkins—Jones, or whatever name she's using this week."

"Your animosity toward the ex-wife is not going to help you at all. If anything, it makes you look as if you are intentionally steering the investigation away from yourself."

"That depends on how well I can substantiate that claim. I can. But I won't risk going to the police with it. Besides, who the hell cares if my behavior toward this woman is socially correct or not? She made our lives a living hell for *years.*"

Tyler figured there was more where that outburst came from. He held her gaze but didn't speak. He patiently waited for her to gather her thoughts.

She shook her head. She was befuddled. She began to say something, but she hesitated when a couple walked by their table on the way out the door.

"Our daughter, Emma, is seven years old. It took five of those years for me to adopt her."

He nodded, indicating he was privy to that knowledge. "She is Kendall's and Damian's daughter from a very brief marriage. It's rare that a father gains full custody of a child as young as she was—less than a year old, I believe. Kendall kept you both in and out of court proceedings several times. You ultimately pursued a 'termination of parental rights' action based on years of neglected court-approved visitation as well as several instances of harassment, but not until it went before a second judge."

It was Mallory's turn to remain silent. He grinned and then added, "I read my research." *I just didn't look at the damn photos.*

She sighed again—this time heavily—and lowered her head. When she raised her eyes, Tyler could see her internal debate of whether or not to share her thoughts. Her teeth raked across her lower lip, a nervous habit that she had kept over the years.

"I need someone on my side that will fight harder than anyone else to prove my innocence and to keep my daughter safe from further tragedy. I strongly believe that person is you. I … I can pay you. Between Damian's company and my web-design business, there is money. Money that won't be tied up in probate."

They both knew, right then, right there, she even sounded guilty.

"Thank you for the confidence. I think. But currently I work for Alexander. At this time, I was hired by him to investigate this case. It is nice to know trust survived our history, though."

A side grin made its way across his face. He doubted it was a smart move to bring up the past a second time, but the words escaped his mouth. *Damn, I'm on a roll today,* he thought.

As if on cue, her eyebrow went up again, but this time when she spoke, her voice was fueled with purpose. "It has nothing to do with history. It's simply a matter of knowing who you are, Mr. McCormack. You have a knack for finding hidden truths. I also know that deep down, you want redemption for whatever still haunts you. You of all people should understand that things are not always as they seem." She hesitated briefly and then added, "Besides, Alexander is retained by me, therefore, through chain of command, you already work for me. You just need to decide which side of the fence you're on."

"Ouch."

"Mr. McCormack." She paused, moved her cup to the side, and then went for the familiar and leaned forward in her seat. "Tyler. Every moment the police department focuses on me is wasted energy. If someone doesn't steer their noses in the right direction, my husband's killer, who every cell in my body believes is Kendall, will go unpunished. This isn't just a case of the police accusing an innocent person. This isn't over. And I strongly believe my daughter's safety is threatened. Kendall killed my husband, whether she was the actual person who pulled the trigger or not. She wants Emma—and she'll enjoy watching me go down in the process."

"What do you mean?" Tyler's eyebrows creased. Mallory now had his full attention.

"She wants me to suffer in the worst way. She will come after Emma. It's not that she has motherly instincts and is desperate to be reconnected with the daughter she lost. She views Emma as a possession. I have something that belongs to her. In court, she lost and I won." Mallory spoke with conviction. "Now that Damian is no longer an obstacle, she won't stop until she gets Emma back."

Their eyes remained in a deadlock. Tyler found himself searching for words to comfort her, not convict her. "Then we better get started."

CHAPTER 3

⌇ ⌇ ⌇

Tyler did not drink very often. He considered it a professional hazard, especially when you were constantly watching your back. This afternoon's mind-blowing interview with his former sweetheart had him thinking a two-finger whiskey was more than a good idea.

He leaned his elbows down on the deck railing of his enormous backyard and stared out at the oak trees that lined the field behind his property while his Labrador retriever, Sami, roamed the grass. He closed his eyes, breathed in the clean air, and rolled his drink back and forth in his hands.

Sami sniffed around but kept looking back at Tyler. He was amazed how his dog understood his moods. She was worried for him and didn't want to stray too far away.

"It's all right, girl. Do your stuff. I'm okay." She whined a little and then moved on to sniffing trees and bushes.

He debated whether or not he should stay on the Jones case. He should definitely tell his chief at the station, but then he'd find himself in more heat over noncompliance. Maybe he should tell Alexander about his past with Mallory and let him be the judge. Professionally, his friend was going to flip out anyway once he figured out today involved more than a few snapshots—a hell of a lot more.

Alexander had given him the chance to start fresh, and he didn't blame him for the things in his past. Maybe it was because the man had always lived life by his own rules. Because of that fact, Tyler didn't want to disappoint him.

But, damn, it had been an uphill battle in an effort to move on. He didn't want to disappoint himself as well. Every case, every detail, he had to fight harder. There was a time his reputation had preceded him and opened doors wherever he went. Now those same doors closed at the sound of his name. Each day, he worked to regain his professional respect without the money and power that had eased his way before. Now he was staring at a forked road because this case could put that progress in jeopardy.

It had been two years since he had walked away. Two long years he had spent trying to rebuild a life and career. And stay alive.

~ ~ ~

Growing up, Tyler lived by the notion that the world revolved around good versus evil. In a perfect world, evil was beaten and good prevailed every time. Now, as a defense attorney, the distinction between the two had become blurred. In his world, good prevailed when he won, not when justice found his clients guilty. And he won. A lot.

This was not a perfect world. This was reality—and reality had rules of its own. This particular battle would end in a San Angelo criminal court building. From the somber and exhausted looks on the jury's faces, the battle between good and evil had been arduous.

Outside the building, the television crews and curious spectators showed up to witness and record the final decision of the most high-profile case in the county's history. This West Texas town had never before experienced such media coverage. As defense attorney of record, this case had made Tyler McCormack famous.

It had all come down to this. Tyler's eyes honed in on one piece of paper. The decision that was written on that piece of paper was held tightly in the hands of the foreman juror. This one decision would either allow good to prevail or evil to triumph. It would also determine whether his client lived or died.

The defendant, Lonnie Jaxon, stood before the court charged with the brutal beating and repeated rape of a young woman, Jennie. She had been found lying in a river, presumably dead (an isolated mistake on Jaxon's part). When she was discovered, any and all hair had been removed from her body. Her nails had been trimmed to the quick, and her skin was scoured clean and had reeked of bleach. He was, without a shadow of a doubt, an evil man guilty of multiple heinous crimes—crimes for which he had cheated justice and eluded punishment several times before. The homicidal defendant deserved not only a guilty verdict; he deserved to rot in hell. Instead of being nervous, he calmly stood before the court in a thousand-dollar, tailor-made, beige three-piece suit. His body was also free from hair on his head, his arms, even his legs. Each ear was adorned with crystal-clear diamond studs. The ring on his pinky finger was polished white gold framing a square diamond as big as one of his teeth. His hands were clasped tranquilly in front of him—his face void of any expression. The only evidence he offered that he was alive and not a statue was the steady, slow rise and fall of his chest. His appearance was a hypocritical resemblance of virtue and innocence.

The prosecuting attorney, an overweight, short, gray-haired man in his mid-fifties, looked across the courtroom, weighing the reaction of the twelve men and women as they entered in single file and took their respective positions. It was apparent to everyone in the courtroom that he abhorred the defendant since he had unsuccessfully prosecuted him twice before. In closing argument, the prosecutor appealed to jury.

"You must exercise your civic duty and protect society from further homicidal acts. Look at him. He sits there in that chair as if he is untouchable. Ladies and gentlemen, he is not. Each one of you possesses the power to make justice prevail in this court-room today. You have been presented with heartfelt testimony, a complex analysis of evidence full of technical and medical terms, but one thing is not complex. You have been asked by this young lady, Jennie Stewart, to do the right thing. Give her the justice she genuinely deserves. Do not allow yourself to be swayed by the other attorney's meticulously crafted defense that was nothing but a smoke screen. Lonnie Jaxon is an evil, brutal man that must be convicted for his unspeakable crimes."

At this moment, several lives would be forever altered. An unbreakable tension filled the air as the final juror took position on the jury panel. The prosecutor glanced at Jaxon and lifted his chin, feeling confident he had finally won.

Tyler feared differently. Over the course of the trial, he had investigated his case to its fullest. He had poured over the previous court cases that his client had escaped either on technicalities, missing witnesses, or exoneration due to lack of evidence. The more he discovered, the more convinced he was that the man he had taken an oath to defend to his best ability was a notorious killer and serial rapist. He had harmed this young lady in the vilest of ways and then left her for dead in a river. It was a miracle that she lived; otherwise, Jaxon would have escaped punishment once again. Tyler was convinced beyond a shadow of a doubt that Lonnie Jaxon would repeat these monstrous acts if given a hint of freedom.

Another fact that haunted Tyler was that the information he had uncovered was not used as prosecutorial evidence. If it had been, the jury would have returned instantaneously with a death sentence.

Tyler had the talent and skills to develop strategic defenses and get his clients off—innocent or not—based on his ability to understand his clients. A good defense from Tyler McCormack, attorney at law, did not come cheap. Word had spread quickly in the criminal world, and his reputation preceded itself. He had been a high-paid counsel for years and put his fair share of criminals back on the street. Tyler justified his actions by hiding behind the United States judicial system—every person deserved a fair trial and was innocent until proven guilty. That was how he had slept at night.

Not this time.

His success had led up to this one high-profile case—a case that, if he won, would provide him much earned prosperity. It was dirty money, and it was a case that he would trade his entire career for if he could extricate himself from it. The more information that Tyler uncovered, the more he had begun to loathe himself for defending the monster.

The very night he had prepared his request to be removed as Jaxon's attorney of record, a message was sent to Tyler's home via a very large, very deadly man threatening his life and the lives of his family. Now he stood next to Jaxon not only as his counsel but also as his victim.

Tyler kept his head facing the judge, but he cut his eyes towards Jaxon one last time before the jury read the verdict. Lonnie Jaxon remained as calm and still as a statue.

The judge spoke in a solemn voice. "Members of the jury, have you reached your verdict?"

～ ～ ～

Tyler was out of his SUV before the engine had fully cut off.

The illuminating lights of the ambulance and police cars decorated the night like a swirling kaleidoscope. The EMTs moved at a slower pace around the victim, which meant only one thing: the victim was dead.

His boots crunched on the sticks as he made his way down to the riverbank. Every step he took was a step closer to self-condemnation. His eyes swept the area. There were no abandoned cars or hints of foul play. Nothing appeared disturbed except for the yellow caution tape that now framed the crime scene.

"She made it five days after the trial." The grim statement that was peppered to Tyler came from the lead crime-scene investigator. His somber expression was reflected on everyone's face. Their eyes condemned him for his knack to free the guilty. He had been tried and convicted by his peers.

"Jennie." Tyler bowed his head and closed his eyes. After Lonnie Jaxon's acquittal, Jennie had turned and looked at her predator with fearful blue eyes. She knew as well as he did that it would only be a matter of time until the fatal hunt began.

Her body lay exposed and lifeless, no longer suffering at the hands of a monster. Tyler felt the pain of each and every shallow cut, rope burn, and devastating bruise she had endured. But most of all, he felt shame and guilt to the depths of his soul. She blamed him. This was his fault. She had never said the words. She didn't have to.

It was in her eyes.

～　～　～

Bark! Bark! He blinked twice before it registered that what he was looking at was the huge yellow tennis ball that Sami had dropped at his feet. She whined at him, figuring his mood would lighten up with a little game of fetch. She began to wag her tail excitedly as Tyler absently scratched behind her ears. Tyler hadn't given his best friend enough attention lately. So he bent down, took the ball in his hand, and threw it to the far edge of the lawn. While watching his most loyal companion speed across the yard to retrieve the ball, he took another drink of his whiskey.

With a shudder, he realized that another set of blue eyes haunted him. He always imagined he would know her anywhere, or so he thought. He wasn't quite over the shock of seeing her again. Of course, the content of their conversation and the investigation it-self required his professional viewpoint—thought over, strategized, and deciphered, but he could not force *her* out of his thoughts.

Halfway through their meeting, he had known he wouldn't be able to shake the need to protect this woman from whatever trouble had surfaced. How could he not step up and help her? It was Mallory. *His* Mallory.

The pit of his stomach turned into acid at the thought of how difficult the quiet vow just might be. He knew the police were looking hard to pin her for the crime, but he also knew he could, and probably would, meet resistance at every turn if he tried to prove her innocence. Not because she was guilty, but because of his past. He was the guilty one. It didn't take a genius to know his job with the APD would be over—he was on thin ice there anyway.

No one who had followed the Jaxon trial had let him forget his part in it. The man was free because Tyler had built a defense so strategic that the cold, hard facts could not prevail. The blood of Jennie's death was not only on Jaxon's hands but on his as well. After that case, rumors and conjecture flooded the news and social media that he and Jaxon had worked together to bury evidence, bribe witnesses, and even pay the jurors off. On the contrary, Jaxon was a very skilled criminal, so it hadn't taken much on his part to discredit any circumstantial evidence of the prosecution and generate reasonable doubt on what trace evidence they did have. And God help him, he had shredded Jennie on the stand. That part would haunt Tyler for the rest of his life.

As soon as Mallory became associated with his name, many would possibly convict her out of spite alone. Trust had not yet been won over at the police station—or anywhere else in the Austin legal society. Maybe it never would.

Tyler would begin to look at possible theories, hoping one would generate a solid lead. It didn't help that the standard forty-eight-hour rule of solving a murder was long gone. Maybe Damian was simply a victim of a random shooting. Maybe someone else had put a lot of effort into staging the act. And if that was true, then the police could possibly be onto something with the murder scenario pointing toward Mallory. Damn.

Romantic past with the suspect or not, his instincts hummed that she and the daughter needed protection. He debated whether he should pursue this through the proper channels and tell Alexander that he had to step back this time. But he only had to look into Mallory's eyes to know he would face the devil himself if she needed him to.

He was so deep in thought that the vibration of his cell phone startled him. Glancing at the screen, he punched the Talk button immediately. "Took you long enough."

"A deposition went into overtime. Did you tail her?"

Alexander rarely wasted time on extended greetings or explanations. He claimed that was what caller ID was invented for.

"Your gut was right. Something's off. It warrants a deeper look."

"You got that by taking a few pictures? What the hell did you do today? I've got four missed calls from her. You obviously didn't feel the need to follow a simple direction."

Tyler could hear the hum of Alexander's latest toy—this one being a black Audi TT. Tyler couldn't help but grin at the vision: he was the epitome of the gray-haired, potbellied businessman jetting around in a sports car.

"We had a little chat."

"I'm not sure that was one of your smarter moves."

"Everyone has an opinion."

"In fact, I'm positive it was idiotic."

Good to know Tyler hadn't miscalculated his reaction. "I had my reasons. I know her."

"That's weak, McCormack, even for you. Just because you know her doesn't mean you had to tip her off. Bottom line is that the police are sniffing hard, and I don't know if I want the case."

Alexander heard the clinking of ice cubes as Tyler took another sip of his drink. He grimaced at the burn of the alcohol and set it aside on the railing.

"Hitting the spirits tonight? It must have been an interesting meeting."

"Not really, it's more of a prop." Tyler lied, initiating a quick inner debate. If he said nothing, it could end up being a conflict of interest. He didn't want to alienate the one person who'd helped him start over. Even though Alexander could be trying at times, he didn't want to risk losing the one person who trusted him.

"Alex … she was the one."

The phone was silent for a moment.

"Shit." After exhaling, Alexander immediately went into

professional mode. "I don't want anything hindering objectivity or quality of professionalism. Do I need another investigator on this? You're already in enough trouble down at the station for going off without regard to rules and procedures. And, well, you haven't even scheduled the first anger-management session."

Tyler chose to ignore the jab. "We were ... look, it's not a problem. I've got it under control." Fake it, 'til you make it, right?

"Explain why this won't be an issue. Investigators have to stay detached and objective. It's the first rule in the book."

Well, if he wanted to consider physical attraction after years apart or the proverbial black cloud that followed him as a *slight* issue, then yeah, there were issues. Instead, he lied.

"That's just it; I am detached. I just thought you needed to be informed. There's no problem."

Alexander's phone signaled another incoming call. "Do your damn job. I'll be in touch." Then the call was disconnected.

Tyler placed the phone back in the clip that rested on his belt loop. He had landed in a living hell before for not following his gut instincts—and now he was grappling with the decision to do so again.

There was no way he wouldn't—no, couldn't—ignore them this time.

His first attraction to Mallory had been purely physical. Even as a teenager, she was overwhelmingly beautiful—not a bad girl, but not completely naïve either.

Their relationship was lust in overdrive. They dated, spent every available moment together, and took each other's virginity. A few weeks later, she was ready to use the "*L*-word." What scared him most was how much he felt the same, but at eighteen, saying it even terrified him more. So instead of telling her he loved her too, he broke her heart and split.

Shortly after that, he graduated high school and deserted their plans to attend UT Austin together and instead headed to Texas A&M in Killeen. Tyler realized too late that she was possibly the best thing that had ever happened to him and he had screwed it up. Determined to find her, he traveled to Austin ready to plead insanity and ask for forgiveness. He had been so confident that they would pick up right where they had left off. He had found her on campus, and before he could approach her, he watched her reach up and kiss another guy. They never spoke again.

Until today.

Tyler whistled for Sami and waited for her to come running. He stepped back into his house and away from the distant memories of his youth—and the not-so-distant memories of his past. His drink sat abandoned on the railing.

He forced his mind to regroup and focus on the objective. He had to make himself disengage and dig for facts, no matter what they might be. He walked into the office and booted up his computer. Immediately, Sami found a cheese-filled bone and curled up at his feet.

As his laptop surged to life, he contemplated the initial direction of his investigation. He began by tapping the name *Kendall Jenkins* in his search engine. He couldn't help but hope that maybe this was his chance to do right and maybe make amends with his own demons.

One thing he had learned through his years of practicing law was that sometimes, more often than not, black and white was not always right. The police were notorious for thinking in the black and white. Mallory had given him the gray.

He was riding on blind faith that the girl he knew had not morphed into a cold-blooded killer. If what she had told him about the ex-wife was true, and he felt deep inside it was, then that's where he would begin.

Risking a breach of security, he tapped into the legal database for "Kendall Kramer-Jenkins-Jones," which proved quite interesting. Her criminal history since the age of eighteen was colorful, to say the least: assault, vandalism, petty theft, prostitution, as well as domestic violence. It appeared that just about every man she had hooked up with ended up with either charges filed against him or lawsuits. She had several civil court appearances with her ex-husband, Damian, obviously over the divorce and custody of their daughter, Emma.

The one thing that caught his attention was the court order that sealed her juvenile records. He jotted a note to himself to get his hands on those. Nothing was ever sealed if you knew who to go to. There was a time he could have had his hands on those by the end of the business day. Now it wasn't so easy. Beside that note, he scribbled another to bring chocolate for the court clerk; she was nice to him if no one else was around, so his timing would have to be critical. It also helped that she had a candy addiction. Addicts never said no to suppliers.

The search indicated a long history of police reports, but more importantly, a long history of court cases. She must love the attention. There were more filed *by* her than *against* her. The latest one was an assault charge. Tyler clicked on the link to further inquire and stared at the screen—no way. Tyler's jaw tightened and he felt instant irritation.

He hit "print" and paced his office as the pages of Kendall Jenkins's criminal hobbies flowed out of his printer. He slapped a label on a new file and, with a Sharpie marker, he scribbled the name *Jenkins, K.*

But before he could make her his primary suspect, he had to get some answers about that most recent police report.

He reached for his phone, swiped it open, and then reconsidered. Once again, doing things the old-fashioned way seemed more appropriate. He needed all parameters of communication to make a true assessment, and that included good old-fashioned nonverbal communication, something that was going by the wayside in this technologically driven society.

Armed with this latest file, he jumped in his blue Trailblazer and headed across town.

CHAPTER 4

⌒ ⌒ ⌒

The last few days had seemed endless, and Mallory wanted nothing but uninterrupted quiet time in her favorite spot: the bathtub. After leaving the coffee shop where she met Tyler, which, thankfully, was on the south end of the city, she had stopped by the church to visit with lingering friends and family. It was short of a miracle that she was able to hold herself together and not cave in to the insurmountable mixture of emotions that flooded her.

It was nearing eight o'clock by the time she had been able to drive to her parents' home to pick up Emma. They lived only a few blocks from each other. With Damian and her salaries combined, they could afford to live on the higher end of Austin's residential areas, which was the only acceptable place, in his opinion. "Residences reflect success," he'd always said. Yet, Mallory had wanted an older, more established neighborhood for Emma. The area where she had grown up was still filled with families, and the yards were landscaped with trees and swing sets.

Her parents' house had been included in the local parade of homes on more than one occasion. Slightly smaller than her and Damian's, it was referred to as a bungalow, with rustic brown trim and off-white shutters. Her mother had remodeled it twice since they had purchased it years ago. Furnished with four rooms, it was the perfect size for them to have Emma stay over, which she did at her every whim.

Feeling beat up from probably the most dreadful day of her

life, she pulled into the driveway, put the car in park, and just sat there. Taking a moment to collect herself, she willed herself to keep it together just awhile longer. As she walked up the flower-framed walkway, she could smell the blooms of the roses and hydrangeas. Before she had a chance to reach for the front doorknob, her mother swung open the door. Without saying a word, she raised her finger to her lips, shushing Mallory before she spoke. Her mother whispered that Emma had fallen asleep on the couch. Mallory immediately entered the house and tiptoed over and carried her daughter to her old room. She kissed her forehead and sat with her awhile, stroking her hair. Against her heart's wishes to crawl into bed and cuddle with her daughter, she knew she needed to visit with her mother. Leaving her daughter sound asleep and surrounded by the protection of her childhood stuffed animals, Mallory quietly left the room.

She found her mother in the kitchen pouring two cups of coffee. Speaking in barely a whisper, her mother's eyes filled with tears as she said, "The funeral service was very respectfully done." Before Mallory had a chance to answer, she added, "Who was that man that wanted to speak with you so urgently and at such an inappropriate time? He looked familiar, but I couldn't place him."

"Yes, it was," Mallory responded to the first statement and hesitated before answering her mother's question. She chose to share as little information as necessary. There was no need to add worry to an already sorrowful situation.

"It was an investigator. Alexander hired him, evidently. He had questions about Damian." She felt the need to ignore the third implied question. Bringing up an old boyfriend would spark a million questions from her mother, and frankly, she didn't have the emotional strength or physical energy to endure them at that moment.

Mallory bent her head and stared into her cup of coffee that she held with both hands. Her mother's voice quavered as she continued. "I still can't believe he's gone."

Nor could Mallory. Everyone who knew Damian was reeling from his sudden death and the shocking violent way his life was taken. Her mind immediately flashed to the steel-gray casket covered with a spray of beautiful yellow roses being lowered into the ground. She had quotes from the emotional eulogies from family and friends echoing in her head. *An inspiration to us all. One of the most respected businessmen I've ever known … kind and loving father and husband.* Sitting beside her on the church pew, Damian's mother and father wept inconsolably, which was incongruous with the dignified composure they waxed.

Her mother reached over and placed her hand on hers. "It will take time, but you will find the strength to live on. We all will. For Emma."

After they sat together and finished their coffee, Mallory assured her mother that she would be back in the morning to have breakfast with Emma. After peeking on her daughter one more time, Mallory drove the few blocks to her house and settled in her office for a quick rundown of her appointment book.

The time taken off to handle funeral arrangements was expected, but still, she needed the escape of thinking about something else, just for a moment. She composed an e-mail to her secretary, Liz, and provided a list of appointments to postpone as well as a list of action items to complete. The simple normalcy of writing and reviewing e-mails calmed her frazzled nerves.

Almost an hour later, she walked through the living room and noticed a huge bouquet of red roses. Her mother must have accepted the delivery earlier that day. She tore open the small envelope and quickly scanned the card. Immediately, she felt the hair on her neck rise. What she read made her stomach wretch. Mallory reread the card again: "One door closes and another opens. Your heart is destined to be mine. L. J."

These must have come by mistake, Mallory thought. Not only was the message awkward and somewhat unnerving, but she didn't even know anyone who referred to themselves as "L. J." Walking to the trash can, she stepped on the lever to raise the lid and began to toss the card. She hesitated and then changed her mind and opened the kitchen drawer by the telephone and tossed the card in the drawer. It was definitely time for the bubble bath. She was probably just overreacting to a bizarre mistake.

At last, Mallory prepared her long-awaited bath with the perfect mix of hot water, bath salts, lavender oils, and bath milk. As she slipped into her comfort zone, her mind began to reel over the emotional roller coaster that the day had been.

Her eyes had witnessed the dirt covering Damian's coffin. It should have solidified what her mind still couldn't grasp: that she had buried her husband. She still felt numb. Shouldn't she have grieved more? It made her feel guilty that she hadn't fallen apart. She hadn't cried inconsolably, as she felt she should have. She hadn't been angry. She had just … existed.

What kind of wife—or human being, for that matter—did that make her? She was intelligent enough to recognize that people mourned differently, so maybe that was it. She had never lost anyone that close to her before, so maybe this was how she grieved. Or maybe she felt guilty because she didn't feel the need to fall apart. She was sad, of course. She would miss him, yes. Alone, by herself, she admitted the depths of her guilt came from the fact that in her deepest, hidden inner self, she knew what she felt: empty.

She bowed her head in shame even though no one could see her.

She felt like a terrible, cold-hearted bitch. Distress radiated through her as she reluctantly allowed herself to relax in the warm water. What kind of woman buries her murdered husband, then feels nothing? She was certainly going to hell.

The hollow feeling mixed with remorse was welcomed like a justifiable penance. Her marriage to Damian had all but become nonexistent. They didn't fight; they just coexisted. They had stayed married for Emma. Well, she did. Damian stayed because their marriage was a business deal that had proved successful. Both of them knew it; they just didn't acknowledge it.

They hadn't made love in almost a year and a half. Prior to that, it happened only once in a while, almost like a quarterly report coming due. He had his routine, and she had hers. Emma was her life, and she wouldn't have entered into a divorce for fear of losing her. So she had stayed in a marriage that had been terminal from the wedding day.

They were friends.

But they weren't in love.

It had taken the majority of the years of her marriage to adopt Emma. It was an exhausting process, almost of battle of endurance. Finally, a few years ago, they had succeeded, and Emma was legally Mallory's. Nothing or no one would take her away—especially Kendall.

That was when she really knew. Damian reacted like he had just completed a business deal with the utmost success. It was like it erased a blemish on his curriculum vitae. Instead of embracing them as a loving family, he celebrated an accomplishment.

She leaned back in the tub, rested her head against the edge, and closed her eyes. She let the warmth of the water soak away her exhaustion in hope of welcoming relaxation.

Tyler McCormack.

He was the last person she'd expected to see at Damian's funeral. It's not every day that a wife buries her spouse and then attends a meeting/interrogation with an ex-boyfriend. Add more guilt to her load—she felt the tingle of butterflies when she saw him. She sighed heavily. She was definitely going to hell.

Sitting across from him in that quaint coffee shop had made her feel off balance. He had barely changed over the years. His face was still lean and handsome; it was like she stared at a memory that had aged like fine wine. The lanky teenager had grown into his large frame. His shoulders were broader and his neck was thicker. He wore his light-brown hair almost too long, but it looked good. Really good. He definitely didn't sit behind a desk all day—the sun streaks were evidence of that. His brown eyes still mesmerized her, but now they held evidence of wisdom and experience instead of the untamed youth she remembered so well. Moreover, his eyes showed no signs of happiness.

She had heard of the trial in which he'd defended a man accused of rape and attempted murder. It had made the news on more than one occasion. She hadn't really thought more of him after that.

When he'd approached her at the cemetery, he had worn a black sports jacket and a blue polo shirt tucked into jeans, though his loafers had seen better days. He had shed the jacket during the interview, so she could see how the sleeves of his shirt stretched across his biceps.

Yes, Mallory, you're going to hell on the fast track.

It didn't matter one tiny bit what the man looked like, or how she reacted to seeing him, because he'd dropped an atomic bomb on her. After leaving the coffee shop, she panicked. When Tyler had told her that the police thought she had hired someone to murder Damian, it scared her to the depths of her soul. The urge to grab Emma and run overwhelmed her. But as easy as it was to get lost these days, it was just as easy to be found. There was really nothing she could do but wait.

Bam! Bam! The sound of pounding on the door jerked Mallory to attention and sent water spilling over the tub. She scrambled out of the tub and quickly wrapped herself in a robe. Instincts had her immediately cringing that whoever it was would wake Emma, but then remembered she was sleeping at her parents'.

Mallory quickly walked toward the door, leaving wet footprints in her path. She flipped the lights on and peered through the peephole, and she realized the instant she saw Tyler that it wasn't a friendly visit. She unlocked the door and opened it while attempting to keep her robe closed tightly around her chest. She remained in the doorway, not quite welcoming him in.

"Mr. McCormack." She didn't even try to hide her shock.

"Explain." Tyler forfeited any pleasantries and jumped right to the point of his late-evening visit. He thrust the file into Mallory's hands as he swept by her side and entered the foyer.

Mallory shot him a look of annoyance and followed him away from the door. "Explain what?"

Tyler pointed at the file he had given her. "I want to know why Kendall Jenkins had enough ammunition to nail you with assault charges as little as two months ago. That does not look good for you, Mallory. You should have told me," he demanded with a distinct bite in his voice.

Mallory didn't need to open the file to know its contents, and she sure as hell didn't *have* to tell him anything. "She showed up at my office, stormed passed my secretary, and barged into my office, ranting and raving that I was going to pay—and pay big—for what I had done. It was like she was totally out of control." Lifting her hand as if trying to grasp the right words, she continued. "Unhinged. I immediately thought it was something about the adoption process, but that wasn't the case. She never said a word in reference to it. She just went on and on about how Damian didn't know the real me, that I was a fake, and that Emma would hate me when she was older. She tossed over a chair, grabbed my laptop, and flung it to the floor. I lurched toward her and tried to stop her before she damaged anything else. That's when my secretary ran into the office."

Tyler creased his brow and shook his head. "That doesn't explain how she ended up with assault charges against you."

Mallory sighed heavily and rubbed her right temple with her fingers. The day had really taken a toll on her. "In a split second, Kendall transformed when she realized she had an audience. It was like a light switch flipped, and she morphed into victim instead of aggressor."

Mallory turned and walked into the living room, tossed the file onto the coffee table, and sat down on the couch. Tyler followed her but remained standing, with the fingers of his right hand hanging from his belt loop. Again, she massaged her temples and went on. "When security arrived, it was my word against hers. She had the witnesses; I didn't."

Tyler stood there for several seconds. He brushed his fingers through his hair, his eyes squinting in thought, processing Mallory's account of the incident and assessing her nonverbal gestures. She sounded quite believable, and knowing Kendall's mental issues, it would be the perfect response. But was it true? Was there something she wasn't telling him?

He looked around the living room. It wasn't overly large, but it was a comfortable place. The furniture was classy and inviting. The room was a toasty color, and the tables and walls were decorated with family photos, several pictures of Emma, and stylish trinkets.

"It still weighs heavily in the negative for you. It gives the police more ammunition for motive." Obviously, he would be talking to Alexander about this—and how this detail was pertinent to establishing character history in the case.

Mallory shrugged, folded her hands on her lap, and stared at him. Her nails were short and buffed, void of polish. "Why are you really here? This conversation could have easily been handled over the phone."

Tyler shrugged. "There are some things I like to resolve with some old-fashioned nonverbal communication. People lie too easily over the phone." *And maybe I wanted to see you again.*

Mallory sat quiet for a moment and studied his face. "You thought I would lie? So you think I'm a candidate for Damian's murder because of withheld information in trumped-up assault charges that never made it off the paper? Here's a hint: it would have made more sense if I had killed Kendall."

Tyler walked over, sat on the edge of the coffee table, and leaned in close, never breaking his gaze. He didn't answer her; instead, he did say, "What you're telling me doesn't make sense. What you haven't told me is what she was ranting about."

Mallory never blinked and held his eyes steady with hers. She succinctly and adamantly stated, "I. Don't. Know."

Again, silence between them. It was her eyes that spoke more than her words, but he couldn't decipher what they were saying. Those were the same blue eyes that used to be ridiculously infatuated with him. He would get lost in the way they lit up when she smiled. There were times he swore she could see into the depths of his soul.

She knew him inside and out, as he had known her. He had panicked because of it. Now he would give anything for her to look at him that way again. And he knew right then that he would sell

37

his soul if he could just look into her eyes and know what she was thinking. Immediately, he wondered how much she knew about his West Texas career—and moreover, her opinion of him, regarding it.

This woman had him scrambling.

Tyler could not ignore the fact that her chest was rising heavily out of anger and it caused her robe to open slightly. Tyler straightened up and took a few steps to regain focus. He inhaled a few deep breaths, but not before silently appreciating the exquisite hint of what was beneath that robe. "There is a possibility that the entire thing was staged."

"Ya think?" she replied. Tyler was not amused at her sarcasm. "I never could figure out why, out of the blue, she would show up and just start screaming and yelling. Through all of her ranting, there was never a concrete reason for any of it. She had no reason to confront me. Her issues were with Damian, not me."

The tone of her voice had changed and her eyes had darted with that statement.

He gritted his teeth because that was a sure sign there was more to the story. He had to proceed carefully. If he pushed, would she shut down? If he didn't, would he be wasting an opportunity for her to disclose more information?

No guts, no glory, Tyler thought. He forged ahead. "It fits, I think." He sat on the ottoman next to the coffee table and leaned forward with his hands clasped between his legs. "Once we start digging, we will be able to connect the dots here. I just don't know all of them yet. She was definitely up to something. I'm sorry, Mallory; unless you can give me more information, I can't see a motive for her committing murder. Drowning him in legal fees, yes, but murder?"

"I can. We just haven't caught on to what finally tipped her over the edge. Like you said, somehow, it all fits together." She gathered her robe again, a futile effort to show modesty. Their eyes met, and an old familiar spark ignited between them. They both felt it.

"Tell me about him." His voice sounded rough, but he never took his gaze off her. It was a justifiable question that any detective would ask. Yet, Tyler's conscience knew damn well that wasn't why he asked. They had built separate lives because of his choice to walk away, but the thought of her married to someone else burned his gut. What had he expected? For her to remain single for the rest of her life until he had come to his senses? Well, hell.

Mallory stood up and walked toward the window. She took a moment to gather her thoughts and then began. "Damian and I met almost six years ago. I had attended a Christmas party with a friend. He was there. Everyone knew him and was talking about his new company. People thought he was kind and genuine. I did too, in the beginning. A few days later, he called and invited me to lunch. Initially, he had mentioned an ex-wife, but he said she pretty much left him alone." She looked at Tyler over her shoulder and shrugged. "I guess that was a bit of wishful thinking on his part.

"He was driven, professionally, and had done quite well for himself. He was working with another small company, merging the two and forming a new medium-sized company—Identity Smart Technologies, Inc. Together, both businesses complemented each other and made blending smartphones, computers, and televisions more lucrative with the new app that monitors identity-theft threats. At the time, I was just opening my own web-design business. He hired me to create a new webpage for the new company. He wanted a cutting-edge designer wall that was interactive with contemporary SVG elements that engaged the user with ease. We sat and talked about it for hours. I was thrilled for the opportunity and threw myself into it day and night to impress him.

"One of the most attractive things about him, though, was the fact that he had custody of his little girl. I mean, any dad that held custody had to be worthwhile. I was smitten with pictures of Emma. Looking back, I truly think I fell for Emma first. She was beautiful. Long dark hair and angel brown eyes. She was tiny and petite for her age. He said she had been born prematurely—around twenty-seven weeks. Kendall was not the type to heed to prenatal care, and when things went bad between them and he had tried to break away, she purposely didn't take care of herself." Mallory paused to give Tyler time to absorb what she was saying. She turned to look at him and saw that he grasped the grave meaning of her words.

He slowly shook his head back and forth and then motioned with his hand for her to keep going.

"Not long after our business arrangement, he mentioned attending a fundraising event. That's when I met Emma. She was almost two." Mallory's eyes sparked for the first time since he had reconnected with her, and her face lit up when she spoke of Emma. Her tone softened. "It was a bonding of hearts. I was immediately in love with her. She had the eyes of an angel and the spirit of a survivor. There was nothing I wouldn't do for that little girl from that moment on.

"I began to see Damian regularly and married him less than a year later. HQ Technologies took off almost immediately. I thought I loved him. I really thought I did, but as the marriage progressed, I slowly realized that it was his little girl that truly held my heart. He didn't spend much time with her; he gave his company 200 percent of his time. She needed me, and I needed her. I changed my work habits and left no later than four o'clock each day and only worked at home after she was asleep. Damian and I never really needed each other. He had his routine, and Emma and I had ours. The best asset of our relationship was a division of responsibilities.

"We only really came together to battle the custody issues, which occurred off and on throughout the majority of our marriage. Kendall never really wanted her and rarely used any of the visitation time after the first eighteen months. Even when she did, she didn't use the full allotment—just enough to keep Emma unsettled. Instead, she sent hate mail, filed random complaints with the judge, and harassed us from time to time with veiled threats of kidnapping. After that, the visits tapered off completely, but the harassing never did."

Tyler's eyes never left Mallory as she paced the floor and shared her story. Her hair had begun to dry, and strands were curling in a messy, sexy way. She tucked a piece behind her ear as she paused to gather her thoughts. It was like she was speaking to herself now.

"Damian worked hard, provided a good home, and never blinked an eye at the legal fees needed to keep Emma safe. But it was really me that took the legal reins by the horn. His company demanded the majority of his attention, you know? My business was important, but, well, you know how it is."

The sadness in her voice could not be disguised. She folded her arms and shook her head.

"Anyway, I was committed to keeping Emma safe from the emotional and physical harm that her birth mother caused and providing the most normal life we could for her. As she got older, it wasn't as easy to protect her from it. Sometimes her questions dumbfounded me by how much a young child could catch on to. I convinced him to look into counseling as a family so she would have the tools to deal with the feelings a little girl experiences in such situations. Damian was too busy, so I took her myself. He was angry after a while because insurance paid for only a few visits. Several times, I thought it would take a toll on our relationship and we wouldn't survive it. But we did. There just was never really time for us. Pretty soon, what little romance there had been dissipated, and we began to simply coexist. In his eyes, though, I don't think he saw that anything was really wrong." She took a deep breath and sighed. "We were great roommates though. He had a successful business and marriage. I was the epitome of the perfect, modern-day Stepford Wife." Mallory shrugged her shoulders and said, "After all that, there wasn't really any energy left to focus on us."

Pausing in front of the window that looked out into the backyard, Mallory bent her head, closed her eyes, and whispered, "And now he's gone."

Mallory did her best to hide the guilt that spread through her like an engulfed flame. She could not and would not voice the relief she felt because she was no longer imprisoned in a loveless union. She hoped he couldn't see through that façade.

Tyler crossed the room to stand behind her. He placed his hands on her shoulder and leaned her back against him. She tensed at first and then relaxed against him. Before even thinking about the consequences, he turned her and took her in his arms. And have mercy; she went willingly.

For the first time in a very long time, he sensed a comfort that had been missing. He wondered if she felt the same. God, he hoped so, because having her in his arms made everything right in his world. Except, he knew very damned well it was not something he should even be exploring.

Or should he?

Mallory had never left his thoughts. Not in all these years. She was the one who had taken his heart and never gave it back. It had taken him a long time to heal his broken heart, even though he was the idiot that ended things between them. He turned tail and ran the very day after she told him she loved him. It was the first time—and the last—he had ever let himself get close enough to be loved by a woman. It didn't take a couch doctor to clue him in that that was why he'd never married.

There was a loud popping sound and then a shattering of the window that jerked him into action. Without warning, Tyler threw Mallory to the floor and covered her with his body. Shards of glass were peppering the living room, and when they showered over his body, it felt like thousands of needles stabbing his skin. Mallory's shoulder was slammed against an end table. The pain struck her hard enough to knock the breath out of her.

As more popping sounds and more glass exploded, Tyler tried to press her to the floor even more to protect her from the tiny, jagged knives that fired across the room. Her screams were terrifying sounds that sent his adrenaline into overdrive and gave him the wits to respond.

"Bullets," he growled into her ear. "We've got to get out of this room. Stay down, and stay covered, but you're going to have to move. Go to the bedroom, and get in the closet. Do not make a sound. Go. Now."

Mallory managed a sharp, jerky nod and did as he asked. Her heart was pounding out of her chest, and every bone in her body was shaking with fear. She army-crawled across the floor as quickly as she could, using only her elbows to raise herself enough to move, keeping as low to the ground as she could. She made it behind the couch and used the furniture as cover until she reached the hallway. Staying down, she moved to her hands and knees and scurried for her life.

When she reached the closet, she closed it tight, stumbled over the pile of shoes in the floor, and hid as far back in a corner as she could. She scolded herself because she didn't think to grab the phone off her dresser to call 9-1-1. Even though she no longer heard the sounds of bullets, she wasn't brave enough to disobey Tyler and retrieve a phone. Instead, she stayed surrounded by the clothes and darkness that protected her from the shooter. The sound of each breath she took was deafening. She grabbed one of her stiletto heels and prepared to stab anyone who came through the door. It was the best she could do.

With all her might, she thanked God that Emma wasn't home.

Tyler edged across the floor, shoving glass and broken vases out of his path. When he reached the corner of the room, he pulled up the pant leg of his jeans and unhooked the handgun from his ankle holster as quickly as he could.

He moved to the edge of the window and tried to peer out. It was dark and he couldn't see anything or anyone clearly, but he heard the screeching of tires as a vehicle sped off.

He ran to the front door and stepped out into the chilly air. The atmosphere seemed eerily calm after the storm of bullets. Cautiously and while taking cover from the front bushes, for a tenth of a second, he thought he could catch a glimpse of a license plate or vehicle model. It was too dark, and he could only decipher the red glow of taillights taking a corner way too fast. When he felt satisfied that whoever had taken the shots was gone, he went to his car and retrieved a flashlight.

Securing his gun in the back of his jeans, he switched on the flashlight with one hand, dialed 9-1-1 on his cell phone with the other, and kicked the door closed with his foot. As he scanned the perimeter of the house, he reported the incident and then gave the dispatch operator his badge number and information. The woman on the phone indicated a squad car would be arriving in minutes. He disconnected once he assured her that no one was hurt.

His heart sank a little bit, because he knew the reception Mallory was going to receive once the police were given his name.

An older gentleman peered out his front door from the house next to Mallory's and asked what had happened. "It's over now, sir. Go back into the house. I'm sure the police will want to talk with you shortly."

The neighbor nodded his head and did as asked.

Tyler flipped the gate open and cautiously examined the area, being careful not to disturb the scene. As suspected, bushes had been disturbed in the backyard. The line of vision was directly across from the window of the living room. A few branches lay snapped in two, accompanied by a partial set of rough footprints resembling hiking boots imprinted in the soft dirt.

Tyler returned to the house and, without hesitating, went searching for Mallory. He called her name, but she hadn't emerged. Entering her bedroom, he said, "Mallory? It's okay. Whoever it was is gone."

He slowly opened her closet door and switched on the light. She remained huddled in the back and looked up at him with huge, terrified eyes. Her hair was hanging in swaths framing her face, giving her a mussed-up look. Bless her heart; she was ready to do battle with the deadly end of a shoe.

Beautiful, he thought, his lips curving into a grin. He extended a hand for her to latch onto. When she did, he could feel her shaking. Slowly, he tugged to pull her up from the mound of shoes she had been crouched on. She stumbled over them as she tried to regain her balance. He stepped back as she slowly emerged from hiding, but he didn't quite let go of her hand.

Some things a guy just never forgot. The feel of her skin was one of them. *Now is not the time, Tyler. Someone just tried to take a shot at the woman.* That thought snapped him back into the moment.

He moved her to the edge of the bed and gently pushed her

to sit. She complied without hesitation. She clasped her hands to-gether to stop them from trembling. She jumped when he spoke. "The cops will be here shortly. We'll file a report and then pack a bag. You're going to need to stay somewhere else tonight."

And I will have a shitload of explaining to do, he thought to himself.

Though the fear in her eyes remained, her back stiffened at his orders. "What do you mean? I have to be here. This mess has to be cleaned up before Emma returns. She's been through too much already! She's *going* through too much. The last thing she needs to see is the house full of bullet holes and glass shattered all over the floor." With every word, her voice pitched higher and shakier.

"It's not safe for either of you here."

She was too in shock to argue with him. She may have had a stubborn streak, but she wasn't stupid. He was right. She reached for the phone to dial her parents' number, but she had to discon-nect at the sound of the doorbell. The police had arrived.

CHAPTER 5

~ ~ ~

Tyler could tell that Mallory's emotions were all over the place. She'd bounced from shocked to furious to concerned to way past scared out of her mind in an extremely short amount of time. At this particular moment, he was pretty sure she was experiencing a fear that she had never imagined.

It didn't take a genius to know that an attempt on her life had just occurred. The bone-chilling thought of what could have happened if Emma had been home would not subside for either of them.

Mallory repeatedly said that Kendall was behind the shooting. She was adamantly demanding her arrest. Honestly, no matter how he looked at it, he could not shake the notion that she just might be right.

"You're all set," the paramedic said as he finished applying the last bandage across her arm. More than once, the paramedic would glance at Tyler and return to what he was doing. He found himself hoping that Mallory would not pick up on the chilly reception of Austin's public servants.

The driveway was swarming with law-enforcement and medical personnel. Onlookers had begun to gather on the other side of the street. Each time someone would take a step in the living room, crunching of glass would crackle beneath shoes, but moreover, the certain tensions in the air battled between criticism and curiosity. The blue and red lights of the patrol cars and ambulance illuminated the walls like a spinning kaleidoscope whenever some-one opened and closed the front door.

Tyler was leaning against the wall of the entryway, staring into the curious eyes of a rather short and stout policewoman. He had seen her around, but they had never been introduced. She sure knew who he was though. Whenever she asked him questions, he felt exposed and under scrutiny. She hung on his every word and nodded her head with wide eyes. She was evidently intrigued and would be sharing her story of how she interviewed "the lawyer cop." He was giving a bullet-point rundown of the shooting inci-dent, attempting to remain as professional as possible. The woman did her best to respond with matching formality, but the underlying tones were not lost.

Officer Meeks stepped through the front door, immediately spouting off remarks as quickly as he could think of them. "Imagine meeting you here. Playing the side of the victim this time? I thought your normal MO was backing up the criminal, not the damsel in distress."

In lieu of answering, Tyler immediately turned his head to see if Mallory had overheard the jibe. She was absentmindedly rubbing the bandage on her arm and speaking to another officer.

"Detective McCormack? Did you hear me?" The woman officer had asked him if he would bring her down for a more formal state-ment in the morning, but he was distracted by Mallory's demeanor.

Turning his attention back to the officer, he replied, "Yes, ma'am. I'll have her at the station first thing."

She nodded and flipped her notebook closed. Using police jargon, she relayed to the dispatch that they were finishing up on the scene. "Around nine o'clock will be fine. In the meantime, I'm sure you're aware that this area will remain a crime scene, so we need you to leave through the front door in order to preserve the evidence." She looked at Tyler and then at Mallory and shook her head. The woman's posture and expression conveyed her thoughts loud and clear as she walked outside. Oh, yeah, she would be gos-siping to anyone who would listen.

Across the room, Officer Meeks had engaged in conversation with Mallory. And there it was, just what Tyler had been worried would happened. It was like a quote his father had always said: "You're judged by the company you keep, son. Be careful who you choose to interact with."

Tyler debated whether to close the distance between him and Mallory or to give her space and hope that the critics and gossips cut her some slack. She made the decision instead and walked over to stand by him. She trembled from head to toe. It was clear she was starting to crumble from the aftereffects of the adrenaline rush.

Officer Meeks snuffled. "Well, I'm not sure we will come up with a suspect, but we will look into things. Looks like you've got someone good and pissed. You know, with the shooting of your husband recently and now this ... interesting." The unprofessionalism of the officer made Tyler want to punch him.

As Mallory absorbed the harshness of his words, dizziness and nausea swept over her. She swayed backwards. Tyler caught her arm and said, "Hey, sit down." He guided her away from the police and led her to the couch.

Out of respect for Mallory, Tyler chose his words carefully as he addressed the remaining officers in the room. "Ms. Jones has had a very traumatic evening. If there aren't any more questions, it's time to let her rest."

"Uh-huh." Officer Meeks turned and addressed the other deputies that were working the scene. "Let's move out. We can continue in daylight." Under his breath, but where he damn well knew Tyler heard him, he mumbled, "Chief's going to have your ass on this."

As the officers walked out, the knowing glances and murmurs were not wasted. And yes, Mallory began to pick up on them. Before Officer Meeks departed, his eyes narrowed fractionally as he said, "We'll be in touch."

Immediately, Mallory turned her head to Tyler and asked, "Am I missing something here, or do some of these people not like you very much?"

Tyler gave a half shrug and sat down beside her. Mallory was an intelligent person. It baffled him that she had not yet made her own inquiries regarding the infamous Tyler McCormack, attorney at law, who defended ruthless killers and put them back on the street. Before he could search for the words to answer her with, she said, "Well, whatever that was, Officer Meeks is a son of a bitch."

Her choice of words had a chuckle escaping Tyler's throat. He pinched the bridge of his nose and wondered where to even begin explaining. He just wasn't ready to confess sins of the past and risk her walking away. She would find out soon enough anyway. So instead, he opted to change the subject entirely. "We need to go on and get out of here."

He stood and guided her to stand by taking her arm. Apparently, he thought she needed assistance walking to the bedroom. "Grab your things and toss them in a bag."

She began to do as he said, tossing shirts, jeans, undergarments, and other items in an overnight bag without thought to style or fashion. Her hands were shaking at will, causing her to drop things here and there. She stepped into the master bedroom, pulled open her vanity drawer, and then just stared at its contents.

Tyler began to zip up her overnight bag that lay open on her bed. "Do you have everything you need?"

"I have to call my father. It's the right thing to do. If he hears about this from someone else, he will go berserk." Mallory didn't even recognize her own voice. The adrenaline letdown had her shaking, not making sense of tasks, but weirdly, her voice was calm.

"I already did. I used your cell. His number was in there. I made the call when the paramedics were cleaning up the nasty scrapes on your arms and face. I haven't told you I'm sorry about those, and I am. I didn't have time to think about the table when—"

"No, don't," Mallory shook her head and replied. "What you did … I can't thank you enough. If you hadn't been there, I could easily be dead." She couldn't try to hide the visible trembling of her body. It was like she threatened to shake completely loose.

Tyler nodded his head but didn't say anything else. Still, knowing he was the reason she was hurt made him feel something in the pit of his stomach that he couldn't put a name to. Of course, he was emotionally intelligent enough to know that if he hadn't, she could have been killed. That thought released an overwhelming surge of savage protectiveness. He shook his head and tried to keep his mind where it belonged. It was just adrenaline on overload—simple as that.

He saw Mallory standing in the bathroom just staring at the open drawer in the vanity. He could read the emotions on her face. He stepped up behind her and looked into the drawer. Her focus was on the set of toothbrushes and toothpaste; a wave of guilt washed over her face as she stared at Damian's lying next to hers.

Moving slightly away from him, she took a deep breath and reached for what she needed and tossed the items in her toiletry bag.

Moments later, she heard her father's voice filling up the living room. "I don't care if you're police, FBI, or Homeland Security! I want to speak with *my* daughter *now*!"

Mallory quickly dashed to the front door and wrapped her arms around him on-sight. "Daddy."

"My God, Mallory! What happened here? I got a call from a Mr. McCormack saying there had been a shooting. Are you injured? Are you hurt?"

Tyler craned his neck around the large man, wondering why the police had lingered after leaving the house. Officer Meeks had been collaborating with two other officers in the driveway. He looked over his shoulder and the two men exchanged an icy glare.

So much for catching a break. Tyler stepped around her father, shut the door, and then extended his hand in greeting. Caleb Tucker, keeping his daughter in his arms, accepted his handshake. The man had changed over the years. He was a softer version of the man he'd feared as a teenager. Now his grip was not as strong. His shoulders were not quite as broad, his hair had more gray than brown, and his facial features showed creases of time.

"Hello, Mr. Tucker. I'm Tyler McCormack. I called you regarding your daughter and the incident." In light of the situation, Tyler was hopeful that the man didn't immediately recognize him.

"Yes, thank you, Tyler … aren't you—"

"Good to see you again, sir."

"Yes, Daddy, it's Tyler from high school. Pretty crazy set of events in one day." Tyler could have kissed her at that moment. Although he could see the headlines running through the man's head, he took his daughter's lead and simply nodded his head once.

"Thank you. You saved my daughter's life. I won't forget that." Gathering his daughter even closer, if that was possible, Caleb said, "So much has been happening lately."

The opportunity to interject his professional opinion and move beyond the moment of awkwardness and reservation he was sure the man felt motivated Tyler to surge forward. "Yes, sir. I am currently investigating the events of Damian Jones's death. This may possibly be connected. I assure you, it will be scrutinized at every angle."

"I thought his death was a drive-by shooting. Open and shut, as far as I've been told. What am I missing?" Caleb looked at his daughter and then at Tyler, and he morphed into the intimidating man Tyler remembered. With an icy glare, he spoke directly to Tyler. "I want an explanation. Now."

Mallory stepped from her father, took his hand, and led him to the dining room. Miraculously, nothing had been damaged. Crystal and china sat safely in an untouched cabinet, and the table, decorated with a flower arrangement that probably cost more than a six-month supply of Sami's dog food, was unscathed. Tyler followed and sat in the dark, cherry-wood, high-back chair directly across from her father, while Mallory sat at the end of the table angling both men.

She rolled her bottom lip between her teeth for the umpteenth time that day. She inhaled deeply and then let her breath out slowly in an effort to gain her composure. When she spoke to her father, her tone was calm and controlled. "Mr. McCormack—Tyler—approached me at the funeral, as you know. He had been assigned by Mr. Blakely, my attorney, to look into Damian's death."

Both men shared a knowing look—a look that clearly communicated that the older man knew damn well that there was more to the story than what Mallory had just shared.

Mallory continued to explain the events from the time of Damian's funeral until the shooting. Her father sat quietly, absorbing the events and implications of her words. *Unexpected*, Tyler thought. He was impressed with her ability to remain calm even though less than a few hours ago, she had been shot at in her own home. Her inner strength impressed the hell out of him, but it didn't stop him from wanting to wrap his arms around her and protect her from harm. Because he knew, without a shadow of a doubt, that she was scared out of her wits. The only sign that she was shaken from the near-death experience was the slight tremble in her hands. The moment she noticed that he was watching her hands, she clasped them to hide the reaction.

She concluded her account of the incident with plans for Emma. "It would be best, I believe, if Emma stayed with you and Mom, just until I get to the bottom of this craziness."

"Absolutely, no problem; you know we love having her. Your mother will keep her with her at all times." Caleb assured his daughter by reaching for her hand. He then turned his attentions to Tyler. "What I want to know is why Alexander Blakely felt the need to question my daughter in the first place. I may not have held as many positions in the legal field as you; in fact, I've held none, but I know that's not the way things work. There's something missing from this explanation. What is it?"

"Mr. Tucker, I assure you, my reasons for questioning Mallory were merely a process of elimination. As you can clearly see, an attempt was made on her life today." Tyler glanced at Mallory, whose facial features gave no indication that what he said wasn't valid. He also noticed that Mallory breathed somewhat easier when she realized Tyler did not feel the need to burden her father with the fact that the police were considering her a suspect in a murder-for-hire scenario. Mallory quietly exhaled and silently thanked him.

Caleb Tucker sat and stared at his hands for a moment. He seemed to be processing the information and probably weighing whether Tyler being anywhere near his daughter was a good choice—hired investigator or not. It cut him to the quick because if the roles were reversed, he'd probably have the same damn inner debate himself.

And here it comes, Tyler thought.

"Your mother and I are scheduled to visit a golf resort in Florida next week. There's no reason we can't leave a few days earlier and have Emma tag along. Your mother will be happier having her there."

"That's a perfect idea. I will get a bag packed for her and bring it over."

Not the words Tyler had expected. Okay, then. He felt humbled, intimidated, and transported back into his teenage years as he breathed a sigh of relief that Mr. Tucker had not tossed him out on his ass. Moments like this were what he lived for these days. Opportunities to prove himself worthy were received on rare occasions. The millisecond of a glare Tyler had received from the gentleman communicated crystal clear that he was getting one chance to prove himself based on the present circumstances, notwithstanding his past. Determined not to let the man down, he nodded his head in agreement.

"In the meantime, Mallory will be staying with you until the house is repaired and safe to return to."

No way was she agreeing with that! Mallory opened her mouth to argue in opposition but was never given the chance. The two men began making arrangements as if she wasn't sitting in the room.

She quickly stood and found her voice. "No way. That's not an option."

"Honey, it will provide you with round-the-clock protection. It's not like the police are on our side here," said Caleb.

"May I speak with you privately, Daddy?" She stood and walked toward the hallway.

Attempting to hide his grin, Tyler watched them rise from their seats. So Mallory was uneasy with the idea of them staying together. Good to know the chemistry he felt before bullets started flying wasn't just one-sided. Talk about complicated. For a guy who walked away from all things remotely resembling complicated, he couldn't shake the feeling that they were in this ordeal together. She had secrets; he'd bet his life on that. But what, exactly?

He'd watch his step. Keeping her close was smart. And, hell, who was he kidding—it was damn convenient too.

Until they settled this situation, it would be smart to find out more about Mallory Jones and her secrets.

He remained in his chair and waited patiently and tried very hard not to overhear the debate on the other side of the room.

"Daddy, this is not a good idea. I can just stay in a hotel. There is no need for me to stay at Tyler's house It's … it's … inappropriate."

"I am not about to leave my daughter unprotected."

"Then I'll check into a hotel with well-established security. Under a fake name."

"Not good enough. You could be followed by whoever took shots at you."

"I'm a grown woman. An adult. I can make decisions for myself."

"Yes, you can. Just not in this situation."

"Daddy," she said in a condescending tone. Tyler swallowed a chuckle as he watched her standing there with her hip cocked, one hand on her hip and her right eyebrow arched.

"Fine, then I will put your mother and Emma in a hotel, and you will stay with me so I can protect you." The muscles in his jaw tightened, and Mallory knew he meant what he had just said. There was no way she wanted her father to be put in any kind of danger.

Silence filled the hallway as they stared each other down. "Okay, Daddy, you win."

Mallory sighed a defeated breath. Impossible. She was definitely living an impossible nightmare.

Seeing Tyler again was a real surprise, so it was only natural that he would have thrown her emotions for a loop after the roller coaster of events. Right? Add to that the incredible fact that he was still gorgeous. She scolded herself that that train of thought would get her nothing but trouble and another heartbreak, courtesy of Tyler McCormack.

Mallory left the hallway and retrieved the overnight bag from the bedroom.

CHAPTER 6

~ ~ ~

As Mallory sat on the edge of the guest bed, tears threatened to spill over her eyes as she spoke to Emma. It was late, but she had hoped that Emma would be awake when she called to check in.

"I miss you, Mommy." Emma's sweet little voice shook. The sadness broke Mallory's heart. "I cried today."

"I miss you too, baby." Mallory did her best not to break into a sobbing fit. She spoke over the knot swelling in her throat. "I cried too. It was a sad day. Mommy's so sorry I can't be with you right now. I have some grown-up things to take care of and then I will come pick you up. If you need to talk about Daddy and the funeral, Gramma is a good listener, or you can call me. Be a good girl for Gramma and Pops, okay? I love you bunches."

"I will. I love you bunches more."

She had spoken to her mother and was told that Emma was enjoying her evening but that earlier, Emma had woken herself up crying. So her mother had promptly decided the best remedy was to break out the baking utensils, even if it was after bedtime. According to her, she was covered in flour and sugar-cookie dough. She smiled at the thought, knowing very well there was more cookie dough in her child's belly than on the pan. Not every grandmother would make cookies late at night, but Mallory's mother wasn't just any ordinary grandmother. She was the best.

Could a heart break any more than hers already had? She

needed to be with her daughter. She needed to keep her safe, more.

Finding her resolve, Mallory clung to the idea that Emma was lucky to have her Gramma. Damian's parents had stopped by for a visit after the service. They had not stayed long—they were both distraught and wanted to rest at the hotel. They were remaining in town long enough to complete the headstone arrangements and then were flying back to Paris. Neither of them had asked to spend time with their only granddaughter. Furthermore, they had not inquired as to Mallory's sudden departure at the funeral services. Yes, Emma was in the best hands possible.

Mallory had never quite met their approval anyway. Yes, Mallory knew she was neglecting certain expected traditions of the mourning wife. One thing Mr. and Mrs. Jones didn't realize was that the events unfolding were anything but traditional.

"She's safe and in loving care," Mallory reassured herself. She placed her phone by the nightstand, settled into the bed, and let the tears come.

～ ～ ～

Tyler was about to knock on the bedroom door to make sure she had everything necessary to rest comfortably, but he hesitated when he heard the sounds of her crying. He never really knew what to do in this situation.

He stood and debated whether or not to knock, until he felt like an idiot. He cursed beneath his breath. The urge to comfort her prevailed and he softly tapped on the door. "Mallory?"

There was a hesitation of silence and then a rustling of sheets. He could hear the patter of her bare feet on the hardwood floor as she came to open the door.

His eyes rounded as his mind absorbed that she was wearing a pink tank top and black-cotton pajama bottoms that had a multicolored pattern of circles, but all of that became overshadowed when he realized she wasn't wearing a bra. It was like being sucker punched. He flexed his hand in an effort to restrain himself from reaching for her.

She looked adorable—and sad.

He forced himself to breathe.

"I heard you crying. Are you okay? Is Emma okay?"

"She's as okay as she can be. This isn't right. We buried her father today, for heaven's sake. I should be with her. Not hiding out here." She shook her head as tears spilled over her eyes. The day's events had taken their toll.

Her hand fell away from the door, and Tyler closed the few steps between them. He placed his hand on the back of her head and pulled her into his arms to offer reassurance.

"She's in good hands. I know you want to be with your daughter, but it's the best thing for her to stay with them. We will figure this thing out. I promise you that much. I know it hurts that you aren't together, but you're both safe tonight. That's most important."

He continued to hold her until her tears subsided. She finally leaned back and attempted a smile, but it never reached her eyes. The sadness and fear he found in them touched something deep inside him. The pull he felt when he was close to her strummed through him like a surge of electricity.

The internal battle waging inside him was in full force. He wanted to kiss her. He needed to kiss her. She needed anything but that.

Mallory gradually backed out of his arms. He should thank her for saving him from the colossal mistake he was likely to make if she had stayed in his arms another second.

"Thank you. For everything. I think I'm going to try to sleep now."

"Good night, Mallory."

"Good night, Tyler."

The few steps it took for Tyler to walk to his room was long enough for him to berate himself in the process. *The woman just buried her husband, for Pete's sake.* One more moment and he would have kissed her. *Not just kissed her—I would have thrown her on the bed and made up for years of separation.* Which, by anyone's standards, would have been the worst timing ever. Lowering his head, he pinched the bridge of his nose with this thumb and forefinger. Chemistry and history aside, he had to keep himself in check. Anything else was not smart. He was the investigator. She was the client, or suspect, depending on how you looked at it. Either way, she was in a lot of trouble, and the last thing she needed was a high school boyfriend making a play for sex. He sighed heavily. "Shit. Shit. And double shit."

Sami raised her head from the spot she had been sleeping in by his bed and stared at him.

"Don't judge me."

Sami huffed and laid her head back down.

～ ～ ～

When Mallory woke the next morning, it took a moment to remember where she was. She looked around and, within seconds, relived the surreal events of the day before. She rose out of bed and padded her way to the bathroom.

The face that appeared in the mirror was shocking. The bruises she had received from the fall were already taking color. Her eyes held dark circles, and her face was tense with stress. Her arm was stiff from the night. She attempted to gently massage the soreness, but it did little in terms of relief. She splashed cold water on her face and brushed her teeth and hair.

As she quietly meandered her way to the kitchen, she took in her surroundings. When they had arrived the night before, she was in such a state of shock that his home had not registered in her mind.

Tyler lived in a custom Hill Country home. Places like this were what gave the city of Austin its reputation and charm. When she looked around, she didn't know what she'd expected, but this wasn't it. The southwest-style fixtures and hardware reflected his masculinity, but the southern dark, custom molding and wood trim throughout the house added to its rustic appeal.

The only evidence found that the house belonged to a person was a few photos of his parents. The rest of the décor could have really belonged to anyone. It could have easily been a showcase for the Texas bachelor.

Since she was up well before dawn, she quietly roamed the house, allowing him to sleep and hoping not to disturb him. She peeked out the windows and decided the home was surrounded by what she guessed was a few acres of land. The property was lined with oak trees and large bushes, which added to privacy.

There was a room adjacent to the living area that intrigued her. She assumed this was his office. The walls were void of any décor. An L-shaped credenza held several monitors, computers, and gadgets. There was a wall lined with file cabinets. The desk in the center of the room was piled with files and other papers. It looked a bit messy, but she figured he had a system of some sort. She stepped into the room and lingered over the files.

With her finger, she flipped through the tabs. She was looking for one with her name but had no success. Would it have changed anything if she had found it? What she feared most was probably not in the file, or Tyler would have already confronted her with that information.

She left the office before he awoke and quietly made her way to the kitchen. There was a back door that led out to the beautiful wraparound porch. She placed her hand on the doorknob and was about to turn it when she noticed a white pad with glowing red lights. A security alarm. She didn't know if it was set or not, but she didn't want to chance setting it off.

Instead, she ventured over to the kitchen window. It was huge with dark plantation shudders. She opened them and took in the scenery. The view was simply exquisite. A river bordered the land and rolling hills painted the background. He kept an immaculate lawn. She wondered if he took care of it himself or hired a lawn service.

There was a dark-stained, wooded deck that seemed to welcome relaxation. A rusty, iron outdoor fireplace sat in the far corner of the deck. A table with green-striped padded chairs encompassed the middle. She longed to go out there and curl up in one of the chairs, sip her coffee, and watch the sun rise—and totally pretend she had no cares in the world.

The house was so quiet that she could hear the birds chirping and trees bustling in the wind. What she couldn't hear were the sounds of the city. She closed her eyes and welcomed the peaceful environment. Yes, she could feel the attraction to this place.

Awhile later, she still sat at the kitchen table, nearing the end of her second cup of coffee. Her mind couldn't help but whirl around the craziness that had occurred in the past few days. She felt like a contradiction to the peaceful surroundings. She made a mental note to call Jamie at the office and tell her she would be taking a few days off. She was pretty sure it was already expected, but she wanted to touch base anyway.

Mallory couldn't help but mull over the idea of who would want to cause her harm. Kendall was the only person that had any reason to want to do something to this extreme. She pondered the recent encounters with the woman, what she knew of Damian's death, and the shooting from yesterday in an effort to grasp hold of what was happening.

Mallory jumped and spilled her drink on the table when she felt a hand on her shoulder. "Oh, my! I didn't hear you."

She had been so absorbed in her thoughts that she hadn't heard Tyler enter the kitchen.

"Sorry. Thank you for making coffee." He walked over to pour himself a cup and grab a paper towel to clean up the spill. When he returned to the table, he stood over her wearing nothing but a pair of unbuttoned jeans. Her eyes became huge and rounded as she watched him take a drink of the brew. She couldn't help but follow the path of his sculpted abdominal muscles all the way down to his bare feet. Holy cow. How did he stay so cut?

He took her hand and pulled her out of her chair. He turned and tapped a few keys on the pad and led her out onto the deck. Sami came running at the sound and bolted through the open door, leaping off the deck and into the yard for her morning routine.

"This is my favorite part of the house. I come out here nearly every morning."

"I was admiring it myself. A person could get addicted to this."

"It's one of the reasons I bought the place."

He motioned for her to sit down, and then he arranged his chair where he could rest his feet on the railing. He tossed a file and pencil on the table and sipped his coffee. His voice was still rough from waking up.

"Did you sleep?"

"A little." She didn't elaborate.

After a few moments of comfortable silence, she caught him looking at her questioningly. "What?"

He found himself wanting to ask her about the moment they'd shared last night. Did he affect her like she did him? *Still not the time, McCormack.* Instead, he said, "You were in deep thought in there. Care to share? It could help us pinpoint where to begin."

"I think you'd need a map to follow the thoughts rumbling in there. My head is basically overflowing with questions. How? Why? *Who?*" She dragged her hand through her hair in frustration. "We were normal people. Living a normal life ... except for an unstable ex-wife ... but it seems most everyone has one of those these days."

"Mallory, I have questions about Kendall Jenkins."

"Okay, but I pretty much told you everything about my encounters with her." Her brow creased in consternation.

"What I need to ask you about is background stuff. Her character. Habits. Things like that."

Mallory deliberated and then said, "All right. I'm happy to answer whatever I can, but I have something even better. Remember the court files I told you about? They would offer a much better profile. There are a few psychological evaluations in there as well."

He inclined his head. "That's excellent. But what I want to know won't be in there. For instance, when she barged in your office, do you remember what she was wearing?"

"She was dressed in black—jeans, I think. She wore heels. She had on a dark leather jacket. I think it was black too. Why?"

"How was her makeup? Her hair?" Tyler was jotting down notes as Mallory spoke.

"Her hair was dyed with one wild red streak. It looked like she had taken a highlighter to it. Not really styled, but straight. Her eye makeup was heavy and dark that day. I remember thinking she looked evil."

He didn't say anything for a moment. He had seen photos of Kendall with blonde hair, red hair, and black hair—just about every color. Photos of her looking professional, looking domestic, or looking like a hooker. It all seemed to center around her state of mind at the time, or what she was after. He scribbled *chameleon* on his notepad and circled it twice.

"Last night, you said she acted crazy at your office."

"No, I said she was unhinged."

"Same thing, right?"

"No."

"Explain what you mean."

"Control. Crazy is not in control. Unhinged is a reaction or a follow-through to something. Pure anger was driving her. She wasn't out of control at all. She knew exactly what she was doing."

Tyler was impressed. She seemed to understand Kendall's psyche better than any paid shrink. Unfortunately, he understood exactly what she was talking about. He had come "unhinged" on that would-be rapist. Something he would forever not regret. Pulling himself back into the moment, he continued his inquiry.

"Something you did, something you said could have sent her over the edge. Had you two had an argument prior to that? Could you have simply misread the situation?"

It was like watching a subliminal message flash on a screen. Had Tyler blinked, he would have missed the split-second change in Mallory's expression. She hid it as quickly as she'd expressed it. That moment sparked Tyler's motivation to push farther, but he also knew Mallory. If she didn't feel safe, it would be a cold day in hell before she disclosed whatever she was hiding.

"Talking it through, I really don't think so. If I had set her off, she would have been ranting about it. Her behavior doesn't fit. She likes to gloat when she has the upper hand. She didn't do that. She just kept ranting. She was furious. Maybe … hell, I don't know. Maybe she just wanted attention. She does that sometimes, but not at that level. She has a need to have the upper hand. When she doesn't have it, she feels a loss of control. With that said, if she did kill Damian, she wouldn't have had the upper hand anymore. My thoughts are incongruous where she is concerned. Think about it like this: if she killed Damian, then game over. But at the same time, if she finally snapped, then maybe she did kill him. I just don't know."

Mallory was talking in circles, but Tyler encouraged her to keep going. "It would make more sense if she would have come after me, not him. You see, in the eyes of the law, an adoption trumps birthright, even after death. If something happens to me, then she has a slim chance at maternity rights, playing on Damian's sympathy. She couldn't have taken Damian back to court for custody, not even visitation. But if something happens to Damian, and it did, Emma remains more legally mine than hers. Adoption is more legally binding than birthrights, so maybe this isn't about Emma. Maybe Damian was the victim of a drive-by shooting after all."

Tyler absorbed her point of view, not feeling the need to reiterate his own legal knowledge because he knew she was processing the situation and outlining her thoughts. He tapped his pencil on the tablet and then considered his next question.

"Is there something about the adoption that would have made Kendall angry? Besides losing, that is."

The moment he put the question out there, Mallory stiffened. "No, not that I am aware of. It was an exhausting battle, but we prevailed."

No eye contact.

Bingo, Tyler thought.

CHAPTER 7

~ ~ ~

It was the best Mexican food Jaxon had eaten since he moved to Austin, Texas. After only one visit with the owner, he had secured preferential seating and customer service. The simple décor covering the walls abounded with framed dogs and velvet Hispanic-cultured paintings, and the ceiling was covered in wooden, painted fish. Random colorful sombreros and piñatas filled the corners of the room. It was not his typical upscale restaurant, but the food made up for that.

He had seen her here. The woman from the website. The fascination began awhile back. First, he simply admired whatever photos he found on the Internet. Then he found her. It took time, but patience was one of his finest virtues. He had watched her for a long time now.

It was in her eyes. The thing that drew her to him. She needed a savior. A strong man to understand the hidden desires she kept buried inside herself. She was a prisoner in need of being set free. The more he learned about her, the more he was convinced he was the one to set her free.

Besides, coming to Austin allowed him to be closer to his new interest. Oh, he enjoyed cat-and-mouse games of the corporate world. She had readily accepted his primary business proposition without hesitation through e-mails, but it was time to make a connection. Explore the chemistry that was sure to sizzle between them.

He sat at his customary table, his back always to the wall, and sipped on a top-shelf margarita. More than once he caught the young Hispanic woman making his flour tortillas from scratch staring at him.

His order of chicken fajitas with a trio of bell pepper and onion, black beans, and rice was served in efficient time. The girl personally brought him his tortillas. Of course, the meal hit four-digit numbers when it came to calories, but he didn't care. He would just burn it off later with a woman—possibly the young, dark-haired, luscious tortilla maker.

He flipped a few bills on the money tray and retrieved his new Mercedes convertible from the young street hoodlum to whom he'd tossed a few twenties to watch it for him and drove down Main Street, across the Brazos River, and into downtown, where his newly furnished penthouse awaited. In less than fifteen minutes, his car was secured in valet and he was exiting the elevator on the top floor of the high-rise building.

The exterior face of the building preserved the historic scene of Austin. The interior fit his tastes much better after he renovated the place completely. The chrome trim and mirrored walls created an ambience of strength and desire.

The echo of his expensive Italian leather loafers clicked on the spotless hardwood floors. He looked around and was satisfied that the housekeeper he'd hired had polished every surface—every inch of metal, glass, and wood. The leather furniture illuminated against the setting sun. When he reached the wall safe, he placed his hand on the security panel to gain access.

In its protected domain lay a single photo of the first and only woman he had ever loved. His beautiful Lena Gonzalez. His heart constricted whenever he reminisced about their short time together. She had been young and beautiful. They'd never fought, because they always enjoyed each other's company. She had been his first. Well, the first woman he had ever *desired* to have sex with. There had been others before her. He hadn't chosen those women.

His mother had sold him for liquor and drugs. Sometimes she had given him to men.

Jaxon's life had changed colors when he met Lena.

One hot summer afternoon, they had entered a newly built house to explore and dream of a future together. As she stood in the vacant living room, his love for her was so overwhelming that it knew no bounds. While he walked over to her, he had visions of her blood decorating the walls and her body exhaling its last breath as he made love to her. That way, they would be forever suspended in time. The love could never end. It wasn't fear that stopped him dead in his tracks. It was need. He needed to love her that much. He needed to be inside her when her heart beat for the last time. When he walked over to her, he took her hand and brought her close to him. She wrapped her arms around his neck and he hugged her. His hold began to intensify to the point that she gasped and said his name. He began to kiss her and touch her everywhere. He had to fight to keep from climaxing when she screamed the first time.

The chime of the doorbell interrupted his memories of Lena. Instincts developed good habits, so as always, he replaced the photo, closed the safe, and approached the door cautiously. When he peered through the peephole, he grinned. His delivery had arrived.

"The woman you requested, Mr. Jaxon."

The dark-haired angel timidly entered the room. Jaxon could smell her excitement as she looked around and took in her surroundings. She knew he was rich, and it did not disturb him, even though it always paved the way for submission. Any attempt to play hard to get was null and void with the gleam in her eye. He hoped she would resist a little; otherwise, it was simply no fun.

The young woman approached him. "You like me?" She smiled up at him and then began unbuttoning her top. He had never had to do much to get a woman's attention until they realized the games he played were much rougher than they expected. That's when he got excited.

"Stop." His brisk command halted her immediately. He placed

a finger over her mouth. There was no need for her to speak. If she did, then it made it difficult to recreate his memories. This is how their love lived on. He didn't always choose women that looked like his Lena. Only when he felt her slipping away.

He grabbed her left breast and held it in his hands. Yes, perfect. With his other hand, he took hold of her hair and examined its color. Close, but a little lighter than he would have preferred. The lights in the restaurant must have made it seem darker. She would still do; her eyes were chocolate saucers, a perfect resemblance.

He pinched her nipple hard through the fabric of her shirt. She wore no bra. She began to continue unbuttoning her shirt. He said, "No worries, you won't need it later." In one jerk, he ripped her shirt open. Standing in the foyer, he pulled her between his thighs and pressed her hard to his center. Then, with a grip on the back of her head, he pushed her to her knees.

The black irises of her eyes widened and her mouth hung open. "This is where you prove to me you are worthy of my time." He unbuckled his belt and unzipped his pants. Without hesitation, she began to take him in her mouth.

"Deep," he demanded.

Her hands trembled as she looked up at him once more with her wide dark eyes and then began to eagerly please him. In and out. In and out.

He let his head fall back and closed his eyes. He needed a moment to fall back into the familiar place he had relived so many times. He thought of Lena. How she felt. The way her skin felt on his.

It was becoming more difficult to reconnect with her memory. Instead, he kept thinking of her. The woman on the website. Only once had he taken a girl that looked like her. She had been the only woman to survive him. His only blemish on an otherwise perfect record.

He never left DNA as evidence. He methodically went through his cleansing routine with precision and expertise. When he was complete, nails would be clipped to the quick, all her hair would be shaved completely, and her body would be cleansed in bleach.

Mouth included. Vital signs were now taken three times to confirm death.

He was becoming agitated. Conflicted with torn desires. He needed to feel connected to Lena. Only images of *her* were taking over. He wanted to do unspeakable things to her. He thought of the many ways he desired to have Mallory Jones.

Grabbing the back of the girl's dark hair, he pushed himself further into her mouth. When she flinched, he twisted her hair tightly around his fist and jerked her bead back.

"Did I make a mistake?" she asked.

Yanking her up by the hair, he finally felt a spark of excitement. The fear in her eyes was unmistakable, and a squeal escaped her throat. "You're hurting me!"

Now he was about to have some fun.

CHAPTER 8

❧ ❧ ❧

The drive on I-35 South to the city was stop-and-go traffic as the morning rush hour peaked. They had only minutes to spare as he pulled into the parking lot for her scheduled nine o'clock appointment with the detectives.

They entered the police headquarters, and it was a toss-up as to which one of them became more tense—Tyler or Mallory. The building was an older place, the walls were dingy and covered with police posters and framed portraits of past chiefs, and the atmosphere was grim. The sound of her heels clicking on the green-and-tan tiled floor echoed throughout the room.

The officer working at the reception desk immediately spoke when he saw them, "Hey, McCormack. Chief's looking for you. Heads up, 'cause he's not a happy man."

No kidding. Tyler knew this was coming and was quite surprised he hadn't been summoned to his office before now. Mallory looked at him inquisitively and opened her mouth, no doubt to ask questions. In an effort to hold her off just a few minutes longer until he could get her to his office, he grabbed her by the elbow and ushered her on.

Before he could completely shut the door to his office, she spun around and cut her eyes at him. She hissed, her voice full of venom, "You're a detective? You *work* here?"

"Hear me out first."

"Absolutely not. You deceived me, Tyler McCormack. You led me

70

to believe you worked for Alexander. So what is this? Some kind of entrapment? I will sue this entire organization!" And with that, she stormed passed him and had her hand on the doorknob before Tyler could reach her.

He slammed his hand on the door above her head. "Before you leave, just listen to me." He could physically see her chest rising and falling. Her breath was heavy and, no doubt, she was furious. Or scared.

"Yes. I'm a detective for the Austin PD. I have been for a few years now, but I also moonlight for Alexander. I've been on what you would call an extended leave."

"What kind of extended leave?"

"The kind they make you take when the head doctor tells them you're overly stressed."

"You lied to me."

"Yes."

"This entire place is looking to put me in jail. You work here, for heaven's sake. Why are you helping me?"

"Because, honestly, my gut tells me it's the right thing to do."

"I don't know if I can trust that."

"Try. Just try." Tyler held his breath, afraid she was about to walk out the door. Making her stay was all he was concerned about; he didn't even care that he sounded vulnerable and he was damn near begging. He would quit the force to make her trust him. What this would do to his job was the furthest thing from his agenda.

After several tense minutes, Mallory took a deep breath and heaved a sigh. What choice did she have? She needed someone to help her. There truly was no one else. How had she ended up in such a situation? If something happened and they did throw her behind bars, what would happen to Emma? Her parents had no biological ties to their granddaughter. God forbid she end up with Damian's parents. Or worse—Kendall. She sure as hell didn't have to trust Tyler, but right now he was her only choice. She pulled her hand back from the knob.

Tyler's shoulders sank with relief.

The better part of the morning was spent going over the events of the shooting with the policewoman from the previous night. They sat and waited while a formal document was processed. After nearly two hours, she had told her story at least four times and was now signing reports. He wasn't quite sure that Mallory had picked up on the fact that the interview had segued into an interrogation. They wanted her to slip up, to mix up her facts or change her story. Mallory did none of that.

Spending the better part of the morning avoiding the chief's office, Tyler inquired on the status of the investigation and why they were still waiting. He was met with resistance and aloof answers. He was finally informed that other than the footprints Tyler had found outside and the bullets extracted from her house, there were no leads. Tyler had the notion he wouldn't get much more than that anyway—unless he found it on his own.

As they were finishing up, another deputy approached them and requested that they remain for an interview with two detectives regarding the events of Damian's death. This immediately put Mallory on edge, and Tyler's instincts went on high alert. Knowing that the police had suspected her of murder-for-hire, she was fearful that her every statement was going to be scrutinized. The only edge she felt she had was the fact that the police didn't know she knew.

That wasn't much.

The instinctive urge to get up and run surged through every fiber of her being. She glanced at Tyler and again debated whether or not he truly was on her side—or was this all part of his plan to have her thrown in jail?

He took her hand and squeezed. It was an unspoken plea for her to trust him.

Tyler was angry that he hadn't foreseen this when the policewoman had so readily agreed to the morning interview. He morphed into a cold, imposing, and authoritative machine. He was punching his speed dial on his cell phone to reach her attorney. He had immediately ordered Mallory to remain silent and not answer any more questions until Alexander arrived.

What seemed like hours was actually only thirty minutes. When Alexander arrived, he was breathless and apologetic for taking so long. He too was in professional mode.

Both gentlemen deliberated outside the room. After nodding in agreement, they both entered the room where Mallory waited. It was apparent to Tyler that she was irked that the two men were collaborating about her *without* her.

"Okay, darling, this is what you are going to do. When you answer the deputy's questions, answer in facts only. Do not give more information than necessary, and do not offer anything not inquired upon. These idiots are barking up the wrong tree, and we are not going to make this pursuit easy."

"I know lawyers say it's better to limit answers, but I don't want them to think I'm trying to hide something."

Tyler interjected before Alexander could respond. "It's okay. Do as he says. When they realize you're answering their questions cooperatively and honestly and that you aren't attempting to hide anything, they will have no choice but to start focusing elsewhere. Just remember: you are intelligent but innocent. Don't let your emotions cloud your judgment. Respond; don't react."

Though his words were meant to reassure her, he found himself reaching for her to comfort himself. He rubbed his hand down her arm and let it linger on her forearm. She straightened her shoulders, took a deep breath, and nodded her head.

They both turned to see two detectives enter the room. They introduced themselves to her as Detectives Johnson and Clark. Tyler knew them but had not had the opportunity to work with either of them. He was almost afraid to remain in the room. Depending on their opinion of him, he could make the situation worse for Mallory.

He found out pretty quickly when Detective Clark issued the first snide remark. "So, McCormack, which side of the law are you on this time?"

"The truth's side." Why he even bothered to respond was beyond him.

"I can appreciate your interest on this one. She's a pretty fine-looking thing."

Tyler stepped forward, ready to slam his fist into the jerk's face.

"It's clear that time off hasn't helped your temper at all now, has it?"

Detective Johnson stepped between the two men. "Enough."

With Tyler's jaw ticking and Clark's smirk on his face, neither moved back. "I mean it," Johnson stated, "Clark, back off. McCormack, go find somewhere else to be right now."

Knowing he would not be allowed to stay anyway, Tyler turned to Mallory, whose eyes were wide in astonishment. He squeezed her shoulder reassuringly and left the room. He quietly made his way to the adjoining room, where a two-way mirror would allow him to watch the interview. He looked around to see if anyone was passing by. He risked turning on the speaker and raising one side of a set of earphones to his ear. If anyone discovered his indiscretion, he would definitely be escorted out of the building, but not until the chief of police issued his permanent walking papers. He honestly didn't care either.

Mallory assessed the detectives that were interviewing her. Johnson was a tall black man with no hair. His height and large frame made him look intimidating. He was very polite and professional. They had obviously decided to play the whole good cop/bad cop routine. Clark was clearly the bad cop, since he'd showed his attitude already. He was shorter and swarthy, and his reddish hair was swept back.

Johnson offered her a drink. She politely declined.

"We just need to clear up a few details." Clark initiated the beginnings of the interrogations—or interview, as they prefaced it. "We apologize for having to detain you and put you through this police red tape, especially after experiencing such an ordeal yesterday."

Detective Johnson's eyes were so dark that the pupils were not discernible. He remained silent, staring and studying every expression and move Mallory made. It was unnerving—so much for the good-cop idea.

They weren't aware that Mallory already knew they had suspected her, but she was still petrified to the bone.

Alexander sat by her right, and the other men took seats directly across from her. The metal table was cold and uninviting. It was funny how it didn't even register on her radar earlier, but now it seemed to be instrumental in setting an intimidating scene for interrogation. She lifted her chin and took a deep breath.

Tyler continued to watch Mallory through the mirror. She could sense his presence. Could they? Probably. She felt stiff as a board and refrained from any hint of emotion. When she spoke, she used manners and professionalism. "No problem, detectives. I'm glad to help and answer any questions you may have." Her calm voice felt like a contradiction to her visibly shaking nerves, but she prayed her façade that she had nothing to hide was successful.

"Are you sure I can't get you something to drink?" Detective Johnson asked.

"No, thank you."

The two detectives exchanged a telling glance. Johnson asked, in a manner that sounded like a poorly rehearsed oversight, "Oh, you don't mind if we videotape this interview, do you?"

Mallory looked at Alexander, who spoke. "No, we do not."

He got up and walked over to retrieve a tripod-mounted camera from the corner of the room. He situated it directly behind the chairs he and Clark were sitting in and aimed it directly at Mallory. Looking into the lens and adjusting the focus, he punched the Record button and took his seat.

Having exhausted the pleasantries, Clark began the questioning. "You last spoke with your husband around ten o'clock the night of the murder?"

"That's right."

"And you spoke only for a brief moment?"

"Yes."

"What was the conversation about?"

"He said he was on his way home. I told him to come in quietly because Emma was sleeping."

"He didn't tell you he had to stop for gas?"

"No."

"Did he indicate where he had been?"

"No."

"Who called whom?"

"He called me."

That could easily be checked, so the only reason for asking would be to see if she was going to lie, Tyler thought.

"How was your relationship with your husband?"

"Our marriage was fine. Why?"

The two detectives exchanged another quick glance. Clark said, "There were divorce papers found in his office desk."

Mallory sat, stunned. Alexander placed his hand on hers. She immediately looked at him for confirmation of that statement.

He didn't make eye contact with her.

Turning back to her detectives, she cleared her throat in an attempt to regain her composure. "I beg your pardon?"

Clark repeated, "We found divorce papers in his office desk. You know, a legal document that he had drawn up suing you for dissolution of marriage."

"I don't know anything about those. He wouldn't have done that. There had been no discussion of separation or divorce. Our marriage may not have been perfect, but neither of us would have split up and caused Emma that pain."

Chime in anytime, Mr. Attorney, Tyler thought. Tyler's hands were fists, and his jaw was tight. He fought the urge to barge into the room and punch the detectives for the heartless announcement.

She blinked at Alexander's sharp tone. "I urge you to tread lightly, Detectives. I will not have my client harassed."

Mallory was vigorously shaking her head. She paused, took a deep breath, and steeled herself to regain composure. "This is not real. This is not happening. You think I killed him because he was divorcing me?"

Tyler winced at her statement. *Don't give them anything, honey.*

Alexander placed his hand on Mallory's shoulder, this time a reminder only to answer questions factually. Not to give them any more ammunition against her.

At that time, Johnson initiated his line of questioning. "Then you admit it is true that you basically stayed married because of Emma?"

"What do you mean?" Tyler was impressed that she did not allow any change in her tone with that answer, considering less than a few hours ago, she had confessed as much to him.

Neither deputy responded. They just stared at her, waiting. Mallory sat as if she was aware of the camera recording every blink, every slight change of expression—even every pace in which she took a breath. Tyler feared that to whoever was viewing the tape, she would look guilty, because, in this part of the interview, she *was* guilty. She did her best to remain perfectly still and to keep her composure. If Tyler had been the attorney scrutinizing the tape, he would immediately be wondering what she was hiding. That bothered him.

"I told you. Our marriage was fine. The divorce papers are highly irregular. Damian had mentioned nothing about divorce."

Clark shifted and rested his arms on the table. "Do you think maybe he was trying to keep it from you until he had a plan for departing? Maybe that's why he was out so late?"

"No," she said adamantly. "When he called, he sounded tired. He had worked a long day. He did so more often than not. His job is not as flexible as mine. He kept late hours several days of the week. There was no reason for me to believe he hadn't done just that."

Johnson snorted. Clearly, he didn't believe her.

Mallory's eyes cut toward him in a silent challenge. *Keep cool, Mallory.* Tyler suddenly wished he could send her mental messages.

"My husband was an executive officer of a cutting-edge technology company. They spend several hours after five o'clock working, Detective. Check the security log; you'll see. I was married to the man. I'm pretty sure I can tell the difference in my husband's voice when he was tired versus distracted. I would have known if there was any indication that Damian was getting ready to leave me. He wasn't."

The deputies paused. Clark looked down and then cleared his throat. "Your husband was seen at a restaurant. With another woman."

And the hits just kept on coming. Mallory would not take the bait. "Then it was a client or coworker. Business was not always conducted from eight to five or in an office."

Apparently, the two deputies thought they knew otherwise. It was Johnson who spoke this time. "They had a private table at The Oasis, Ms. Jones. A cozy little corner. Witnesses said the two had their heads together like nobody else in the world existed. They were deep in conversation."

Witnesses? Cozy corner? The words struck Mallory like a baseball bat. Tyler watched as her temper snapped. When she spoke, it was quickly. "I refuse to honor that with a comment. Where is this line of questioning going? This is nothing but a fishing expedition."

"Here's where this is going." It was Detective Johnson's turn to go in for the kill. "Your husband was leaving you, Mrs. Jones. You would have lost everything, lost custody of your daughter. He didn't want you anymore; he obviously found someone else. And that just pissed you off. So you hired someone to take him out before he could leave you. Then, to make yourself look like a victim, you have your shooter stage a little action at the house. Suddenly, you're no longer a suspect but a victim. Perfect plan."

"Unless you are arresting my client, I will not allow you to badger my client with these insulting accusations. This interview is over." Alexander stood, took Mallory by the arm, and walked out of the room.

～ ～ ～

Hidden in the shadows of the parking garage, directly across the street from the police station, Lonnie Jaxon watched as Mallory and the man who he presumed was her lawyer emerged from the building. Through the telephoto lens of his camera, he could see the concerned crease of her brow. Both she and her counsel were deep in conversation as they headed toward the small, uncovered but convenient parking lot.

Jaxon allowed his interest to sway as he considered how well Mallory Jones would accentuate his life. It was time for him to settle down, and she fit perfectly into his plan. The sun reflected in her blonde hair, and he noticed how she walked with confidence and poise. He wondered how much of that confidence was exhibited behind closed doors or if she would submit quickly to a stronger, more efficient man. One day soon, he would find out. Because he had zoomed in to get a better view of her face, he hadn't paid attention to the gentleman walking toward them.

"What the *fuck* is he doing here?"

Jaxon's hand clenched a death grip on the camera as he watched Tyler McCormack wrap his arms around the woman of his desires. The life expectancy of his current informant just shortened drastically. How this tidbit of information eluded him was unacceptable in every aspect. He was a successful man in all endeavors because the standards he set were of high expectations. Yes, he had been informed that the ex-attorney was currently residing in the Austin area and working as a lowly detective. The fact that he was working on this case was completely and insufficiently omitted from any report he had been given.

The instant he recognized his former attorney, he had to almost physically restrain himself from reaching in his glove box, pulling out a pistol, and putting a bullet between his eyes. Killing the son-of-a-bitch based on principle would be satisfying. One thing he'd learned through his career, however, was that rash responses caused accidents. He calmed himself by choosing a more calculated response to the situation.

Jaxon had warned him after the trial that he would always be watching. To-date, to his knowledge, Mr. McCormack had no idea that they were sharing the same town again. If McCormack had let the prosecution know about the evidence he had pieced together during the last trial, Jaxon would most likely be residing behind bars in the state penitentiary waiting on an execution. And for that, he had decided to let the man live. Besides, he considered him a friend of sorts. But now, well … now he was going to have to reconsider his act of kindness. Tyler was getting involved with Jaxon's projects—and that was simply inexcusable.

It didn't take a genius to figure out that Mr. McCormack had negated his suspension from the department. He simply could not walk away from his curious nature. What Jaxon did find quite interesting was that he seemed to be on her side. Now, that just wouldn't do. They were standing entirely too close. He would need to be eliminated immediately.

Unless … yes, that's it! Since he enjoyed a high-quality game on occasion, he figured it would be interesting to see how this all played out. McCormack had obviously been a quality member of the justice system as a lawyer, so it would be interesting to see how well his friend performed his investigative skills. Yes, calculated responses were much more efficient than reaction. He would look forward to their reunion.

Satisfied with his decision, he repositioned his camera and continued to watch and take photos of his beautiful subject.

～ ～ ～

It had only taken seconds for the heat to begin pulling the sweat out of Alexander's pores. He reached for his keys, unlocked the door to his car, and tossed his briefcase in the passenger seat. He began to summarize the interview, but Tyler told him he had heard it all.

"They don't believe me, do they? They really think I had my husband killed." Her voice was shaky, and her bottom lip quivered. She stood with her arms folded, and her hands gripped her arms. It was an attempt to keep herself from unraveling.

"They're just following the leads in front of them. It doesn't mean they will unfold. Eventually, we will show them they are wrong." Tyler's attempt at consoling her was not working—on her or on himself.

Moving one hand up and rubbing her forehead, she responded with a tired sigh. "I suppose you're right. But divorce papers? I don't believe that. Damian would not have given up on our marriage. I was the one that was unhappier than he was. And I kept that deeply hidden. He seemed content with the way life was, and besides, he would never admit to failure. Especially not twice."

She took her hand away from her face, squared her shoulders, and confronted Tyler. "Wait a minute. Just last night, I told you everything about my marriage. What did you do?"

That hurt. How could she think he would betray her like that? Tyler was irritated that she questioned him, but he tamped down on his temper. Barely. His face turned to stone as he growled back at her. "Not a damn thing, Mallory. I've been with you the entire time—remember?"

Not wanting to argue with him further, she turned to her attorney. "Did he, Alex? Did he file the divorce papers?"

"Not to my knowledge, he didn't." Alexander continued to analyze the interview in his mind, knowing that the police were not done pursuing her. "We need to look into whether there might be more evidence of him planning a split. I will call the courts and see if he had officially filed anything, but if not, then we won't know anything more unless we get our hands on a copy. The cops seem pretty confident about what they found, but let's make sure. Tyler, see what you can find out about the woman who was at the restaurant. That's going to be our key lead at this time."

"I want to head over to Damian's office as well. See what trail he left there." Tyler reached into his pocket for his keys. "I can drop Mallory off at my place. She needs some down time."

Alexander gave Mallory a reassuring hug before settling into his car. He leaned his head out the window and looked up at Tyler. "I'll be in touch once I see what I can find out."

"Looks like you were right about this, but I don't think she's good for it." Tyler mumbled under his breath so Mallory couldn't hear him.

"Looks like it."

CHAPTER 9

~ ~ ~

Kendall opened her bedroom door in time to see him pulling off a pair of jeans and climbing into her bed. After noticing his new tattoo on his right forearm, a skull and crossbones of needles, she immediately became irritated. He probably wanted money to pay whomever was responsible for the artwork.

"What the hell are you doing here?"

"Now, come on. Is that the way to talk to your best guy?" He scratched this chest and rested his head on her pillows.

"How long have you been here? How did you get in?" Kendall tossed her keys on her dresser and kicked her shoes off. "We agreed not to see each other. That doesn't mean you can just show up whenever. Get the hell out."

Unruffled by her irritation, he rested his hands behind his head. "No."

The unexpected visit from her fuck-buddy, Nick Hanson, put a kink in her afternoon. He needed to leave; it wasn't a good idea for him to be there. She stepped into the room, tossed her keys on the dresser, and kicked off her spike-heeled shoes.

"Besides, I'm not into it. I just finished up with a new john. He was very generous today too. Paid double for a massage and my talent, but he stunk, and I want a shower."

Nick's expression grew hot. His hand clenched into a fist. "Then you're warmed up for me, so get over here, bitch. I don't care what you smell like."

She blew off his warning and turned to head to the shower. In an instant, he leaped off the bed, grabbed her arm, and held it high behind her back. He shoved her face against the wall and spoke in a low, growling voice so close to her ear that his whiskers scratched her cheek. "Don't forget that you belong to me. Or what I did for you. Got that?"

She could smell the whiskey on his breath. "Got it. Now back off, asshole. You're hurting my arm." She flinched, trying to loosen his grip on her. When she did, her chest became exposed. He grabbed her between her legs, hard. When she jerked back, she rubbed back against him.

"That's more like it." He took hold of her black-and-purple streaked hair and unbuttoned his jeans.

Later, the musky smell of sex permeated the room. Kendall eased off the bed while he snored beside her in an after-sex coma. She looked at the inside of her thighs. He had bruised her this time, and it ticked her off. She should shoot the bastard, or at least take out his knee with a baseball bat.

He was right though; he had done her a favor, and she still needed him.

Damn Nick for breaking the agreement and showing up here. She tiptoed her way to the shower, looking back to make sure she didn't wake him. His arms were painted with tattoos; it was strange to see the new design. His back had new scars, probably from another motorcycle wreck. He was menacing to look at and even more so to fuck.

As she stood under the spray of hot water, she knew he was trying to rile her by showing up. It unnerved her that she couldn't control him. Most men she could, especially with sex. But, Nick, well, there was something about him—he had a wild, almost crazy look. When he was in that frame of mind, there was no controlling him.

If she kept him with her, fucked him whenever and however, and kept a steady supply of his drugs and alcohol within his reach, he would be more manageable. Usually, when he was thinking he was getting his way, she could get him high and he would get right into it with her.

She turned in the shower and began to wash her hair. The cheap, temporary hair dye tinted the water as it flowed down her body.

Thoughts of the time she "lost" began to flood her memories. Whenever this happened, she would usually drink or get stoned. But for now, she let them reel through her mind, because it was important to stay focused. It's how she planned to win.

She was alive without a soul. What the hell did it matter anyway? She tried the so-called "normal life," and it just wasn't for her. As the counselors and psychiatrists had told her parents when she was a teenager, her mind was wired differently, and without constant and habitual therapy, she was not a candidate for rehabilitation. A conscience only messed with her focus in getting what she wanted, anyway. And she *always* got what she wanted.

She was sick to death of people taking what was hers. Sick. To. Death.

Her moment of truth came when she got the crap beat out of her one night. She had a session with a local banker. He liked his stuff kinky, always wanting her to dress up and shit. He was just getting into it when the baby woke up, started crying, and interrupted his blow job. The guy had gotten pissed and knocked her into a coffee table. He took her money and left her needing stitches in her left temple.

The blame was Damian's. It was his fault she was turning tricks. She wasn't good enough for him and he had tossed her and the kid out like trash. That was when she decided no man was going to leave her weak with no way out again. Not ever.

Starting with Mr. Kinky, she got revenge. She hid and waited for him to return home one night. She met him coming into his garage and put a gun to his head. She made him strip naked and then tied him up to a dining chair in the middle of the living room.

As he watched, she taped 8x10 photos of their sessions all over the walls. She knew keeping hidden videos of her sessions would come in handy one day.

He was now divorced.

Her plan to make Damian pay was much more involved. It was strategic and required patience and planning.

A few months later, she had run into Nick again at a nightclub on Sixth Street. He experienced a newfound appreciation for her body, which had been clad in fishnet stockings and a teeny leather skirt. With a few rounds of coke and whiskey in his system, her plan kicked into high gear.

After rough sex and a little weed, he was agreeing to do anything to help her out.

She was sure having Nick's assistance helped to put the ultimate revenge against Damian and Mallory in motion. Damian was now dead—what a shame. It didn't mean her plan had to end. There was still a way to get what she wanted. She just needed to shift her focus.

A grin spread across her face as she stood in the shower and let the water beat down on her sore muscles.

The day she waltzed into Mallory's office and tore it up was one of her favorite memories. She closed her eyes and let the water run over her as she replayed the scene in her head. She snickered at Mallory's reaction that day. She played into it well. As soon as that snotty little receptionist walked in, she immediately went into victim mode. She couldn't have planned it better herself if she had written them a script.

She returned to her apartment flying high after that performance. Once Damian got wind of the situation, he was putty in her hands. She was so grateful to Nick for helping her set it up that she did him twice that day.

Dammit, why did Nick break their promise? Showing up here went against their plan and threatened to ruin everything. That was dangerous. Anyone could have seen him enter the building.

He had been rougher than usual in bed too. When he got like that, it was smart to keep a distance. Kendall glanced down and examined the inside of her thighs. Those bruises were going to hurt for a while and be bad for business.

It was time to find out why he had shown up. She turned off the shower and squeezed the excess water from her hair. Wrapping a towel around her, she went to wake Nick up.

When she entered the room, the only thing she found was a picture of Emma tossed on the bed. Nick was gone.

CHAPTER 10

～ ～ ～

It had been a grueling day. Tyler had pulled out of the parking lot and turned into oncoming traffic before Mallory had overcome her shock of the day's revelations. He had taken side-glances at her several times and knew that she was debating on whether or not she could trust him. Why he felt that was so important, he couldn't really pinpoint.

Who was he kidding? He wanted her faith and trust more than any other person's.

"His appointments, everything, will be on his external hard drive." Mallory explained her sudden insight to Tyler as he navigated the vehicle to her house. "Damian habitually backed up his information every few days. He, of course, used the cloud-storage services daily, but he still liked to have a backup plan."

Taking it as a small victory that she had chosen to move past her initial mistrust, he pondered her statement and then responded. "Hopefully we will find a solid lead to go on. If there's any appointments with an attorney, we'll hopefully find that too."

Tyler's thumb tapped the steering wheel as he drove. Knowing she wasn't going to want to discuss it, he went ahead and added, "It's critical that we find out the identity of the woman at the restaurant before the police do."

Mallory turned and stared out the window. She had nothing to say in response.

Tyler immediately felt like a jerk for bringing it up. He placed his hand over hers. "Hey, I'm sorry. I know you feel blown away. We'll figure it out. Don't draw conclusions just yet."

They didn't exchange any further words until they reached her house. He didn't let go of her hand either.

When he pulled into the driveway, he turned the ignition off and waited for her to make the first move. She just stared at the house. From the outside, it looked completely normal. Without a word, she exited the vehicle and walked up the steps. Finally, she spoke. "This is our home. Our safe place. I feel anything but safe here right now."

"You're safe with me." He placed a comforting hand on her shoulder.

"He keeps his external drives in a locked file cabinet in the office, but he kept the keys in the den."

"We can go through the front hallway and avoid the living area."

She unlocked the front door and began to step inside. Tyler stopped her and went ahead of her. He guided her through a path to avoid tampering with evidence from the previous night. After retrieving the key, he took her down the short hallway to the office and watched while she unlocked the black file cabinet. She reached into the drawer and pulled out three external drives.

"The majority of his information will most likely be on one of these. Any current documents would still be on the cloud."

He took the small electronic devices from her and cradled them in one hand. "Let's take them back to my house and pull the contents up on my computer. I don't want us here longer than necessary."

"I don't have the passwords."

"Not a problem." Tyler had acquired many skills being an investigator.

"Let's take the court documents as well. We need to go through them and see if there is anything that can help figure out how and if Kendall is involved in this mess."

"Good thinking. I have copies of the main court proceedings, but not of everything."

Mallory checked her cell phone for the time. "I have to pack a bag for Emma. Their flight leaves in a few hours."

"You go pack her up, and I'll fix us a couple of sandwiches."

About fifteen minutes later, Mallory came into the kitchen. She had changed out of her business attire and into a pair of dark jeans, a bright-blue sleeveless shirt, and gray ankle boots. She had pulled her hair back into a ponytail. She looked more like the Mallory he knew. Tyler couldn't seem to take his eyes off her. Damn, she had the ability to tie him up in knots.

She sat down two medium-sized suitcases packed with Emma's things. Tyler's eyebrow rose, undoubtedly questioning how much luggage a seven-year-old could possibly need.

"Most of her toiletries are already with her, but I wanted to make sure she had the right clothes for the trip. With my father's profession, dressing the part for any event is crucial, even for a little girl. She needs everything from a swimsuit to a party dress."

Tyler considered himself a smart man, so he simply nodded in compliance and then shoved the rest of a sandwich in his mouth. He spoke around his chewing. "Sit and eat. It may not be much, but you need to keep your energy up."

Mallory didn't think she could chew a single bite. She was physically and mentally exhausted, but she did as instructed. When her mouth tasted the turkey and ham, her stomach growled in response. Clearly, her mind and her body disagreed.

"This is good. I didn't realize how hungry I was." She took another bite of her lunch and then stood to grab a paper towel. "So fill in the gaps. What have you been up to between now and the last time I saw you?"

Tyler leaned back against the kitchen counter and crossed his legs, debating how much of his past he wanted to share against how much he figured she already knew.

"Well, when I obtained my law degree at A&M, I had ambitions of becoming a famous lawyer with visions of defending famous criminals. My goal was to be rich."

"But you're a detective now." She continued to nibble on her sandwich but never took her eyes off him. She left the elephant standing in the room.

He shrugged and said, "I kept digging in my own cases and figuring out most of my clients were guilty." The truth simply would not come out of his mouth, so he hedged around it. Explaining how he became a ruthless attorney who essentially sold his soul for money wasn't something he wanted her to hear.

"So why not flip sides and prosecute?"

"The courtroom just wasn't a place I wanted to be anymore, to be honest. I was better on the front lines than debating a criminal's justice. I ended up here, back in Austin, a few years ago after Dad had open-heart surgery."

"I'm so sorry. Your father's okay now?"

"Oh, yeah. He's wreaking havoc around the house whenever he's not causing trouble on the golf course or fishing somewhere."

"What about women? Marriage?"

He looked at her without blinking. "Just disposable dates. No one serious ... since you."

Mallory immediately rolled her bottom lip between her teeth. "Oh."

Silence filled the room, both wondering what the other was thinking.

Tyler finally cleared his throat and decided it was time he sucked it up and said what he had needed to say for years. Once the truth did come out, he might not get the chance, so timing be damned. "I was stupid."

She creased her eyebrows. "About what?"

"When you told me you loved me that day. I was young and stupid. I'm sorry I hurt you."

Mallory sat still for a moment, not really knowing what to say or how to react. Her heart skipped a beat and her breath quickened. "Tyler—"

He held his hand up to stop her. He had to get this out. He had to know one way or another, because he didn't want to turn his back on fate. Not a second time. She was the one woman he could never forget, and *bam,* here she was in his life again. "I loved you right back. I was just too stupid to know what to do about it. When I left, nothing felt right. I came back for you."

The look on Mallory's face was of utter bewilderment. She had never known. He continued with his confession. "I searched you out at the university. When I found you, you were with some guy. Apparently, you had moved on. I figured my chance was blown."

"Some investigative instincts you had back then." She stood and walked to him and reached for his hand. "I wish you would have talked to me. Things might have been so different."

"Well, in my defense, I didn't become this smart until much later in life." They both chuckled. He was about to ask her another question, but he realized that the answer had the power to burn a hole in his gut. Timing was not on their side. His job was twofold. He had to find a murderer and prove Mallory innocent in the process, and he had to keep them alive while doing it.

She grinned up at him and softly said, "Well, things happen in life for a reason. I wouldn't change anything because then I wouldn't have been blessed with Emma." She dropped his hand and took a few steps back. "And speaking of her, let's get going. I want to be able to spend some time with her before the plane departs."

She quickly cleaned up their lunch while Tyler packed the luggage and banker boxes in the car. As they backed out of the driveway, she looked over at him and said, "I've thought about you too … several times over the years."

CHAPTER 11

~ ~ ~

It was payday. He climbed over the chain-link fence, dropped to the ground, and took off running. The humidity soaked his T-shirt, damn it. He gasped for air as he dodged between cars and pillars.

He took a quick glance around and concluded that no one was paying any attention to him. He just looked like another passenger running a little late. He slowed to a walk and proceeded into the airport.

Out of the corner of his eye, he spotted his partner sitting in his car waiting at the designated pickup location. The jerk had better not fall asleep.

The female member of this operation had alerted him that their target was sitting in a café near the security checkpoint. He had promised her a shitload of free drugs if they were successful today. If she did as she was told, he'd gladly supply her.

Since no one in life could completely be trusted, and there was always a chance of something going wrong, he had taken the precaution of creating a backup plan. That plan was sitting in short-term parking currently flirting with a trashy blonde. That asshole better stay alert too.

Good partners were so hard to find.

If all went as planned, phase two of his project will be put into motion. This time that bitch Mallory would pay big.

With that thought, he couldn't help but whistle while he walked, because he was going to impress the hell out of his boss.

～ ～ ～

"So, Pops, what are we going to do in Florida?" Emma had asked this question about three times in the last hour. She swung her feet beneath her as she sat at a café table between her grandparents.

Caleb took a sip of his coffee and smiled down at his grand-daughter. He tugged one of her long brown pigtails and grinned. He had been adamant that they arrive several hours early in order to avoid the traffic as well as to secure the boarding passes, check their luggage, and find an accommodating place for Emma to visit with her mother before they left.

He knew that this long of a wait in an airport would be difficult for a child. It was difficult for him, and he was an adult.

His wife, Joan, snapped a picture as their granddaughter took a huge bite of ice cream. He figured his granddaughter could be in the running as the most photographed child in America. Joan had snapped photos of her getting out of the car, walking into the airport, standing in the ticket line, picking out magazines. *This trip will be successfully documented*, he chuckled to himself. He figured she would send them to Mallory later to keep her connected and as reassurance that her daughter was fine.

"We are going to swim in the ocean, eat all the unhealthy food we want, stay up late, and visit with a lot of people." Her grandpa answered her once again with the patience of a saint.

"Gramma won't want to get in the ocean, and she won't let me eat that much unhealthy food. She says it's bad for my digestion. Isn't that right, Gramma?" Emma looked up at both of her grand-parents as she dug into a very large ice cream sundae. "Besides, if you eat unhealthy foods, it clogs your heart-tube thingies. Right, Gramma?"

"Well, within reason, sweet girl. This is a special vacation, so we may break the rules just a little." Joan took a napkin off the table and swiped a portion of chocolate syrup that hadn't quite reached her granddaughter's mouth. "Just like having ice cream before lunch is a very special treat."

Emma looked around again, her pigtails swinging and coming dangerously close to being dipped in chocolate syrup. "When's Mommy coming? I need to hug her before we get on that big plane."

With that question, Caleb checked his phone for the time again. He discreetly shared a look with his wife and noticeably shrugged a shoulder. They were starting to cut it close to when they would have to proceed through the security screening.

He patted her sticky hands and said, "She should be here soon. Why don't you run to the restroom so you can spend all your time with her before the plane takes off?"

"Okay, but I don't have to go," Emma frankly responded.

"Be quick, and don't forget to wash your hands," Joan reminded her.

They sat and watched their grandchild's long dark hair bounce as she scampered toward the ladies' room, which was less than a few feet away from their table.

~ ~ ~

The highway felt like one long parking lot. They crept along so slowly that Mallory figured she could walk to the airport faster. She was beginning to take the stress out on her nails.

"We're not going to miss them. Stop worrying," Tyler told her.

"I know. I just wanted to get there with enough time to sit and visit with her before they had to take off."

Almost as if a wish had been granted, the traffic began to move, and shortly thereafter, they were turning into the newly remodeled airport in South Austin.

Tyler navigated through the parking lot and chose the short-term parking ramp. After slowing long enough to grab a time-stamped parking receipt, he tossed it into in the console and drove through the gate.

Mallory quickly sent a text message informing her father they had finally arrived. By her calculations, she had lost twenty minutes of quality time with her daughter. She willed things to move faster.

They weaved in and out of the lanes through nearly the entire parking level until, finally, a spot opened up at the far end. Mallory quickly hopped out, opened the trunk, and grabbed Emma's luggage before Tyler even had the car turned off. She checked her phone again and groaned because they hadn't received a response from her father.

"Hold up there, speedy. Chivalry isn't dead just yet." He jogged to the back of the vehicle and reached to take the luggage from her hands. "Where did your father want us to meet him?"

"They're flying Southwest Airlines. With the heightened security, we can't get past the checkpoints, but there is a small café located just before that. We agreed to meet there. The flight doesn't depart for a few more hours, so as long as they pass through an hour before, we still have time."

"Let's hustle, then." He quickly tightened his grip on her hand as a nonverbal show of support. Their eyes met, and she nodded her head. He knew this was hard for her. Too much had happened in a very short time. Having to separate from her daughter had to be extremely difficult. It went against her basic motherly instincts. They should be curled up at home talking about all the insecure and scary feelings a child must be experiencing after losing a father.

As they reached the concourse level, Mallory heard a screeching voice. "Mommy!" It stopped her in her tracks.

Automatically, she looked in the direction of the voice. "Did you hear that?"

"Hear what?" Tyler looked around but kept walking.

There it was again. Mallory halted, almost yanking on Tyler's hand as he took a few extra steps. She looked around some more. This time the voice was more panicked. *"Mommy! Help!"*

She zeroed in on the voice, and her eyes almost didn't register what she saw on the other side of the road leading into the airport's main entrance. Time froze, and so did the blood flowing through her veins. Unmitigated fear crept up Mallory's spine.

A tall, long-haired man wearing jeans and big black boots had Emma and was rushing past a crowd of people. She could see Emma's shoe fall to the ground as she struggled to get free of him. He was losing his hold on her as he was trying to reach a parked brown sedan.

Mallory witnessed Emma open her mouth wide and take a huge bite out of his hand. He almost dropped her, so she began kicking and screaming with all of her might. He grabbed onto her upper arm and tried to regain his hold on her.

People were looking and staring, but they just kept on walking.

An airline employee who was accepting luggage for check-in took a double take and radioed for security.

"Stop him! Tyler!" She dropped her things and started running toward them as fast as she could through the pedestrian and vehicle obstacles. It seemed that no matter how fast her feet were moving, it wasn't fast enough to get to her and save her little girl.

In front of her, she could see that Tyler had taken off running must faster than she. He had veered in another direction, hopefully in an effort to block the man who had Emma. *Please, God, don't let him take her!* Mallory prayed with all her soul. *No. No. No!*

"Stop that man! Please! Somebody, stop him!" Mallory was almost hit by a passing car. She swerved out of the way and kept running. When she was a car-length away, the man suddenly yanked the back door of the car open. When he tried to place Emma in the vehicle, she began to kick frantically.

"No! Mommy!" Panic surged. Emma was reaching her hands out, shrieking at the top of her lungs for her mother.

The airport security guard approached the man and said something. The man who had snatched Emma immediately raised his leg and kicked the guard, sending him tumbling back on the concrete. Out of nowhere, Tyler leaped into the air and tackled the man, causing Emma to be flung out of his arms. He had to take a chance, even knowing Emma could be badly hurt.

The little girl had fallen to the ground, crying, as Mallory skidded to a halt and grabbed her daughter. "I've got you, honey. Mommy's here. I'm here." Mallory picked her up and scrambled back toward the security guard who had taken a nasty fall.

Too many things were happening at the same time. The driver of the car scraped another as he bolted from the parked spot and took off, leaving his partner behind. Another, elderly security officer was peppering Mallory with questions. Tyler was fighting the kidnapper. Emma was screaming and crying from panic and fear. Mallory was hysterically checking every inch of her daughter for injury.

Crowds of people began to either scatter or stop and stare at the sudden volley of punches and fighting, but no one tried to help Tyler. She witnessed the man throw a punch at Tyler's jaw. Tyler's head swung back. Though he tried to keep hold, his grip wasn't strong enough to detain him. The man fled, running at full speed.

Tyler jumped up, glanced at Mallory to verify that she had Emma, and then took off running after the kidnapper. His breath was pounding out of his chest, his lungs burned like fire, and his jaw hurt like hell. His mind was reeling in fury. He kept running. It seemed to take a thousand years to cover the distance to the perpetrator. As the man leaped onto the chain-link fence, Tyler dove to grab his calf and ankle, pulling him down. They both lost balance and tumbled down the embankment, half sliding, half throwing punches. The man kicked Tyler in the knee, causing him to utter a sharp cry, and he went down, hitting his head on a rock.

Stunned by the pain, he had lost his edge. The man pulled a knife from his belt and started to swing it back and forth. "I'll cut you, you son of a bitch." Then he laughed in a manic, crazy kind of way.

A second car screeched to a halt, and someone yelled for the man to get in. Tyler immediately registered that it wasn't the same car as earlier. Those insane eyes focused on Tyler once more. He was sure the man was going to take a stab at him. It was as if he had to force himself into the getaway car.

~ ~ ~

Word that there had been a kidnapping attempt spread quickly, and the airport was swarming with police officers. Bystanders were loitering, as if the entire scene was being played out for entertainment.

An officer had wrapped Emma in a blanket. Caleb and Joan had been ushered to them as quickly as possible. They sat with her as they waited for the paramedics to assess any injuries Emma may have received. Mallory refused to let her go, so they did so as she sat in her lap.

Her parents were distraught. "Mallory, it happened so suddenly. We were sitting right by the bathroom. We watched her go in and then she just didn't come out. When I went in to check, she was gone. She wasn't in there for more than a few minutes. We watched the door the entire time!" Joan explained over sobs and tears flowing down her face.

"It's just a miracle that we saw them. We have her, and that's the most important thing." She was furious, scared, and as freaked out as she had ever been in her life.

A thousand questions were demanding answers. There was no time for Tyler to dwell on the pain and defeat of losing the culprit. Almost immediately, two officers had reached him right after the perp disappeared via the second vehicle and offered assistance. One officer stayed with him while the other sped away, trying to detain the vehicle.

Tyler needed to assess his physical condition, and he wanted Emma to be checked out in a hospital. More importantly, he felt certain they needed to get away from here and figure out what the hell was happening. One murder, one attempted murder, and one attempted kidnapping. If they didn't get out soon, the assholes that were behind this might return and follow them, and he didn't want them to be sitting ducks.

When the police officers started asking questions, Tyler gave them the basic details and then issued a command of his own. "I want you to contact Detectives Johnson and Clark at the Austin PD. They are familiar with the case. They have my number."

He was going to give them a message for the chief as well, but he figured there'd be no way to avoid that meeting anymore if he did. There would be a right time to man up and face it.

Right now, there was something about this entire thing that didn't sit well with him. He just hadn't figured it out yet. He couldn't think clearly. The anger that he felt that someone would try to take such a sweet, vulnerable child came close to making him lose it. He had approached life emotionlessly, and he allowed no room for error. Right now, at this moment, he was ruled by emotions that he was not accustomed to.

Reaching across, he took Emma out of Mallory's resistant arms and handed her to Caleb. Not wanting to distress the women any further, Tyler gave him a look that he hoped he understood. Quietly, but firmly, he stated, "Let's go. I want out of here. Now."

Without hesitation, Caleb and Tyler began to usher Mallory and her mother to the car.

CHAPTER 12

～ ～ ～

Tension hung in the vehicle as Tyler, lost in thought, navigated through the airport terminal and headed toward the safety of his home. He was missing something that obviously was the key to this entire mess. Being cautious about anyone possibly tailing them, he took side roads and doubled back on the interstate before feeling secure enough to arrive at his residence. There was no way to know for sure if the perpetrators knew his identity, so it was better to be safe than sorry.

Whoever was behind this had upped the ante with the kidnapping. Tyler no longer held any niggling of doubt of Mallory's innocence. Now it was just another matter of convincing the police and pointing them in the right direction.

Looking in his rearview mirror, he glanced at Emma. What a brave little girl. Had the kidnappers succeeded today, things could have been a nightmare. He didn't want to think about what would have happened had they shown up seconds before, or even a split second later. The fact that Emma had seen her mother had been a chance in a million. Tyler was somewhat baffled that the kidnappers had not drugged the girl.

His head pounded and his leg was sore. He reached up and tenderly felt his swollen jaw. His adrenaline was in overdrive. Damn, he wanted his hands on that guy again. He wouldn't walk away next time.

Whoever the hell he was.

His description was sketchy at best, but he did remember the basics. The guy was about six feet tall with long, stringy dark hair. Both his forearms were tatted up. There was no way for him to zero in on what they were, but the one on his right forearm was relatively new. He remembered it being the shape of a skull with needles that made the crossbones. And the asshole could throw a damn punch.

The tat could be a lead. If the guy had it done in a shop, there were ample tattoo joints in the Austin area. It would take time to check them all out. If it was done privately, it wouldn't be easy to track.

The guy had had help today. The list of leads was growing, but it was just as muddled as before. The only sure suspect he had was Kendall, and he still had no way of connecting her to the kidnapping or the murder. Yet.

There was also the driver. Male. Who was he? None of them got a good look at the guy. Cameras at the airport might be helpful. Once the police scanned and interviewed the bystanders, maybe someone would get a lead on him.

Emma, bless her brave little heart, was a huge help. She informed the police that it was a woman in the restroom that had taken her. The only details of her description were that she was shorter than her mother and her hair was white-blonde. The woman had held a knife and had scared Emma by saying if she uttered a sound, she would gut her like a fish. Tyler cringed at that thought. He was going to make sure Emma received counseling. She would need help dealing with the aftermath and fear of what she had endured. A lot had happened to this little girl.

When asked by the police what door they went out, the grandparents had a look of utter shock. There was a second entrance to the ladies' room that neither grandparent had realized. That's when Joan had broken down in tears. There was no doubt that fact would haunt them both. He held Mallory in high regard that she refrained from lashing out at her parents over the careless error.

Emma said that after they had left the restroom, the woman had handed her off to the man that tried to escape with her. He had whispered in her ear that if she tried to get away, tried to scream, that he would pull out a gun and shoot everyone. Then he would hunt her mommy down and kill her too. Just like Daddy.

Just like Daddy. Those three words were the best lead he had. Whoever the kidnappers were, they knew about Damian's murder—or were involved in it.

He glanced back at the little girl again and made a silent vow to himself. If anyone harmed a hair on that child's head again, he would kill him.

The most important question that circled in his mind, though, was how in the hell had anyone known the plans for Emma to even be at the airport?

A half hour later, they arrived safely at home. He hit the remote and closed the garage door before allowing anyone to exit the vehicle. As soon as the luggage was unloaded, Tyler instructed them that he was going to engage the security alarms. He wanted Emma to feel safe; besides, he had fears of his own. He just didn't feel the need to share those.

It took less than a minute for Emma and Sami to become good friends. Sami sniffed and licked her hand in a welcoming gesture. Almost instantly, Emma stroked Sami's back over and over. Their bond was almost immediate.

"Hey, Emma. Why don't you walk with me and let me show you my security gadgets? It's pretty cool."

Emma didn't say a word, but she placed her tiny hand in his and followed him to his office. Sami loyally trotted behind them.

He pointed at the keypad and said, "When I punch in these numbers, it turns on a security system that protects not only the entire house but the property as well. See?" He turned and pointed to two computer screens that sat on a table behind his desk that immediately hummed to life. Pictures of the property and views of the house appeared on the screens.

She nodded her head but didn't let go of his hand. She hadn't said a word to him either. Her eyes were still swollen, but now they appeared curious and intrigued as she took in the unfamiliar surroundings.

"Come here; I want to show you something else." He walked over to the window and pulled open the blinds. He pointed to a small wire that was attached to the windowsill and frame. He bent down to talk to her at eye level. "Those wires are hooked up to all the downstairs windows. That way, I'm alerted even if someone tries to come in through the window. But guess what? I'll know before they even get here because my property line is secured with cameras and wires. If anyone trips them, I get an alert before they ever reach the house. Then I can punch buttons that immediately send a signal to the police station."

"Why do you have all that? Are you afraid too?" She had finally found her voice. He was glad to see her start talking, but he wasn't about to answer her question truthfully—that he hadn't felt safe since the day he'd walked out of the courtroom in West Texas.

"Well, I work with the police. Sometimes I catch bad guys, and I like to know that my home is safe." Basic truth, nothing more, nothing less. He just hoped it was enough.

"We have a security alarm too, but Mommy forgets to set it. Other times, she sets it off and forgets and goes outside. It makes Daddy irritated sometimes. It's not as good as yours, though. My daddy is in heaven now."

Tyler's heart couldn't help but break just a little. "Well, I'll remind your mommy not to go outside unless I turn it off."

"But don't you have to be in this room all the time, watching?"

Smart girl, he thought. "Not anymore. It was like that in the past, but technology has gotten better." He pulled his cell phone off its holster clip. "When I want it to, the alerts go right to my phone." He navigated through his cell phone and pulled up the application to show her.

"What if your phone is off?" She was a hard sell. Impressive little girl. "Mommy sometimes doesn't hear her phone. That frustrates Daddy a lot too."

"Because of my job, I never turn my phone off. It's with me all day and all night."

He looked up to see Mallory leaning against the doorframe to his office. "Emma and I were just checking out the security system."

She walked into the room and placed her hands on her child's shoulders. "I can't keep myself from touching her." Emma leaned back into the safety of her mother. Mallory waited for him to look up and make eye contact with her. "I owe you. You saved her life."

The words she wanted to say were blocked as tears threatened to spill over.

He stood and placed his hands at the base of her neck and pulled her into an embrace. "Shh ... she's right here, safe with you."

Emma looked up at both of them and said, "I'm okay, Mommy. Don't cry." Then she hugged her mother's leg tight. "Mr. Tyler has top safe stuff."

Tyler couldn't help but chuckle at her assessment. He thought to himself that Mallory may not have given birth to the child, but she was definitely her daughter. She had the same inner strength and the ability to overcome her own fears and console her mother. It was motivation for him to not fail either of them.

Wiping tears from her eyes, Mallory took a step back and inhaled a deep breath. "Well, let's go run a big bubble bath and clean you up, baby."

Tyler and Mallory held each other's gaze for a few moments. Then Mallory turned and exited the room with her child.

As he watched them leave, Sami stood and followed. Tyler shook his head and couldn't blame his dog for abandoning him for two pretty females.

~ ~ ~

"You've made the news," Alexander said.

Tyler leaned back against his kitchen chair, paused, and closed his eyes. He pinched the bridge of his nose with his finger and thumb in frustration. Damn news, they would sensationalize the story, and if any photos or video of them appeared on television, it could lead the kidnappers to his residence. Not to mention, they would link him to past news clips. Damn.

Alexander had arrived shortly after Tyler contacted him about the incident at the airport. He had already heard about it through the police grapevine and had attempted to gather facts of his own.

He appreciated Alex stepping up, but he appreciated more that he was sober with a clear mind. Too many times, he had "needed" his partner, only to be faced with the fact that he was drinking or doing some recreational drug that impaired his ability to perform.

Everyone had gathered around the kitchen table. Joan had offered to put a meal together, and he gratefully gave her reign. She had managed to find her way around and made a meal of scrambled eggs, cheese, and peppers, potato wedges, and biscuits. Tyler was impressed that he had the rations to feed that many people. He didn't even know he had the paper plates.

Being alone the majority of his days, especially since living in Austin, it felt odd having several people around his table. He realized, too, that he liked it.

They ate and spoke in hushed tones in an effort not to wake Emma, who had fallen asleep on the couch in the living room. Sami kept guard on the floor next to her.

Mallory was not about to move her to a bedroom until she could retire with her. She was still shaken and couldn't be out of the same room with her. A plate of food sat waiting for when the innocent child woke.

"Only basic details were reported today. Video was only of a crowd of people and police. The clip didn't include anything that truly identified anyone." Alex took a sip of coffee. "It won't take long for names and cell phone video to begin to leak, and then Internet news and bloggers will pick it up. The press is more like a Hollywood scene these days. They'll keep coming until they get what they want."

"Did you get anything from the detectives?"

"No."

The vibration of his cell phone made his plate rattle. He swiped the screen to turn off the notification without even looking at it. There were three missed calls from the chief of police.

"You're going to have to respond sooner or later," Alexander said.

"I know."

"Respond to who?" Mallory asked. Impatiently, she reacted to the exchange. She was an intelligent woman, and she was growing weary of the men keeping her out of the loop.

"The chief," Alexander offered without hesitation.

"Do you need to talk to him? What you're doing for me ... I don't want it to cost you your job." Her look of concern made Tyler want to put his arms around her and reassure her that there was no job more important than her.

"Not now." Tyler's response didn't put Mallory at ease, but the look he gave Alexander was a warning to let it drop. The chief was going to be asking for his resignation or firing him. Either way, it could wait.

Picking up his fork, he continued to eat. In an effort to steer the conversation back to more pressing matters, Tyler stated, "It's time for a new strategy. We are in the position that we keep responding to situations. It's time to get out in front of things and be more prepared. First off, it's time for me and Kendall to have a chat. I can read people pretty well; if she's behind this or has any information, I'll know."

Mallory's entire body sagged with dread. She stated with concern, "Be careful. If she feels threatened in anyway, she could turn violent."

Tyler nodded; he figured he'd be an ass if he tried to remind her that talking to bad people was something he held years of experience with.

Caleb spoke up in a gruff voice. "Of course Kendall is behind this. She's the only person out there that would want to harm our granddaughter. The police need to haul her butt to jail, and then, you'll see, no more trouble."

"It was two men and one woman that tried to take Emma today, Caleb. If the female kidnapper had been Kendall, Emma would have recognized her." It was Joan who spoke this time.

"It's time we get the paper chase started with the case files that Tyler and Mallory brought over. If we're lucky, we will find a lead, a photo, or something that points to whoever may be helping her," Alexander said as he stood and carried his coffee cup and silverware to the sink and tossed his plate in the trash. He turned to Joan. "Thank you. That was delicious."

Mallory stood as well, "I'll help you. Mom, will you sit with Emma? I don't want her to wake up alone."

"Of course I will." She hugged her daughter, moved to the recliner, reached for a magazine, and settled in to watch over her granddaughter.

"I'll come with you. With three sets of eyes, this paper hunt is bound to move quicker," Caleb offered as he cleared his dishes.

The men moved to the office. Mallory hung back and followed Tyler to the garage.

As irritated as she was at him for intruding on her husband's funeral proceedings, she was now just as grateful that he was there to save her daughter today. How could she ever thank him? Neither of them were the same people they had been when they were in school. It was happenstance that had put them in each other's lives again. Even after all he had done for her in the past few days, she still was afraid to fully trust him. She could not afford to trust anyone. She hadn't even trusted her husband with the truth. Had someone figured her out? Was someone out there holding a smoking gun on her? If so, then she was putting lives at stake by keeping the truth hidden. She needed Tyler to help keep her daughter safe. Would he turn on her and walk away if he knew what she had done?

She silently watched him as he checked his pistol and his cell phone battery and began to input Kendall's last known address into his GPS. Estimated travel time was twenty-five minutes with good traffic. Like everyone, his demeanor had changed. He was more focused. More ruthless. He could and would protect them. She owed him the truth. He was putting his life on the line. Something in her heart shifted. An emotion she hadn't felt in a very long time spread through her, but the guilt of what she had done seemed to suffocate it.

"This whole thing is my fault." Mallory leaned against the front fender of his SUV with her arms folded into her waist and stared to the ground.

His hands hesitated on the screen of his GPS, and he looked up at her. "Not unless there's something you're not telling me. You didn't plan your husband's murder. That much I know for sure. You didn't shoot up your house. And you most certainly aren't responsible for the bastards nearly taking your child."

He could tell that she was waging one hell of a debate over how much she was ready to share with him. He thought she was going to turn and go back into the house.

When she looked at him this time, tears shimmered in her electric-blue eyes, making them even more magnetic. Her voice cracked as she said in a querying tone, "Why is this happening, then?" She pleaded silently, *Please don't let this be my fault.*

"You can't do this to yourself."

He exited from the seat and closed the small distance between them. He reached for her and rubbed both his hands up and down her arms. He noticed her bruises had taken on different colors. He ground his teeth together because it still pissed him off that he had hurt her, though unintentionally, and he knew damn well things could have been worse. She was lucky nothing was broken and even luckier to be alive.

"Tyler?"

"Yeah?" he prompted.

Slowly, Mallory leaned her forehead against his chest and mumbled, "Don't get dead."

He threw his head back and laughed. "I'll do my best." Then he couldn't help it. He pushed her chin up to him and kissed her. It was a simple, soft kiss. Neither of them moved. When he leaned back, the flash of heat in her eyes undid him.

Never in his life did he think he would be kissing Mallory Tucker again. She stood in front of him. His second chance had finally come. He knew the absolutely very last thing he should do was kiss her again, because he had to be careful. Take things slow. The last thing he wanted to do was push her away.

But, damn, it felt right.

Her face had flushed with shades of pink. Then her hands were on his face, pulling his mouth back to hers. Her lips opened for him; her tongue frantically sought after his. She was a contradiction. She tasted sweet and her lips were so soft, while her fingers threaded up through his hair and formed tight fists that tugged his hair by the roots.

He angled her head and deepened the kiss, moving his hands to the small of her back as he pulled her closer to him. The feel of her body, smaller and softer than him—have mercy. It was like his body suddenly remembered how well hers matched his.

She continued to kiss him, her body pressing into his. Then a soft moan escaped her. It was too much. It was consuming him. Damn, it had to be the most selfish moment of his life, because at that second, nothing else in the world was even a blip on his radar.

A siren was sounding inside his head, though. It took all his inner strength to heed that warning. Yes, this would happen, but now was not the time. He had to stop. With every fiber of his be-ing, he pulled back. His heart was pounding out of his chest. He wanted her, and from the look on her face, he could take her right there against the garage wall. Which was exactly what he wanted to do—and exactly what he shouldn't do.

He knew he needed say something. It was like he had lost the ability to speak. He just hoped she could hear everything he wasn't saying. He held her for another moment, exhaled a slow, deep breath, and then dropped his hands and stepped away.

"Do us both a favor and go back inside." His voice was gruff and sounded angry. He actually felt everything but that.

She opened her mouth to speak but then changed her mind. She took a step up to the garage door and placed her hand on the knob. When the engine roared to life, she looked back at him one more time. Their eyes met as Tyler backed out of the garage. She smiled at him and then went inside and locked the door.

CHAPTER 13

～ ～ ～

"**D**ammit!" He pounded his fist on the dashboard and immediately regretted it. "Son of a bitch!"

He tried his cell phone, but it had been crushed in the melee. He was fuming with rage. How in the hell did they not take into account that the mother hadn't shown up yet? He was still breathing hard. His muscles were vibrating with the urge to pound something, or someone, to a bloody pulp.

"I had that brat in my hands." He inspected the bite marks on his hand. "The little shit nearly drew blood when she bit me."

"It ain't that bad," the driver replied. "You need to focus on finding a car so we can ditch this one. It won't be long before every cop in the damn city is looking for this one."

"Well, if that bitch hadn't shown up with her new man, we'd be hightailing it out of town with that kid."

"I still get paid. My job was to drive the getaway car. I drove. I got you away. I want my money."

"Whatever." He leaned his head back against the headrest. He was so pissed. His plan to snatch the kid had gone to hell. Now he had to come up with plan B. It was now or never. The chance of a big payoff wouldn't last forever.

He realized they were close to a small, cheap, used-car lot. He told the driver to turn in and lose the car in the back of the lot. As they left, his buddy lifted a license plate off one of the used cars. They jogged a few blocks back and found an unlocked old

Mustang. It took seconds to switch the plates. Perfect—at least something went right today.

"Where to?" his accomplice asked.

"Nowhere." He pulled the trigger and shot the guy right in the heart.

Nick jumped back on the interstate and headed south.

～ ～ ～

"Nice spot you got there," Detective Johnson remarked as he opened the passenger-side door.

"It's cozy." Tyler chugged the rest of his coffee, which had lost its heat hours ago, and tossed the thermos in the backseat. He glanced at his watch and realized he had been on stakeout for almost six hours. It was early morning, and hunger and sleepiness were start-ing to settle in. Investigative work was not all it was cracked up to be. Long hours sitting and watching, and just as many long hours following paper trails.

When the detective closed the door, the smell of greasy burg-ers and fries filled the vehicle. Stakeouts were a common chore for private investigators, but they were rarely entertaining, so he welcomed the company, although he was cautious of his intent.

As soon as Johnson handed him a burger, he bit off a huge por-tion and reached in the bag for a napkin. Both men ate in silence and watched the apartment complex. They ate the entire meal within minutes and dropped their wrappers into one of the bags.

Slurping on the remains of his soda, Tyler let out a loud burp. His eyes never left the building across the street.

"Pretty good burgers." Johnson finally broke the silence.

"Hit the spot. Thanks."

"You've had better?"

"Not recently, but the joint on Sixth Street has the best burger in town."

"That's a matter of opinion."

"Is that why you drove out here? To discuss burger joints?" He knew he was being rude. He had been told many times in his life that he lacked manners and patience. There was no reason for him to start changing now. He didn't have time for pleasantries anyway.

As Johnson stared out the front window, he assessed that the security lights around the apartment were inadequate, to say the least. The glow of the moon gave off enough light to make out the images of men and women occasionally coming and going from the three-story shack that looked like it would succumb to the slightest storm. It was shelter. That's about all it was. There was nothing fancy to describe.

"Chief's been looking for you."

"Yep."

"It'd be in your best interest to call him."

"Again, opinion, as well as none of your damn business."

"Hey, don't shoot the messenger."

"Message received; you can go. Thanks for the burger."

Johnson didn't take offense to Tyler's demeanor, which actually impressed him. Instead, his colleague chose to continue the conversation. "After today's kidnapping attempt, I started to look at the case from a different angle. I checked the docket and pending divorce cases. I found nothing regarding a recently filed divorce from Damian. I couldn't confirm the attorney of record either. The name was bogus."

"And?"

"I smell a hell of a setup."

"No shit."

Minutes passed as they sat and watched the building.

"Problem is, the setup could be coming from Ms. Jones herself. I can't discredit that as a possible lead."

A growl escaped Tyler before he could pull it back. An urge to punch the guy overcame him. He knew cops had to follow all leads, but there was no way he could defend Mallory just by pleading his gut instinct. He kept quiet and controlled.

"There's something else."

In lieu of answering, he removed his eyes from the apartment and looked at the detective.

"Jaxon left West Texas."

"Good riddance." Tyler retrained his eyes on the building.

"Word on the beat is that he's relocated and is venturing into other, more lucrative business ventures."

"They had their chance to put his ass in jail." Tyler gripped the hand of his steering wheel and squeezed as the habitual anger that rose inside him whenever he thought of the inefficiency of the justice system. Knowing his own life was saved because the man walked, he sometimes thought it would have been worth dying if the vicious criminal was rotting in a cell.

"They didn't know as much as you did." That comment took Tyler by surprise.

Johnson continued. "Come on, dammit. I didn't make detective based on my good looks. I'm an intelligent, good-looking black man. You seem to be a stand-up guy. The system is flawed. They couldn't get him for that rape or the other crimes he obviously committed. It's clear the burden of proof had not been achieved by the prosecution. You did your job well. Everyone knew it. Had you given up that information, you would have been disbarred, at the minimum, and dead, if Jaxon had his way. Not to mention the mistrial."

Not wanting to dwell too much on his humbleness by Johnson's admission, he said, "He killed that girl. He'll do it again. Whatever his new ventures are, he will always come back to what he does best. Torture. Rape. Killing." Tyler gritted his teeth and leered at nothing in particular. "The worst of it is, he'll mess up just enough to get indicted again and then it will be the same circus, different day. Question is, how many bodies will accumulate before he slips? It doesn't matter what DA's office he'll be up against. No one will ever be able to convict him. To stop him, you'll have to kill him."

"It's not Jaxon that haunts you." Tyler shot the man a piercing glare as soon as the words were said, but the man unrepentantly didn't let up. "It's the fact that you figured it out and your hands were tied."

"Shut up."

"You prove every day that you are good at this job. You're earning your way here."

"It's not enough. Everyone in this city—or anywhere, for that matter—blames me for his acquittal."

"You're your own worst enemy. You blame yourself more than anyone else does."

"Don't let the door hit you on your way out."

Tyler retrieved his camera and zoom lens out of the console between the front seats. He positioned himself behind the camera and zoomed in on the female that was walking toward the front door of the complex. Noting that it was not Kendall, he placed the camera on the dashboard.

"Officially, I'm informing you to be on the lookout for any information indicating that Jaxon is in the area." Then, followed by a heavy sigh, the detective added, "In regards to Mallory Jones, we are looking to arrest her—and soon."

Johnson stepped out of the vehicle, shut the door, and then leaned into the window. "Call the damn chief."

When Tyler finally spotted Kendall entering the apartment a few hours later, the sun was low in the morning sky, but the heat was already rising off the pavement.

The building was old and cheap. He circled to the back of the building to check out the exits. Other than a fire escape, there were no back exits. There weren't many tenants populating the complex. The parking garage was scarce; many probably hadn't made it back because of shift work or partying. He heard a baby crying from a second-story apartment window. Through another, he heard a couple arguing.

When he entered, he noticed the lobby was small and smelled musty. The green paint was old and chipping in the corners. Water stains spotted the ceiling. The fake plants that stood in the corners were coated with dust. He crossed over to the mailboxes and double-checked to make sure his suspect still resided in the building. "Yes. K. Jenkins in 3C."

He turned to assess the two elevators. One was in transit, and the other was parked with the door open. He stepped in and hit the button for the third floor. When the door closed, he immediately regretted it. The stench in the boxcar reminded him of spoiled fish. While the elevator rose, he checked his pistol and clicked off the safety.

Kendall Jenkins's apartment was at the center of the hallway. Tyler positioned himself to the side of the door. He rapped three quick times on the door and called out her name.

A woman's voice called out, "Go away! I'm not expecting anything from anyone."

"I got your address from a friend. Said you were the best massage in town. I pay better than him too. Come on; it's been a long night." Tyler silently begged for her to open the door.

"What friend?" Money always spiked curiosity for someone like her. He could hear it in her voice.

"Just a friend. He didn't want me to give his name. Wife and all. But, hey, if you don't want to make some quick hundreds, so be it. I got a backup girl who likes my dollars just fine."

She took the bait and immediately jerked the door open. She stood with her foot braced against the door and stared out at the man who was requesting her services but also holding an official-looking badge at eye level.

"Detective Tyler McCormack, Austin Police Department. Nice and easy now, Kendall. You have two seconds to open the door and let me in, or this little visit turns very unpleasant."

"What the hell?" She quickly tried to shut the door, but Tyler blocked her from being successful. "Who the fuck are you? What do you want?"

"I advise you to step back and open the door."

She hesitantly stepped back and Tyler entered the apartment. Kendall immediately copped an attitude. "Is this how you operate, Mr. APD?"

Her hair was black with pink streaks down both sides framing her face. Her eyes were painted up with thick black eyeliner and a dark shade of lipstick. From the look of her outfit, massaging clients was not the only service she offered. She wore a tight, pink shirt that was covered in black lace, and it showed more chest than it covered. Her skirt was so short that Tyler didn't think it would leave anything up to the imagination if she bent over. Fishnet stockings covered her legs, and she wore platform heels. She looked down right skanky.

Tyler said, "Tell me what I want to know, and I'll consider changing my approach." He swept the room with his eyes as he kept his peripheral vision trained on her. "Let's check the rest of the place and make sure we're alone."

Tyler kept Kendall in front of him as he followed her into the bedroom and tiny bathroom. Once he was satisfied that no one else was present, he ordered her back into the living room. She swayed her hips and walked as seductively as she could, glancing at him over her shoulder.

"Now, let's have a little chat."

"Well, you obviously aren't here for a massage, so there's nothing to chat about," she replied.

As Tyler shoved her down into a kitchen chair, the legs scraped the dirty tile floor. He grabbed her wrists and had them in a zip tie before she could move. Then he yanked the back of her hair and squeezed. The more he thought about what this woman had done to Mallory, the more he had to check his temper. The fury in his mouth tasted like acid. The desire to hit this woman was almost too much to resist. Besides, what he was looking at could make the term *woman* debatable.

He bent down and got right in her face. "I want your attention right here, right now. Look at my face, Ms. Jenkins. That's right. Look at me. I want you to tell me, right now, who you hired to murder Damian Jones and kidnap Emma. Who is it, and where do I find them? Your murder plot was a success, but your little kidnapping plan was foiled today. Start talking. Now."

"What? Whoa … back up. What kidnapping?" She creased her brow and shook her head. "I don't know the first thing about that. And I know nothing about Damian getting killed. Where's Emma? Is she okay?"

"It's not like you to care about either one, now, is it?" Tyler didn't release her hair, but he grabbed the zip tie and pulled up, making her arms stretch unnaturally—an efficient reminder of how serious he was. "Let's get something straight. You don't fool me. I know there's not an ounce of regret or remorse flowing through that poison blood of yours. Whatever you touch gets destroyed one way or another. I won't let you hurt Mallory or Emma ever again. I'm getting impatient. Talk."

"I don't know what the hell you are talking about." She lifted her chin belligerently.

"Give it a rest, Kendall. I could fill up an entire computer's memory with your history of crappy dealing and illegal ploys against the Joneses alone. Don't try the I'm-innocent-and-life-is-hard trick. You can either tell me what I want to know, and when this goes down, I can get you a lighter sentence—or you can make it harder on yourself, and I will make sure the book is thrown at you so hard that you end up in the worst prison cell there is in the state of Texas."

She was breathing hard and her mind was reeling. He had her attention now. By the look in her eyes, she didn't like the fact that she was on the losing end of this heart-to-heart.

"I'm waiting. Tick tock."

"You can't do this. There are rules cops have to follow. I'll have your job for this. I know people." Her nostrils flared as she tried to take in breaths.

"Trust me. Losing my job is the least of my worries, but here's where you're going to lose if you try. There are no witnesses this time. And you don't like to lose, do you, Kendall?" Her eyes were throwing daggers at him now. "See, it's your word against mine. So don't waste your time trying to play me. I can see right through you. So talk."

"I have nothing to say without a lawyer." She snapped her mouth shut and looked straight ahead.

"Most of the time, a lawyer is a good thing to have, but in your case—well, a lawyer isn't going to help you this time. You're in too deep. He'd just advise you to cooperate and tell the truth, since we all know you're guilty. That little show at Mallory's office? A setup. I'm pretty sure it was you that was last seen with Damian in a restaurant. Another setup. You've been a bad girl, plotting to destroy. Guess what? You're going to lose. You've not been as slick as you think. Today, you screwed up. I will prove it, Kendall, so save us both some time."

"I don't know anything. I—" Tyler yanked her head back so far that the chair tipped back on two legs and made a screeching sound on the floor. She froze, her chest heaving with each breath, her eyes wide with a mix of anger and fear. "Asshole! You don't scare me."

"You've never shown one ounce of remorse for any of the miserable crap you have put Damian and Mallory through. You and I both know you are a lousy mother who uses her kid as a pawn. You make me sick. But know this; hear this: if you ever lay one hand on that child again, or come to cause her harm or anguish in any way, I will use every bit of my resources, and I will hunt you down. You will spend the rest of your pathetic life looking over your shoulder and wondering."

Kendall shook her head back and forth, back and forth, but she said nothing.

"One last chance, Kendall. Think about your future. A jail cell is a pretty lonely place. You. Will. Lose," Tyler said in a voice that was quiet and scary.

Still, she said nothing.

"Well, if you do find the mood to share, here's my card. Call it. It might save your life." Tyler flipped the card onto her lap, and as quickly as he had tied her up, he reached in his pocket, pulled out a switchblade, and freed her hands. He took the cut zip tie and left her sitting there.

Within seconds of his exit, Kendall picked up the cell phone with shaking hands and hit the contact on her speed dial. It went directly to voice mail.

"What in the hell have you done?" she said and tossed the phone onto the kitchen table. She sat there with her head bent and her shaking hands threaded into her hair.

Her head was reeling. What had just happened here? How in the hell had things gotten so out of control? She was on the verge of collapsing. She didn't need this shit. It wasn't too late. She had to get a hold of Nick. Where the hell was he?

"Christ." With a death grip on the white business card, she covered her face with her hands and fought the urge to throw up.

～ ～ ～

Later that morning, Detective Johnson leaned over and adjusted the files that were spread out on his desk. He glanced at his partner and said, "This case is getting weirder by the day. Murder. Attempted murder. Kidnapping. What's the motive of the day?"

"I still think we know who killed Damian: his wife. She may not have pulled the trigger, but she set it in motion." Detective Clark eased back into his chair and stretched. "She's smart enough to make it appear she's the victim. Don't rule her out."

"Yeah, it's a good theory, but there's absolutely nothing connecting her to anyone. It's all circumstantial evidence. The only solid evidence is an unidentified shooter in a black Escalade with no known plates. Hell, we don't even know for sure if the kidnapping is connected. I can't shake the idea that we need to look closer at the ex-wife, Kendall. We haven't checked alibis anywhere because of the security tape from the gas station and facts of the shooting. She had motive to kidnap the kid. Think about it; she went from living off a successful businessman to back to living shady. I doubt she has the financial resources to hire anyone to do anything, much less a murder-for-hire. What we can't ignore is her chronic history with arrests and courtroom theatrics. Maybe she met someone along the way that would help her with this." Detective Johnson tapped his fingers on the desktop.

For a time, only the sounds of the air conditioner from the aged vents hummed in the room. Johnson picked up the remote control and pointed it toward the flat screen that held an image of their prime suspect. He clicked the Play button and studied the images as they flowed across the screen.

As he scrutinized Mallory's movements, he remarked, "The one thing that concerns me is that she's not the typical nervous person being questioned about a murder. Look at her; she didn't sweat or show any physical signs of apprehension. Not once did she fidget, cross and uncross her legs, or shift in position. She just sat there, poised and in control. Eyes straight ahead and steady. Not the composure of a guilty woman who just buried her husband."

As they watched the playback of the interview, Detective Clark commented, "She has a definite attitude beneath all that composure."

"Yeah, and don't forget that control is an illusion. She may just have the wits to manage nerves better than the average person."

Both detectives studied the screen and pondered their assessments. Finally, Johnson said, "Let's keep our options open for now. Check alibis and dig deeper. Follow the leads we find. There's still an unidentified 9-1-1 caller. The clerk and the female. Let's see what we dig up there. It might lead to something."

"Yeah, you'd think businesses would actually make sure their camera equipment worked. It's a deterrent, yes, but it sure would help if it actually worked when something did happen." He shook his head. "I guess it wouldn't hurt to have a chat with the ex-wife either."

On the way out the door, Clark added, "So what do you think about McCormack being involved? Interesting how he seems to always be linked somehow with the bad guys."

There were times that Johnson wondered what he did to end

up with a partner like Clark. He wasn't always an asshole, just the majority of the time.

"I think the guy got himself into a bad situation and did his best to get himself out alive. Cut him some slack."

"Don't be a damn fool. The guy's a ticking time bomb. He has more anger issues than a caged tiger."

For that reason alone, Johnson did not share the fact that McCormack had already followed the lead on Kendall, or that they had had a conversation about the case.

"Man, seriously, it would be the best day of my career to bust that asshole wide open as a dirty lawyer and now dirty cop."

Instead of telling his partner to shut up, he just headed out the door.

~ ~ ~

When a series of three quick, high-pitched warning beeps signaled that a main door had been opened, Mallory quickly went to the garage door. As she reached the hallway, she was met with Sami, who wagged her tail in anticipation of greeting her master. Tyler entered the code to reset the alarm with one hand and reached down to pet his dog with the other.

"Hey, there. Did you have any luck on the hard drives and files?" He reached over and gave Mallory a quick hug. He relished the fact of how good she felt.

"As a matter of fact, we found information overload. Damian was very thorough with backing up his appointments, meetings, documents, you name it." She followed him into the kitchen and took a seat at the bar.

Tyler reached into the refrigerator and pulled out two bottles of water. He offered her one, but she shook her head no. He leaned against the counter and downed half the bottle at once. As he stood there, he realized just how much he liked coming home to her. It hit him square in the gut. How could he be having thoughts like this? There was a very big chance that she could be guilty. Of what, he had no idea yet. He did know for certain that there was something she was keeping from him. He just hoped like hell it wasn't murder.

"Well, are you going to keep me in suspense?" He blinked twice, bringing his attention back to her as she spoke.

"She was at the apartment. We had a little chat. Let's just say, my intentions were clear." Not feeling the need to share details of his visit with Kendall, he chose to change the subject. He tossed the empty water bottle into the trash and rounded the bar to stand beside her. "How's Emma?"

"She woke not long after you left. She ate most of her dinner and then I went and snuggled with her until she fell back asleep. Sami hasn't left her side until just now, when you came home. My mother is in with her now. I can't believe how resilient my little girl has been. Our worlds have been turned upside down in a matter of days. I'm almost on pins and needles waiting for her to wake screaming from a nightmare. So far, she hasn't."

Tyler closed the distance between them, placed his arms on her shoulders, and then began to rub the knots out of her shoulders. "She has a mother who loves her very much and grandparents who would lay their lives down for her. She knows she is safe."

Lowering her head and relaxing into the comfort of his hands, she sighed and said, "Yes, she does. At some point, we have to let her talk to someone—a professional that can help her through this. She has had so much to deal with in such a short time. Losing her father, and then experiencing the fear of almost being taken. It's too much for a little girl."

"I think that's an excellent idea." Tyler took her by the hand and led her to the office. "Let's go see what y'all found out last night."

He found Caleb and Alexander with their noses to the grind, looking exhausted from having spent the night researching. Caleb sat in a chair slightly angled to the corner of the desk. He had filtered through just about all of the paper contents of the banker boxes. Alexander was scanning through the hard-drive files on the computer.

"Tell me something good." At the sound of Tyler's voice, both men raised their heads. Alexander and Tyler exchanged a look that informed him they hadn't found much. He was tempted to call it a day—or morning, rather—but time was something they didn't have to waste.

"Well, I just found something interesting on the hard drive. Damian kept his appointments logged regularly." Alexander clicked the mouse a few times and brought up a calendar screen. "Here, the night he died. The appointment was for 8:00 p.m. with *K*."

"That's it? *K*?" Tyler questioned.

"Kendall," both Tyler and Mallory said at the same time.

"That's what we think too," Alexander elaborated. "You see, every other entry either has a first name, last name, or organization. This entry is the only one that is logged with an initial."

Tyler envisioned the woman he'd seen, and in comparison to Mallory—well, there was no comparison. Why would Damian link up with her again? She obviously had information that he wanted, or she was up to no good again—or maybe he was thinking with his dick.

Caleb shared his insight. "If he was meeting with her, then there was a damn good reason. She was probably blackmailing him or something. He wouldn't have met with her for any other reason."

Alexander nodded in agreement and blew a deep breath out of his mouth. "Well, there's something else."

"When I clicked on this appointment, it's a recurring entry. This meeting is logged back for six months and is set to continue."

"Were the calendar details filled in?" Tyler inquired.

"Only on the first entry."

"Meeting with K. Time: 8:00. Date: February 8. Place: Mezzaluna Italian Restaurant on Bratton Lane."

"This information definitely gives us a place to start." Tyler turned toward the whiteboard that Caleb and Alexander had begun to use to map out information. There were so many facts that they didn't know. So many theories of what was happening. Now he must concentrate on what they did know and go from there.

Although Kendall revealed no information, her nonverbal reaction to the things he said to her definitely gave him query. The way her teeth had cringed when he mentioned "losing," or the way her eyes threw daggers at him when he mentioned Damian's murder. She wasn't sad he was dead; she was pissed off. In fact, he was pretty sure "pissed off" didn't begin to cover it.

So the question remained, was the kidnapping connected to her? Did she try to take Emma because Damian was dead?

He went to his desk drawer and pulled out a dry-erase marker. He added the meeting and information and circled it. He stood at the board and studied it. This was his resource. Limited, yes. Incomplete, obviously. The information about the kidnapping attempt, including best descriptions of all involved, was listed. The description of the woman that Emma gave was also listed. The facts regarding Damian's death and the shooting at the house. All were listed as sequence.

What wasn't listed was the secret that Mallory held deep within. He knew it was there, and she was, at some point, going to have to come clean.

"We know—or at least, we suspect we know—what she's trying to do, assuming she wants Emma back or she wants to use her for revenge. Then the pattern was becoming clear. She stages a scene at Mallory's office. She sets up meetings with Damian over months, making sure she's seen in a public place. Then, conveniently, he's 'accidentally' murdered."

Tyler paused and contemplated his thoughts. Everyone stayed silent and let him process. He clicked the lid of the highlighter open, shut, open, shut. "Mallory stated that Damian had not given her any reason to think he was considering divorce. She's right. I was informed by Johnson, who paid me a little visit on the stakeout, that the divorce papers were, in fact, bogus."

Everyone commented at once.

"What?"

"When?"

"They believe that?"

Tyler explained the basics of the conversation, feeling it prudent to leave out the warning about Jaxon or the fact that they were looking to arrest Mallory. There was no need to scare her more.

"Alexander, did you find anything else?" Tyler asked.

"No, not that I found," Alexander confirmed.

"Good to know they've gotten something right," Caleb said with gusto.

"All right," Tyler said. "If that's the case, then the papers were planted as a ploy to give Mallory motive for murder. But I just can't reason why she would try to kidnap Emma so soon afterwards. If she had waited until the police arrested Mallory, then it would have been easier to grab her."

"No one's arresting my daughter!" Caleb had remained patient long enough.

Mallory went over to stand behind her father. She wrapped her arms around him and leaned over to hug him tight. "It's alright, Daddy, he's just theorizing right now." She hoped.

Caleb patted her hand, but he fixed his determined eyes on Tyler. "You better do your job, boy. I don't want my daughter and granddaughter to suffer any longer."

"Yes, sir. That's exactly what I'm trying to do."

Alexander stood and walked to the whiteboard. He tapped his finger on the list of men described in the kidnapping. "We have to find out who these men are. I will check my contacts at the police station and see if anyone assigned to this case has any leads."

"Sounds like a plan." Tyler walked over and booted up his own laptop. "We also need to have Mallory's cell phone checked for tracers and her house swept for bugs."

"Tracers? Bugs? Why?" Mallory asked incredulously.

"Because it's the only way someone would have known that Emma would be at the airport. But right now, I've got to get a few hours' shut-eye." Alexander answered for Tyler as he gathered up his laptop and files, gave Mallory a quick reassuring hug, and headed out the door.

Caleb leaned back in the metal chair while examining a police report. In spite of the recent years of his retirement, the way his glasses sat on his face reminded Tyler of the business shark he had been. The scowl on his face made him wonder what he had found.

"Damn," he sighed, blowing out his frustration. "This woman really is crazy." He shook his head and handed the report to Mallory.

She scanned the report. It was a public intoxication and disturbance report. Kendall had been involved in an altercation with a man. He had hit her across the face, causing her to fall into the street. A motorist had to swerve and hit a light pole to avoid hitting her. When the driver of the vehicle got out to check on her, the man she was with had grabbed her by the arm and yanked her back to him. The report indicated that Kendall and the other man engaged in a loud argument. The cops arrived and arrested both.

"Yes, Daddy, there are several of these reports. It's a pattern. She's good for a while and tries to hold down a job and live accordingly, but it never lasts. She doesn't have the ability to sustain the rules and regulations of society."

Tyler turned and encouraged her to continue. "You see, people who have antisocial personality disorder, or APD, usually exhibit levels of instability in moods. Kendall often has episodes that manifest themselves into unsocial behavior or chaotic relationships. This particular report fits her pattern. She does not have the ability to sustain rational and responsible day-to-day living. She rarely accepts responsibility for her actions. She will always be the victim."

"So why the hell didn't her parents get her clinical help?" Caleb asked.

"Most of the time, this behavior pattern doesn't show up until after the age of eighteen. As with any disorder, there are levels of intensity. In Kendall's case, the first time she was institutionalized, she was in her early teens. However, she was not diagnosed with APD at that time. She was just considered an unruly teenager. With counseling, she was released back to her parents. Then, as she became a young adult, she acquired the ability to fool counselors. In all of these reports, counselors all considered her a manageable patient, but her psychiatrists differed in that opinion. Where she beat them at their own game was that they didn't diagnose her with enough of the tendencies to be considered true APD. She was labeled histrionic, however. Most of her police arrests and social disturbances all occur within a year to eighteen months of each other. She can't keep her life together any longer than that."

"Sounds like hogwash to me. The woman's crazy and has turned to criminal means." Caleb took the report back and placed it in the appropriate file. "She has to be stopped."

"I agree," Tyler said. "That's an interesting profile."

Caleb thumbed through the files awhile longer, and he paused on the fifth police report. "Wait a minute. This is the same guy who she was arrested with earlier." He quickly navigated back through the files and found the police report he had shared with Mallory earlier. "Yes, see, right here. Who is this guy?"

"Who, Daddy?"

Tyler reached for the reports. He glanced at both of them and then looked up at Caleb. Although the hair was slightly shorter in the picture, and the man had a beard, he knew exactly who it was. He was looking at the photo of the guy at the airport. It was the first solid lead they had since the mayhem had begun.

"Nick Hanson."

He pulled out his cell phone and quickly dialed Alexander to try and reach him before he traveled too far from the house. As it rang, he assured them all, "It's the asshole from the airport."

CHAPTER 14

❧ ❧ ❧

When she stepped out into the streets of downtown, the night air was still sweltering. The clicking of her high-heeled boots echoed as she headed toward downtown.

Kendall couldn't kick her foul mood. After she spent an hour or so brooding after Nick didn't return any of her calls or texts, she decided to go find the jerk. She knew he wasn't thinking right. She had needed him to pull her plan off, but he wasn't thinking straight right now. What had he done? She was so wrong to think she could control him.

So if you don't want to die, think! The only way to get free and clear of this mess was to make sure she left no evidence. The idea of splitting town seemed like a pretty damn good one. But she didn't have enough money to get lost. Not anymore. Nick had taken that too.

Her nerves were shot. She had taken a few pills and chased them with cheap vodka to calm herself down. It wasn't working. She was pretty damn sure she hadn't seen the last of Mr. APD either. She had to get control of this situation. The only thing she could think to do was find Nick and fill him full of alcohol and sex until he passed out. Then, she would tear through his computer and phone until she got some answers.

She had only made it three blocks from her apartment when her stomach began to wretch. She leaned against a building and puked her guts out. A homeless guy stopped and applauded her efforts. Kendall flipped him off. The guy chuckled and said, "Anytime, anywhere."

She took a few deep breaths and then tried Nick's cell phone again. No answer. Best-case scenario: he was dead somewhere. Since Kendall's luck was not running so hot, she figured it was the worst-case scenario: he was in hiding and letting her take the rap.

～ ～ ～

Tyler's car slowly crept down the street as he checked addresses until he found the one he sought. It had only taken Alexander a few clicks on the computer to find the last known address for Nick Hanson. He pulled to the curb and put his car in park in front of the house. It was a dangerous, high-crime neighborhood, not far from Kendall's apartment. The location of her building was still considered downtown, but this house was in the heart of the slums. Every house on the street showed signs of neglect and years of hard living.

Cars were parked on lawns; old, torn furniture sat on sidewalks. Rusty bicycles and toys littered the block in neglect. None of the scenery could be considered landscaping, unless "ramshackle" fell into the latest home and garden magazines. Trees were sucked dry and brittle from the heat and lack of water. Several bushes were overgrown but brown and crisp from neglect as well. Tyler considered it a fire hazard—one flick of a cigarette could send the neighborhood up in flames.

He slid his weapon from its holster. He wasn't trigger-happy, but he wasn't stupid either. With the pistol secure in his right hand, he exited the car and took in his surroundings. The house appeared to be deserted, and the street was quiet. He doubted most of the residents worked from eight to five, if they worked at all, but it was unnervingly quiet. *Abandoned* might be a better word to describe the eerie feeling.

As he stepped toward the house, he had to side-step more than one portion of the uneven concrete that resembled a sidewalk. Weeds were growing up between the cracks, and some portions were missing chunks of concrete completely. He paused and examined the house as he stood at the edge of the yard. There were no lights on inside, and the front door was closed. The security screen was swinging open, as if the latch was broken.

The few streetlights that weren't busted or burnt out cast barely enough light to decipher between shadows and darkness.

He began to contemplate his decision to be there alone. He acknowledged it was probably not one of his better ideas. *Reckless and stupid* actually came to mind. But he had left the house on an adrenaline rush. They finally had a lead that even the police had not discovered, and he didn't want to wait. Maybe he should have contacted Detective Johnson, but every minute that passed put Mallory closer to being arrested. He considered getting back into the car and waiting for the background search that Alexander was running, but he was here, so he might as well take a look around.

Cautiously, he took the driveway up toward the house and followed the short path of a pebbled walkway to the front door. He glanced over both shoulders but saw no movement—and, more disturbing, he heard no sounds. Concrete crumbled beneath the soles of his shoes, which sounded almost amplified on the quiet street. He studied the house more closely. It was entirely dark.

The warning tingle at the base of his neck was in full force. He knew immediately that he could be walking into an ambush. Hanson and his crew could possibly be waiting inside. He slid the safety off his pistol and held it ready.

When he approached the front door, he listened for sounds inside the house. Nothing. He decided not to knock but to carefully recon the perimeter and back entrance. Again, he checked his surroundings for any activity on the street. Still, there was nothing. He took the few steps that led him around the house to the backyard. He approached a rusty chain-link fence. There was no need to look for a gate; he simply walked through the man-sized, gaping hole.

Taking a deep breath, Tyler cautiously, with his gun raised and ready, approached the back porch. He reached out and tested the sliding glass door that was barely hanging by one hinge. It was unlocked. He slowly and quietly slid the door to the side just enough to let himself in. In reality, what took seconds seemed to take eons. He waited a few heartbeats to make sure he had not alerted anyone in the house and then stepped across the threshold and went inside. The air indoors was as stifling as the summer heat—obviously, the air-conditioning had not been running. The stench of stale cigarettes and long-term use of marijuana filled his nostrils.

He had not ignored the warning tingle at the back of his neck, which was now in full vibration. He listened intently for any sound. It was so quiet that he could hear the blood rushing through his veins. He looked around to orient himself with the interior. The Formica table and folding chairs sat in the middle of the kitchen area. No pictures or mirrors on the wall. Old pizza boxes and other fast-food takeout trash littered the small bar. The tiled floor was filthy with missing pieces. Nick Hanson did not live cleanly.

The open doorway led to a small living area that held one ratty, torn sofa, a well-used brown recliner, and an old television that had the screen cracked. A coffee table was filled with empty beer bottles, dip cans, and overfull ashtrays.

He followed the interior wall holding his gun with both hands, raised and ready for intrusion. In past years, when the neighborhood thrived, it had probably served as a sitting room or study. He moved his head to where he could catch a glimpse of the room. Ragged mini-blinds covered the window, with spider webs covering the corners. When he rounded the doorway, he stepped fully into the room and came face to face with someone.

Kendall Jenkins was standing in the far corner of the room.

His heart lurched in shock, but he raised his gun and pointed it directly at her chest.

"Damn you!" she hissed, full of anger. "What is it with you? You make a routine of showing up places unwelcome. Bad habit, dude."

"What the hell?" Tyler responded, but he didn't lower his gun.

"Well, we are obviously both looking for the same asshole, but I doubt this means we're on the same side now."

"Here to tip off your buddy?" Tyler took in her appearance. She was strung-out, and her eyes darted like she was running scared.

"Not likely. More like trying to figure out what he's done."

"Something tells me you know exactly what he's done."

Kendall didn't answer, but she didn't act like she was about to bolt either. She was paranoid, though. Her eyes kept darting around. Tyler studied her for a few moments and then lowered his pistol. He stayed where his back was against the wall and kept her in full view.

"He's not here. He's ditched me and won't answer my calls or texts," she said.

"Why is it so urgent you find him?"

"Like I'm going to share that info with you? Not." She let out a sarcastic laugh and kept searching through papers on a makeshift desk.

"This Nick Hanson, how close are you to him?"

Kendall took a second to consider answering him. She shrugged her shoulder and gave him little information. "We have history."

"Enough history that he would try and kidnap your daughter for you?"

"You aren't going to trap me into saying something stupid, Mr. APD."

"Looks like he left in a hurry."

Kendall nodded in agreement, as though that explained everything to her. It explained nothing for Tyler, just poured more unanswered questions into his head.

"He's a suspect in the kidnapping and possibly involved with Damian's murder. So let's be straight; why are you here?"

"It's not a matter of why I'm here; it's what I need from him. I'm a little desperate for answers myself since your uninvited visit."

He negated any feeling of guilt for scaring her earlier. He reminded himself that she was not a person to play nice with. She was unstable and had a history of sudden, violent outbursts. He wondered just how deeply involved she was with Nick. Had they planned the kidnapping together? Had Nick skipped out and let her take the heat, like she said? Was Nick the guy that murdered Damian? So many question, not near enough answers.

"You're here. Nick's not. Why?"

"Would you put the damn gun away? I'm not going to do anything. I'm trying to find him too, you know."

"No."

"Seriously, you've got nothing to worry about."

Only my life, he thought.

"I'm the one who should be afraid. You ransacked me earlier, remember?"

"Yes. You've still not given me any reason to consider you anything but a threat. Nothing's changed."

He caught a whiff of her breath. It reeked of vomit, and her skin was pale. She had bloodshot eyes and her hands were shaky. Kendall was not looking good at all.

"You can't keep this up, Kendall. Things are out of control. You play games with people's lives as revenge. It keeps your victims off track and afraid of you. How many times have you actually won? You couldn't keep your marriage to Damian. How many men did you go through before him? You lost custody of Emma. You don't like to lose, but that's all you really do, isn't it? Damian divorced you because he knew who you really were. You can't stand that—when someone sees the real you. It makes you crazy. These games are your way of making sure they knew you could always be in control. But that's not what it's really about this time, is it? You made sure they could never forget who Emma's birth mother was. You didn't want to be forgotten and not important. What you didn't count on was me. I will prove that Mallory is innocent, and I will bury you in the process."

She tensed and her shoulders stiffened as if she had been struck. Her chin raised. Yeah, he'd struck a nerve.

"Why don't you believe me that I know nothing about Damian's murder? Get it through your thick head, asshole. And what makes you think Nick and I are involved in anything illegal?"

"The answer to both of your questions is simple: because you're lying. You and Nick have quite the legal history."

"So, then, you know he beat me up. That's not a secret, but it doesn't make me his criminal partner."

Okay, now she's going to play the victim, Tyler thought. He didn't remember all the details of the report, but he knew enough to bluff. "Oh, yeah. It was an interesting read."

"Well, it wasn't me who filed those charges, believe it or not. We both got busted. I would never have ratted him out. He loves me."

"Really? From the looks of that report, you weren't his favorite person that night."

"Nor he mine."

"In fact, he referred to you as a crazy, psycho bitch—and worse."

"What?"

Tyler knew he had her now. Crazy people don't like to be called crazy.

"I'll spare you the recount, but that's the gist of what he had said to the cop. I don't think the love is that deep between you two. He was more than happy to let you take the rap that night. Today, he obviously took off and left you behind to take the blame. Again."

"No, he wouldn't do that. If he's taken off, he'll be back for me."

"He also said that night was your fault. If it weren't for you and your psycho, violent ways, he wouldn't have been arrested. According to him, he only hit you to stop you from going crazy." Tyler knew nothing of the sort, but it helped that she didn't know that.

"He's a lying bastard," she simply stated. "He lied then, and he's a lying coward now. If he blew a kidnapping attempt, it's because he's out of control and didn't think anything through. That's what he does. He goes off without planning and organizing. He cuts and runs too." She thought about the photo of Emma Nick had left on her bed.

Tyler remained quiet and cautious. He had her talking.

She paced back and forth across the worn carpet. "Nick is out of control. Whatever he has done, he's done without me. Get that? I killed no one. And I sure as hell had nothing to do with trying to take Emma."

"Tell me what you do know, Kendall. Don't go down for that guy. Tell me what else his motive could be. Damian's your ex-husband; Emma's your daughter."

"Just shut up! Shut up!" Her shoulders slumped forward and she bowed her head.

Tyler took a few steps toward her, placed his hand beneath her chin, and yanked her head up. "You are going to fry for this, Kendall, unless you talk. Is that what you want?"

"Screw you; just do it!" She thrusts her hands in his face, wrists pressed together. "Handcuff me, asshole. Take me to jail. I could use a good night's sleep to figure this shit out. At least I'll be safe there."

"From Nick?"

"Yes!"

"Because you think he'll come after you too?"

"Yes. No. I don't know!" she exclaimed, shaking her head. "I don't think so. He's not that dumb. But I can't figure out what he's up to. If he wanted to hurt me, he had his chance the other night. He came over, screwed me, and then left while I was in the shower. When I came out, there was a photo of Emma on the bed."

"Why?" Tyler growled at her.

"I guess ... I don't know. He didn't want her around when she was just a baby."

"Why now? Why the sudden interest now? Think!"

"I can't tell you why."

"Because you don't want to incriminate yourself."

She shook her head violently. "Not like this. Yes, I've messed with Damian and Mallory. I admit that. I was pissed! They stole my daughter from me and they took what was mine! I messed with them, just to make them pay. But I never, never, killed Damian or tried to take Emma. I don't know anything about that. Trust me."

"Trust you?" He laughed. "No way in hell, Kendall."

"What do I have to do to prove it? Turn up dead?"

"That would be a start."

She jerked her head back like he'd slapped her.

"In the meantime, whenever you turn around, you'll be looking for me. Like I said before, I will do whatever it takes to prove Mallory's innocence. But you? You are not innocent. Not by a long shot."

CHAPTER 15

~ ~ ~

Tyler walked back into his bedroom wearing a pair of unbuttoned jeans and a towel wrapped around his neck. It felt different because he was used to walking around his house free from cover. At the same time, he realized he didn't mind at all.

Early-morning light broke through the cracks of the blinds in the windows. He pondered his conversation with Kendall and then studied the background information on Hanson that Alexander had e-mailed. His mug shot proved he was definitely the guy at the airport, which put stronger weight on the theory rumbling in his head. He had contacted Johnson and had an APB and arrest warrant issued.

He reached into his closet and pulled out a T-shirt. In the midst of pulling it over his head, he stopped head in his tracks. He smelled coffee … and breakfast? Oh, yeah, he could get used to having Mallory in his house.

His chest warmed at the thought. The more he was around her, the more his need to keep her safe from harm grew. He was now absolutely certain that Kendall was up to something that even she couldn't handle. Nick was bad news, and he was more than convinced Mallory and Emma needed protection from them both.

Mallory knew something too. He was sure of it. The more time he spent with her, and the deeper he delved into things, it became more and more clear. She trusted him, but not enough. Not nearly enough to let him in on the one key fact of this entire case. How could he protect her if he didn't know the truth?

The question that warred between his head and his heart was why she wouldn't trust him enough to tell him her secret. He had vowed not to fail her. He had sworn to her that he would protect her and Emma from harm. But he didn't know if he was going to be faced with protecting her from herself. He had learned in life that evil was found everywhere. It was a prevalent part of every living thing. Just how bad was this thing she was keeping hidden?

He walked toward the living room, and he could see her standing at his stove cooking breakfast. It looked right. It felt damn right. He may have lost her once, and he'd be damned if he let it happen again—secret or no secret.

Just then, Mallory raised her head and caught him staring. She tilted her head in question and smiled at him.

Aw, hell, he had made a serious breach in his professional ethics. He had crossed so many lines that there was no way to step back and gain any distance. He was in deep.

A security notification beeped on his phone. They had company. He tapped the screen to verify the visitor. He gritted his teeth. "Mallory."

"Yes?" She was continuing to work her way around the kitchen, but before Tyler had a chance to warn her, the front doorbell rang.

She swung around toward the sound. She had turned skittish, and her eyes were alarmed. She immediately took the pan off the stove and walked over to stand by Emma, who had been coloring at the counter.

"I'll take care of it. You stay there." Tyler moved toward the door.

The person outside had abandoned the doorbell and was now knocking. *What a jerk,* Tyler thought. He looked through the peephole to make sure there were no surprises and then decided to deactivate the alarm system. He glanced back toward the kitchen area, composed himself, and opened the door.

"Good morning, officers."

He was sure these guys were catching hell from the chief for not having someone in custody by now for Damian's murder. If they were here to arrest Mallory, it would be over his dead body.

Detective Johnson reached his hand out to shake Tyler's hand before he removed his sunglasses and spoke in a professional tone. "We have a few questions for Ms. Jones. We've been informed she is temporarily staying here."

The other detective, Clark, didn't attempt to hide the smirk on his face. Tyler thought—no, Tyler knew—that one day soon, he and Detective Clark were going to have a serious disagreement. Tyler's expression was blank as he stepped back to let the men enter the house.

"Yes, she's here. I would like to remind both of you that so is her daughter."

"This shouldn't take long," Detective Johnson said. Neither officer seemed phased by the little girl's presence. That gave Tyler a slight bit of reassurance that maybe they weren't here to arrest her—yet.

Tyler led the men into the living room, where they remained standing. He began to walk toward the kitchen to alert Mallory, but she met him at the doorway. As she approached, he could read her expression. His hopes for her not panicking were shattered.

As Mallory could do, she gathered her wits and presented herself with confidence. Without preamble, she demanded to know, "What questions do they have for me?"

"I don't know; let's find out together." He motioned for her to take a seat on the couch. He sat next to her but remained on the edge of his seat. He was sure his demeanor appeared protective, but he didn't care.

The detectives both sat forward in the recliners that were separated by a small table. The coffee table served as a battle line drawn between both parties.

"How are you doing, Ms. Jones?" It was Detective Clark that had begun the questioning.

"I'm fine, thank you."

"We have just a few questions to ask. As you know, our investigation has continued."

"Yes."

Tyler interjected with caution. "Shouldn't we alert Mr. Blakely of this questioning?"

"We don't see that as necessary at this time, but if it makes Ms. Jones more comfortable, then by all means, please do."

"I will answer as long as I feel comfortable," Mallory decided.

"Nothing continues until I have him on the phone." Tyler knew it was highly out of the ordinary for detectives to approach a suspect who had representation without the attorney present, and it irked him that they would even try. Then again, if they did end up arresting her, she might say something that incriminated herself.

Within a matter of minutes, Tyler retrieved his laptop computer and engaged the attorney in the conversation via video conferencing. Alexander's image appeared on the screen as he sat at his desk in his office.

The discussion resumed, with Detective Johnson confirming with Mallory that they had been considering the kidnapping of Emma a possible connection to Damian's murder and asked if she could share any light on possible reasons why.

"No, I'm sorry."

"We can inform you that the body of the driver was found in a used car lot." Both Mallory and Tyler looked at each other.

"Is there an ID on him yet?" Tyler inquired.

"Not quite yet," Detective Johnson answered.

"Did you and your husband have separate bank accounts?" Detective Clark inquired.

"I'm sure you already know the answer to that question, but yes. We have three, to be exact. One for his business expenses, one for mine, and one joint account for family purposes." Her abrupt answers impressed Tyler, since he could see her hands trembling.

Alexander's voice came over the speaker. "What, specifically, do you want to ask my client?"

"Ms. Jones, how often did you and your husband review the accounts?"

"To be honest, I rarely, if ever, looked at his business account. I mainly managed my account and the joint household account."

"Okay. What about—"

Mallory interrupted him. "Is there a discrepancy with the business account?"

Taken a little by surprise that she redirected the questioning, the detective answered. "*Discrepancy* may be a weak word. For the past six months, there has been a monthly cash withdrawal of $5,000 from his business account that does not appear in either of the other accounts."

No one said a word for a long moment.

"I don't understand." Mallory's forehead creased, and she shook her head, as if trying to process the information.

Tyler's mind, on the other hand, was quickly doing math and connecting dots. Meetings with *K* started about the same time. Monthly too. Son of a bitch. Damian was paying Kendall off!

"Here's how this looks, Ms. Jones." Detective Clark leaned forward, held his hands together, and pointed them in her direction. His nonverbal communication seemed to be directing a guilty verdict toward her. "It looks like someone had a plan for a while. Six monthly withdrawals of $5,000 totals $30,000. That's enough to pay for, let's say, shooting someone? And now we have another dead body. Maybe to keep them quiet?"

"That's enough, gentlemen." Alexander spoke in a quick, domineering tone. "Tyler, see them to the door. This interview is over. Gentlemen, in the future, I strongly suggest you make an appointment via my office to see my client."

Tyler stood and began to lead the detectives to the door.

Mallory sat frozen, staring at Detective Johnson. Confusion had struck her paralyzed. As he stood up, he abandoned his cop routine. He breathed heavily and said, "Ms. Jones, this isn't looking good for you. If you have any information that could help us clear this up, please come forward. Any information at all, because as it looks now, you're one guilty woman."

"Out. Now." Tyler spoke in a determined voice.

Detective Clark's phone rang as he reached the front door. He took the call and dismissed any efforts at offering departing words. Johnson hung back a few feet. He turned to Tyler and spoke in a hushed tone.

"Look, I know you feel responsible for her; otherwise, I can't imagine why you would be putting your career on the line to help her. You obviously believe she needs protection, but I'm urging you to be careful. Don't get yourself into another situation that can get you killed."

"I know what I'm doing." He shook the detective's hand and wondered what it would be like to actually have an ally he could trust.

As Tyler closed the door, Emma came into the room and asked, "Mommy, who were those people?"

Like a light switch, Mallory snapped to attention and rose to comfort her daughter. "They are detectives who are working to find the bad man that hurt Daddy, sweetie. They were just here doing their jobs."

"I finished my breakfast and coloring pages. Sami and I didn't want to come in here. They talked kinda mean to you, Mommy." Emma had a small crease between her eyebrows. She was concerned for her mother.

"No, baby, they weren't mean; they were just serious and using their work voices. Did you put your plate in the sink like a good girl?" Mallory spoke to her in a soothing voice and tucked a piece of Emma's hair behind her ear.

"Yes, ma'am."

"Hey, Emma, while Mommy and I talk, would you and Sami like to watch a movie on my very large, very awesome big-screen television up in the den?" Tyler figured it might be best if the little girl was preoccupied. It was pretty clear to him that she was as intuitive as her mother.

"Can I please, Mommy?"

"Of course. Just don't mess with any of Tyler's things."

"I promise!" Emma darted up the stairs, and Tyler followed to help get her settled. Sami looked around, grabbed a bone from behind a chair, and took off after them.

Mallory sat back down on the couch and turned the monitor to face her. She could see Alexander writing something on a piece of paper. He glanced up and said, "Mallory, don't let them get to you. We are working diligently to clear your name and resolve this situation."

"I know, Alex, and thank you. I just don't understand what Damian was up to. Why had we not considered looking into his accounts ourselves? What else are we overlooking?"

"It's not that we overlooked it, dear, we were just analyzing a different angle of the puzzle. We will put it all together. That's what we do."

"Why didn't you tell them about Nick? The cops obviously need to know that we figured out who he was."

"It's already done. An APB and arrest warrant have been issued."

Once Alexander asked her to have Tyler contact him later, he disconnected the call.

Mallory sat and waited while Emma chose a movie and took a moment to calm her nerves. She smiled as she listened to Tyler tease her about not wanting to watch the sports channel or news coverage. It wasn't long before Mallory heard the sounds of Nickelodeon coming from the room.

~ ~ ~

"What do you mean, you don't know where she is?"

"Sir, we have looked everywhere. She's not staying with friends, her family, or in a hotel."

"It's rather simple. Find her, or you become useless to me."

"Yes, sir."

"As a general rule, I do not offer second chances. You have not proven yourself worthy to my organization."

"Yes, sir. We will find her."

Jaxon stood and peered out the window of his high-rise downtown residence. The only silver lining in this mess was the comforting fact that the stakes in this cat-and-mouse game had risen. He was, however, beginning to grow antsy.

CHAPTER 16

~ ~ ~

Tyler came back down the stairs and found Mallory with her hands fisted together. She was abusing her bottom lip again. He knew her mind was racing and that she felt everything was closing in on her. It frustrated him that he had not been able to put all the pieces together, but his instincts told him they were looking in the right direction.

"It was late when you got back last night." Mallory immediately cringed because she sounded like those jealous and obsessive women she couldn't stand. She followed up with a clarifying statement. "You must have found something."

"More like some*one*."

Mallory's eyes became curious. "You found Nick Hanson?"

Tyler shared his findings at Nick's residence. When he finished, Mallory could hear the birds chirping in the trees and Emma's laughter upstairs.

"Meeting up with her a second time cannot be a coincidence, Tyler."

"When I first saw her there," he said in a low voice, "I was instantly concerned about her state of mind. It was like ... like ..." He paused to search for the words. "She was desperately seeking a way out of something. She was trying to find him. He had skipped out on her. I'm not quite sure she's the mastermind anymore."

"Don't be so quick to fall for her theatrics," Mallory reminded him.

"I'm not, but this Nick guy has a lot of questions to answer."

Tyler studied her Coke can sitting on the coffee table, watching the condensation drip and how it created patterns in the metal. "To be honest, Kendall looked truly desperate. I know I hit nerves the first visit. I scared her. But there was more—something or someone that she is truly afraid of."

Mallory pursed her lips and nodded her head. "Yeah, I know how she feels."

He almost reached out to take her hand but caught himself. "I know it looks like evidence is piling up on you, but it's all circumstantial. You are innocent. I will prove that."

She raised her head and looked at him with her blue eyes that had turned cold and hard. "I'm not so sure that's as easily done anymore. Someone has gone through a lot of trouble to set me up. The one person I believed is behind this is now being second-guessed, even by you. The police aren't even looking at her."

"Hey, I never said I didn't think she was involved. Just that maybe she's not the one pulling the strings."

"Whatever." Mallory stood and began to pace across the floor. She dragged her fingers through her hair away from her face. "So much is happening, and I can't get my head around why."

"But you're afraid you know why." Tyler held his breath and waited. This was it. It was now or never. Whatever it was that she kept hidden could obviously be the key to this entire thing. His heart barely beat. He silently willed her to come clean, to trust him. It was something he needed from her. Not just to solve a crime but to reconnect them on a deeper level.

For several seconds, she remained staring out the window and then she sighed heavily. When she dropped her chin to her chest, she folded her arms and rolled back on her heels. Still, she said nothing for a long moment. Her conscience was waging strong.

Finally, she spoke. "You think Damian was silenced, don't you?" She turned and looked at him. "He was killed to punish me somehow."

"Possibly."

"Then to make my punishment worse, they tried to take Emma." Her voice quavered.

"Maybe."

"Those shots at the houses weren't meant to really kill me, then, just to scare me."

"I think whoever took those shots was ordered to miss. We were both sitting ducks in that window that night. I think if the shooter was ordered to do so, you would have been killed. I also believe the attempt to take Emma would have occurred anyway."

Tyler stood from the couch and went to her. He took her shoulder and turned her to him. He couldn't help it anymore. The look on her face was a mixture of exhaustion and fear. Tears began to spill over her eyes. He tucked her hair behind her ear and rubbed his hand down the side of her arm. She wasn't going to confide in him, but she was getting close. It was enough. For now.

"You're safe. Emma is safe. I'm going to keep you both that way. I won't fail you, Mallory."

As soon as the words were out of his mouth, she reached up and pulled his face to hers. Her lips frantically began to seek comfort in his. She threaded her fingers up through his hair and moved a few inches to close the distance between them.

The feel of her next to him made his blood hum through his veins. His arms closed around her. He angled his head to deepen the kiss. When he did, her lips parted. When their tongues touched, aw, hell, he was lost. His hands went lower and pulled her into him. She smelled good, she tasted even better, and she was as into this as he. He couldn't get enough of her.

He groaned and broke the kiss. He kept her where she was, close to him—almost touching everywhere. He rested his forehead against hers. Their breaths were heavy and mingling together. An incoherent string of curses mumbled out of his mouth.

"Whenever we do this, I suddenly forget everything around me." He gave a light kiss on her nose. "And everyone."

"Emma."

"Yes," he took a deep breath and said. "Things are not finished between us, but I want better timing. I want all night with you. I want it right."

Huskily, she said, "I ..." She hesitated, cleared her throat, and tried again. "Me too. I want it to be right too."

∾ ∾ ∾

"Well?" Alexander had summoned Tyler to his office after the impromptu visit from the detectives. Mallory's parents had returned to his house to be with her and Emma.

"What?"

"What did you think of Mallory's demeanor during the interrogation?"

"Come on, Alex, they waylaid her. They seem to get off by doing it. Especially Clark."

"Let me play devil's advocate for a minute here. If you were the cop looking at her as a prime suspect, wouldn't you think it's an obvious connection that within days of the husband getting popped at a gas station, bogus divorce papers are found, and then a repeated withdrawal of money from an account is discovered?"

"Whose side are you on? Defense or prosecution?"

"You're jaded. I'm trying to look at this from all angles. I asked you once if Mallory was going to be a problem with your objectivity."

"She's not. I just think sometimes the obvious is not what it seems."

"They had a history of unhappiness and stress."

"So do you and I!" Tyler raised his voice. "There's no way, dealing with an ex-wife as crazy as he had, that it wouldn't take a toll on a marriage. I consider it a huge feat that they hadn't divorced."

Alexander stubbornly shook his head. "We're missing something."

"Financials? Life insurance policies?"

"Yeah, she's going to inherit substantially as well as gain

controlling interest of the company. He doubled his policy after the company started expanding."

"Damn. That's more motive stacked against her. It won't take long before the cops connect that—if they haven't already. But Mallory is a successful business owner. She has money of her own."

Both sat silently considering. Tyler continued, "Damian contacted his wife, said he was coming home. He stopped for gas and food. He was shot three times in the chest while exiting the convenience store. Witnesses confirmed seeing a black Escalade. Wallet was found on his person. Nothing from the car taken. There were two 9-1-1 calls."

"It appears clean and random. Perfect drive-by scenario."

"So what got the cops started asking questions and suddenly everything is stacked against the wife?"

"Don't forget the bogus evidence."

"Stay with me here." Tyler rose and began to pace. "Number one: the cops almost immediately find divorce papers. It didn't take long to confirm they weren't legit. So why do it? Number two: they discover his last meeting was with a woman at a restaurant. We figure out that whoever he was meeting, which might be Kendall, was recurring. Number three: there's the monthly withdrawal from the business account that's unexplainable. It doesn't take a genius to figure out he was paying off someone."

"That helps to diminish the motive on Mallory's part," Alexander offered. "What did you get from your visit with Kendall?"

"She's guilty; I just don't know of what yet. She has a lot of hatred. She lost custody. She lost income with the divorce from Damian. If she was getting money from Damian, killing him wouldn't make sense. I just don't know where that money is; she's not living off it. She does have some pretty expensive, if not illegal, habits. Maybe she's using it for drugs. She has the intelligence and warped personality to pull off the bogus papers. Then again, I can't ignore the mental status. Something simple that we don't know about could have made her snap."

"The shooting at the house. That puts an entirely new spin on things. Not to mention the kidnap attempt."

"There's no way they can pin either of those on Mallory. I was with her both times," Tyler said.

Alexander opened his mouth to speak, but Tyler cut him off. "Just don't go there."

"It can't be ignored. They will throw that in your face, and you know it."

"Which brings us to Nick Hanson."

"No leads on his whereabouts."

"The guy's split. His buddy is dead. No trace of the female at this time."

"Do you think Kendall was in it with them?"

"Oh, yeah. Just how much, I don't know."

"No evidence found at the house?" Alexander asked.

"Like I told you. Nothing. She was definitely strung-out. It hadn't been that long since I paid her a visit. It put her in motion, and she went searching for him. He's in deep hiding, though. Honestly, I don't think this guy is smart enough to organize this level of activity."

"Which circles us back to murder-for-hire."

Frustrated, Tyler locked his hands behind his neck and stretched. "Damian never had any lawsuits, other than the custody battle. Hell, not even a traffic ticket. No outstanding debts. The company was operating in the black and cutting-edge technology was about to explode. The only known enemy was Kendall. And I've just got a gut feeling about her and this Nick guy. I need time that I'm afraid Mallory doesn't have."

"You can't ignore the obvious facts, Tyler. She might be guilty."

"Quit trying to go there and help me figure out who is setting her up!"

Alexander blew out a heavy breath. "Christ. What a mess."

~ ~ ~

Driving away from downtown, Tyler noticed his SUV was almost out of gas. It would be an annoyance to get off the freeway and fill up but even more of an inconvenience for the tank to run out and stall traffic. He checked his watch. He spent almost two hours with Alexander, hashing out evidence and forming a plan of action. After their discussion, he was more motivated to do a drive-by and see if there were any signs of occupancy at Hanson's house.

He veered off the exit that lead to Loop 1 and wheeled into the first service station he came to. As he filled the tank, he noticed Emma's jacket lying in the back seat. He couldn't help but grin.

Thoughts of his past spun quickly through his head. Once he had gotten over losing Mallory, his career became his entire focus. He had been content to be alone. He had made decisions to not let people into his private life. He was grateful for that choice now. The path his life had taken would have drastically affected anyone he had allowed himself to love. It still could. Jaxon would always haunt him.

Besides, it was easier to not have to answer to another person when he was on stakeouts or unplanned trips out of town to pursue evidence. He could spend long hours at the computer or tail a suspect without the worries of having someone at home. He was working hard to build his investigating profession and to overcome his past. In order to do that, he lived an emotionless life. No strings. No attachments. It was best. And that's how he liked it.

So why would a jacket have him standing there all sappy?

He knew exactly why. After waiting all these years, he finally had Mallory back in his life. Most certainly not the way he planned it. Ever. But nonetheless, she was back, and with a child too. He could relate to how Mallory was immediately taken with the little girl. The same thing had happened to him. There's nothing he wouldn't do to keep Emma safe—although doing just that might not be so easily done at this point. Both of them gave him motivation to be a better man.

He could not fail them. It wasn't an option. It wasn't the courage to keep her safe that he was lacking; it was the knowledge of who he was up against. A smart investigator didn't go off half-cocked. He didn't react. He was patient, and he gathered intel and proof. And since he didn't have any, the next best thing was a solid witness who could corroborate events and suspects.

It irked him that the police had found evidence of the money transactions before Tyler had even had a chance to look. He berated himself for not being more accurate, focused, and quicker to the lead.

On the other hand, he had set things in motion. To Kendall, it might appear he had threatened her. But what he did do was light a fire under her. The fact that he would find her so quickly at the Hanson place only proved a connection, not a plan. The only way to figure this out was to delve deeper into that relationship, because at this point, he wasn't even sure which of the two conspired to have Damian killed.

Both Kendall and Nick had been in on a plot to harm Mallory; although the evidence was circumstantial, it was strong. Kendall destroyed her office and was more than likely the woman at the restaurant with Damian. Nick tried to take Emma. Though each had resources to fight dirty and mean, they didn't necessarily possess the intelligence to link it all together. Besides, there hadn't been a money trail linked to either—unless the money had been given in cash.

Whoever was in charge of this entire thing was accustomed to machinations and complexity. The person involved was intelligent and controlled. He or she had to have an inside connection to Mallory's day-to-day life.

There had to be a trail. One he'd overlooked.

He realized he had been standing there, staring at Emma's jacket. He turned, repositioned the gas pump, and got back into the driver's seat. He pulled away from the station, but as soon as he was about to turn onto the highway, he hit the brake. The passing police car gave him pause.

Tyler had to find a way to get Emma to a safe house. It wouldn't be long before the detectives arrested and booked Mallory.

Honestly, she might be safer behind bars until he could prove her innocence. She would be all right. She was tough, but he had to prepare her for it. Mallory would need time to get her mind straight and find her courage. Emma, however, needed to be secluded and away from any danger.

With the decision planted in his mind, he quickly hit the speed dial on his phone as he entered the feeder road to head back in the other direction. Several phone calls later, Tyler had a plan to hide Emma until the ordeal was over. The one thing that could throw a kink in this well-collaborated plan was Mallory's reaction.

～ ～ ～

"Absolutely not!" Mallory stood with her arms crossed and her head shaking back and forth. "You cannot be serious. I stood back and did as I was told when you made decisions for me the first time. Not again. The last time I agreed to send Emma away, she was nearly kidnapped! I am not letting her out of my sight. No."

"Mallory that was not an event we saw coming." Tyler pinched the bridge of his nose with his thumb and middle finger. "Now that we know what we are up against, these events could continue until we figure things out. We have to keep her safe. I promised you I would. This is how to do it."

"Listen, sweetheart." Caleb took his turn to try and convince her. "This plan that Tyler has is a smart one. We hadn't taken enough security measures last time. No one will know where we are or when we leave."

She was adamantly holding her position.

Her mother walked to her. "Mallory, we let you down last time. Please trust us to take care of our granddaughter."

"Oh, Mom." She immediately took her mother into her arms and hugged her tight. "It's not about that. You didn't do anything wrong. You have always taken very good care of Emma, and I know you will in the future. I don't blame you."

Both women held onto each other. "Let Tyler do his job. Let him protect her, and you, the best he knows how."

Mallory was so saturated with fear, panic, and anger that she didn't recognize herself anymore.

"I need time to think. Please."

She walked out of the kitchen and went upstairs to be with her daughter.

CHAPTER 17

~ ~ ~

Tyler was passed out by the time his head hit the pillow. He was reaching twenty-four hours without sleep, and his tired muscles needed to recharge. At first, he thought the sound of his cell phone was a dream. No such luck. He picked it up and answered in the form of a grunt.

"She what?" His eyes shot open and he was immediately alert.

"You heard me. She inherits millions."

"What kind of insanity is that? She's a kid!" Tyler swung his legs to the side of the bed and checked that his door was still closed. "You're the probate attorney. I thought you had all this information."

"He went to the life insurance company on his own. I just received copies for his file today in the mail. They were changed last week; he doubled the values."

"When?"

"Immediately."

"No, I mean, when did you find out?"

"Honestly, about ten minutes ago."

"Son of a bitch."

"Yeah. Tell me about it. Why the hell Damian put little Emma as the recipient of the life insurance is beyond me. The original policy bequeathed everything to Mallory. Any guesses as to why the revision?"

Tyler muttered a string of curses. "What if this is the secret Mallory has been hiding?"

"Here's the nail in the coffin: Mommy controls the money if something happens to Emma."

"Shit."

"Mallory has some explaining to do," Alexander said.

"I really hate it when you overstate the damn obvious."

"There might be a reasonable explanation. Don't jump to conclusions."

"She's been lying by omission about something. I hope to the ends of the earth that it's not about this." Knowing there was really nothing else to say, Tyler disconnected the call.

He sat there for a moment staring at nothing. He was a professional. He could handle pressured situations. He had survived and escaped from evil. But this? How in the hell was he supposed to handle this? Had the Mallory he had known and loved staged a murder and kidnapping to get her hands on money?

~ ~ ~

Throwing herself into her work, Mallory spent hours on the computer and managed to create the layout of a bakery webpage before reality sank back in. The house was quiet, and when she looked at the clock, it was nearly two o'clock in the morning.

She saved her file and stored her flash drive with the few business belongings she had brought with her. Earlier, she had checked on Emma and couldn't help but feel amazed at her child's resilience. She was sleeping like an angel with Sami curled up next to her.

The overwhelming silence in the house hadn't really spooked her. She felt an odd sense of comfort in Tyler's home that she'd never experienced in her own. Holding her arms wrapped around herself, she walked over to a window and looked out into the darkness. She rubbed her temples in an effort to stimulate blood flow and ease the tension.

She looked at her bed and knew with the oncoming headache, she wouldn't be able to sleep. A bubble bath would be nice, but she didn't want to wake Tyler. Instead, she quietly headed toward the kitchen for a cup of tea and ibuprofen.

She waited on the coffee pot to heat the water; it was the quietest way to make tea without creating a disturbance.

"Mallory."

Startled by the sound of his deep, low voice, she reminded herself to breathe. "You have got to stop doing that."

"Sorry." The clipped tone of Tyler's voice told her that was far from the truth.

He approached the counter where she was assembling her tea and reached for a cup of his own. They both stood in silence as her cup filled with heated water. She added the tea bag to steep. He followed her actions but went to the pantry for honey to sweeten his cup.

She moved away then, but she glanced over her shoulder to see if he would follow her to the table. Something had him distracted and his face was tight with tension. Something was wrong; she was sure of that.

"Do you wake often at night, or has something happened?"

"Huh."

Okay, that wasn't much of an answer. They both sat and sipped tea. He wasn't in the talking mood, so she didn't feel the need to pressure him and make things worse. He was generous to allow her to stay in his home. Maybe he needed alone time. She would do her best to accommodate him; it was the least she could do. She began to rise and go to her room.

"You haven't been honest with me." There was no indication of a question, just condemnation in his tone.

Mallory froze for a second, then two. Her tank top had ridden up from her pajama pants and revealed a fine line of skin. Tyler closed his eyes and made a fist to stop the need to reach out and caress the bare skin. No more. Get a grip. He had to know why she kept withholding information. Especially if he had been allowing a murderess to stay in his home.

She calmly seated herself again in the chair and regarded Tyler warily.

"What do you mean?"

"You know why Kendall is after you. You have very good ideas of why Damian was killed. Yet, you don't feel the need to come clean with information that will protect your daughter. Information that makes you guilty, perhaps?"

His words struck her like weapons. But moreover, his words hit home.

"What do you think I have hidden from you, Tyler?"

The double-edged sword hurt like hell. It was a small victory that she didn't up and leave the room. It cut deep that she didn't deny that she was, in fact, hiding something.

She had to know about the insurance money; there was no way Damian wouldn't have told her his plans. He had begun to admire her tenacity. He had thanked fate for bringing her into his life again, only to have to face reality that she just might damn well be guilty of murder.

He could no longer deny the evidence that was staring him in the face. Her denial hurt. Leaving his career as a lawyer and his roots in West Texas had hurt like hell, but nothing came close to the heartache he was feeling at this moment. There was a pit deep in his stomach that seemed to get deeper with every second. He wanted Mallory to come clean. He needed it. But, dammit, he feared the answers he might get.

Their eyes connected. His mind willed her to tell him the truth. She closed her eyes and took a deep breath. He could see the battle in each breath she took. So he waited. He watched her every move. He knew the exact moment she decided to come clean. And his gut sank—because she was guilty.

Fuck. In the next moment, he wished like hell he had never returned to Austin because the words that came out of her mouth were like a modern-day Pandora.

"I withheld information in order to win the custody battle and secure the adoption process. I did it to protect Emma."

He was still as stone. He hoped he had heard her incorrectly. He knew this was going to be a bombshell of information, but this changed everything.

"Emma is not Damian's daughter."

"Say that again?" Tyler blinked in confusion.

"I withheld evidence that proved Damian was not Emma's father."

He wanted her to stop talking. He was seriously speechless. He took a moment to absorb the information Mallory had just revealed. She began to look agitated, and he was afraid she would bolt for the door.

"Why are you telling me this? This evidence implicates you in so many ways."

"You wanted the truth, right? That's it."

It's possible she knew nothing of the insurance-policy change, or it's possible she wanted to get her hands on the money before the issue of paternity was revealed and this was a way of throwing him off track.

"You're right. I do want the truth. All of it."

"I am going to jail, aren't I?"

Tyler sighed heavily, rubbed his hand down his face, and settled it on his chin. He might as well throw all the cards on the table.

"At this point, I honestly don't know. How much had Damian shared with you about his life-insurance policies?"

Not a single flinch at his question. No stiffening or looking away.

"We took the policies out together. I know the house, the money in the bank, all that goes to me, of course. The company and stock will be handled separately. Why?"

"He altered his policy last week. Emma inherits everything. Six million, to be exact."

The incredulous look on Mallory's face could not be faked. She stared at him, aghast.

"What on earth are you talking about? I was with him when we generated those documents."

He explained the connection that the police would make once this information surfaced and how it would implicate her.

"Why would I have my own daughter, who I fought tooth and nail for, even broke the law for, kidnapped?"

"The majority of children kidnapped are done so by close family members."

"Screw you." She got up to leave so quickly that the chair scraped on the floor.

"And it will make you look even guiltier regarding Damian's murder."

As she took in the new information, she tensed. Tyler knew her mind was reeling. His was too.

This new information needed to stay between them for now—especially until he was able to put more clarity on this situation. Sometimes a man had to go with his gut, and his gut kept urging him to protect her, not convict her.

"We keep your little revelation between us for now. Got it?"

Her eyes were filled with relief, as if a sudden weight had been lifted.

"You still believe me? A minute ago, you were ready to turn me over to the police."

"Yes, I believe you."

He ignored every warning racing through his mind and reached over and put his arm around her bare midriff. She closed her eyes and rested her head on his shoulder. Tyler noticed that her hands were fisted. He took both of her hands in his and coaxed them open. He stroked both her palms with his thumbs.

They were both aware now that every angle was beginning to implicate her. Tyler had uncanny talent for reading people's non-verbal communication. She kept it together and fought the urge to simply break down and cry, even though that was exactly what she wanted to do. She continued to impress the hell out of him.

"Come on." He led her out of the kitchen.

She followed without argument. When her steps hesitated, he looked over his shoulder at her.

"Thank you."

"Mallory," he admonished. "Don't say that. I don't deserve it."

"We've taken over your space, your time, and your life."

"True," Tyler said with a slight grin. "But Sami adores Emma. They made fast friends, and until recently, she would get bored during the day. Now she has company."

It was not the right time to tell her how his feelings had ignited for her again. Not that they'd ever fully extinguished.

"No one enters my space and home that I don't invite willingly." He tipped her chin up. "You're here because I want you here."

He placed her hand in his and continued the path to her room. "Try to sleep."

He truly meant to walk away. Instead, he stood there, still holding her hand and ever so lightly rubbing his thumb back and forth across the back of her hand.

As she stared into his eyes, she involuntarily took a step closer to him. Mallory could feel his breath on hers, she was that close. Neither knew who made the first move, but their lips met. His lips demanded hers to open more. She did so willingly. He held her so close that he could feel her heart beating against his chest. He had every intention of walking away. Really, he did. It was a colossal mistake to be kissing her. Evidence usually spoke the truth, and it was pointing straight at her. He was going to listen to all of the screaming warnings in his head. Until, dammit, she pulled his bottom lip between her teeth. Then he had her up against the door. He lifted her legs and wrapped them around him. He angled his head to deepen the kiss. His hands found her waist and started to slowly travel upward. She broke the kiss and leaned her head back against the door to give him access to her neck. He trailed kisses and love bites down the side of her neck.

He could tell the moment she wasn't with him anymore. He nibbled one last kiss on her chin and then leaned back. They were both breathing heavy. Her eyes were heated, which he figured reflected his own. But then hers began to shine, threatening to fill with tears.

"Easy," he whispered. "We keep ending up in this situation."

"I know. It's just all too much."

"Yeah, I know. Timing is a hell of a thing."

"I know, so I guess I should warn you," she said.

"About what?"

"That I really want you."

~ ~ ~

Once they were in the SUV and underway, they rode in silence. He wasn't used to an awkward morning after. Especially when sex had not been involved. After his heroic exit last night—and yes, he considered it heroic that he did not charge her into the bedroom and make love to her all night—he had gently kissed her and sent her to bed. A few hours later, she was excitedly chattering about an idea. She shared her insight with Tyler, and he hurried her to the vehicle as soon as day broke.

For Tyler, it had been another night of a fitful few hours' sleep. He had never in his life wanted someone to be innocent. He had lain there recounting the conversation with Mallory in his head. Any other time, he would not have hesitated to move forward with an arrest. He would have turned the case over to the detectives of record and recused himself. Instead, he found himself searching for a tiny thread of hope—any one piece of evidence that would turn the focus in this case to another suspect.

He had watched the clock until he was sure Mallory had at least a few hours of sleep. Then he went into the room and woke her. Even in her sleep, she seemed stressed. The space between her eyebrows was clenched together, as if she couldn't escape her thoughts. Her hands were in fists. The urge to crawl in beside her and hold her until she relaxed almost won.

Now he glanced at her as they drove and wondered what she was thinking. She was staring out the window of the passenger's seat, deep in thought.

She couldn't breathe. Her lungs felt like a brick was smashing them. Please let the information be in there. Why had she not thought of it before? Damian was a computer geek, for crying out loud. He backed up his computers religiously, and they had found his external drives. With all of the pressure and stress, she hadn't even thought of it. He kept a second computer that held all of his personal business. That computer was not at the house, and it had not been returned along with his other things from the car. There was only one place it could be.

Damian had been distracted lately, but he had given no indication of what it was, other than the business merger. Insurance policies putting Emma in the position to inherit millions? It just didn't fit. Why would he have done that? Had things gotten so distant between them that she had no idea he had changed future plans? The idea of it scared her to death, but it also reminded her that unless they figured things out, she could very easily end up in jail—or dead.

Mallory looked at Tyler. As he drove, he kept his eye on the rearview mirror. She was more than grateful for him. She also had to admit to herself that she had missed him in her life. Once this was over, she had to tell him that—if she got the chance. She turned to stare out the window again.

Tyler suddenly shifted to a more alert position while now watching his side mirror.

"Are you buckled up?"

She didn't have a chance to answer. The impact of metal scraping metal jerked them both forward, causing their necks to whip. Tyler kept control of the car, but they swerved into another lane and almost hit an oncoming car.

"Hang on!"

The black, tinted-windowed car that had slammed into them was now swerving up on the right. The taillight made a popping sound as it crashed onto the pavement. Tyler's hands were quick and skilled behind the wheel. The sounds of tires screeching and metal scraping together were louder and scarier than any noise Mallory had experienced before.

"Son of a bitch!"

They were lurched forward in the car when they were rammed from behind. Mere seconds later, they were slammed from the right side again. That was when Mallory figured out there was more than one car after them.

As an intersection quickly approached, the cars had begun to trap them on either side.

"Hang on tight, honey."

Tyler slammed on his brake and took a hard left heading down the wrong way of a one-way street. Call it divine intervention, and Mallory was sure it was, but there was not another car heading down the street at the moment.

Tyler immediately navigated through the downtown streets and found a parking garage in which to hide the vehicle. He turned off the headlights and steered through the dark garage until he found a somewhat hidden spot. He unbuckled his seatbelt quickly and reached over to unbuckle hers.

"Can you move? Are you okay? Are you hurt?"

Mallory could hear him speaking to her, but she couldn't find her voice to answer him. She nodded her head in affirmation.

"Good. We need to move, and move quick. It won't take them long to start searching."

He watched the mirrors and waited, and then, when he felt confident that the two cars were not coming, he turned off the SUV.

"Wh-wh-where are we?" Her voice was shaking, probably as much as every bone in her body.

"We're in a medical-center parking garage. I doubt very seriously that whoever that was will come looking for us in this type of place."

But let's not take chances, he finished silently.

Looking behind him into near pitch-black, he stepped from the car and looked around to see if anyone had followed them. He walked around the back of the damaged vehicle and opened the door for Mallory. He guided her out of the car, placed his hand on her elbow to steady her, and then steered her to the nearest elevator.

He pulled out his cell phone and punched his speed dial. The tables were turned; the sun was barely coming up, and this time it was Alexander getting woken up. Tyler took a split second to relish that fact.

After explaining the circumstances, Alexander told him he would have a car sent immediately. They agreed on a pick-up point, and Tyler quickly disconnected the call. As they stood near an elevator, Tyler took in his surroundings. Making a quick recon, he changed his mind. Soon, cars would start to enter the garage for the business day.

Taking her hand, he said, "Come on; we're sitting ducks like this."

He led her down a few flights of stairs. Cautiously, they entered the third level of the parking garage. Once he found a janitorial closet, he tested to see if it was unlocked. Of course, it wasn't. Mallory immediately assumed they would keep looking, but he dropped her hand and reached for something in his pocket.

"A credit card? Seriously?" Mallory raised her eyebrow and looked at him incredulously.

He simply shrugged and said, "It's a simple lock, no need for fancy tools."

He slipped the card between the doorframe and lock. Within seconds, he had the door open. The closet was dark and cool. He clicked the flashlight on his phone for a small amount of light.

"I'm surprised you're willing to run your battery down."

"Extended battery. Best purchase I ever made."

She checked her own phone as she put her purse down on the cement floor. She had one bar of battery left.

"I need to look into one of those."

She reached her hand up to rub the back of her neck. She ached in several places from being jarred in the car. But she wouldn't complain. They were alive.

Tyler had shifted a few things around and presented two

five-gallon buckets to sit on. She lowered herself down and sighed out of pure exhaustion.

"You saved my life. Again."

"We got lucky, that's all."

Mallory knew better, but she let him be humble.

"Someone tried to kill us," she whispered.

Wanting to calm her fears, Tyler reached over, placed his arm around her, and tucked her close to him. He knew she had had an enormous shock. It didn't hurt to have her close to him. She never ceased to amaze him; her endurance was bottomless. Any other woman would probably be crying uncontrollably, maybe even getting sick after the adrenaline rush.

She looked up at him, full of resolve.

"I may be guilty of hiding Emma's paternity results, but I'm not guilty of murder."

Somewhere in between trying to keep the car on the road and dodging getting them killed, he had already come to that conclusion. Insurmountable evidence made it appear as if she was guilty, but there was no way a selfish murderess would put her own life in danger—not once, but twice.

"Yeah, I know."

Mallory took a deep breath of relief. She nodded once and then remained thoughtful. She finally said, "Okay."

"Okay, what?"

"Okay to moving Emma to a safe house."

He nodded. "I know it's hard, but it's the right thing to do. Especially now."

His concern humbled Mallory. For a split moment, she looked back on her life with Damian and realized how much time they had truly lost in their marriage. She knew they hadn't loved each other. Really loved each other. Of course, they had cared, and if Damian hadn't been killed, chances were, they would have remained married. Being with him had brought Emma into her life. That was a choice she simply could not make herself regret.

Watching Tyler's features creased with concern for her and for

Emma suddenly made Mallory want to hang on tight to the feeling that was simply overtaking her: love. At some point in this mess, her feelings for this man had become no longer buried deep in her heart. They were free again.

Tyler laced his fingers with hers and gave her a gentle squeeze. She was about to tell him—the words were on her lips—but then Tyler's phone buzzed with a text message saying a driver had arrived to take them to safety.

CHAPTER 18

⌣ ⌣ ⌣

The car had barely come to a stop when Tyler opened the passenger door. They needed to get out of there quickly and not be seen. He wasn't sure what pissed him off more: the two idiots that had tried to run them down or the fact that he hadn't figured out the source of danger yet. No one other than the detectives knew that Mallory was staying with him. So how did they get exposed? There was a leak at the damn department.

Tyler walked close to Mallory as they approached the front door. He unlocked it, scanned the area as the driver rode away, and ushered her into the house. He tapped the keypad to disarm the alarm and then immediately reset it. After securing the locks on the door, he headed straight to his laptop.

"You're going to work more? You need rest, Tyler."

"Honestly, I don't think I could string two thoughts together right now. I just want to have the security monitor set up next to the bed. Just to be alert."

Tapping the keys on the computer immediately split the screen into four window sections. Illuminated pictures of the grounds around the house appeared.

He caught her concerned expression. Reaching for her hand, he said, "It's just a precaution."

"You think of everything. Has anyone talked to you about paranoia?" A small smile appeared on her face.

"That's a huge can of worms."

He didn't reach for her. He simply held her hand. He was grateful that she didn't move closer. If she did, he wouldn't have the strength to stop. Somehow, he knew being with her this time would be different, and he knew damn well once wouldn't be enough.

After he walked her to her bedroom, she hesitated outside the door. She parted her lips as if she was about to speak. But she didn't. Instead, she rose up on her toes and kissed him lightly. It was over quicker than a blink. His body still reacted though. He wanted her. Soon.

~ ~ ~

Lonnie Jaxon was beyond livid.

Was good help that hard to find? Not once, but twice, his orders had been failed. His eyes were cold, hard as steel, and he looked at his lackey as if his eyes alone could rip him apart. Killing the useless man that sat with his head down and his eyes averted would be easy. Yet, the man would feel no pain. He liked people who disappointed him to feel pain. He just didn't have the time right now.

"When I brought you into this organization, you assured me that you would be an asset."

"Yes, sir," he answered obediently.

"Yet, you have failed me. Twice." Jaxon spoke without emotion. "That's more chances than any of my former employees have ever received before."

"I can make it up to you." He spoke nervously. He licked his lips, and his eyes were as wide as silver dollars. He knew if he didn't convince his boss, he was a dead man.

"You were asked to find my Mallory, not try to kill her."

"Yes, sir. I will do better, sir." It was his last words; he was dead seconds later.

CHAPTER 19

~ ~ ~

Mallory sat quietly in the overstuffed chair in the den, her chin resting on her knees and her hands clasped around her ankles. It seemed as if she had been sitting there forever. She checked her cell phone for the time—it was just after two. Which meant her parents had probably arrived at the cabin Tyler had arranged for them to stay at.

Her gaze tracked over the stuffed animal that lay in the chair across the room. It was Emma's. Her heart broke a little more each moment her daughter was gone.

Tyler had wasted little time putting his plan in motion to move Emma and her parents. She'd had only moments later that morning to prepare her daughter and convince her that it was going to be a wonderful adventure. In her head, she knew it was the right thing to do, but in her heart, she wanted her child back. She let out a sigh that, given the silence in the room, echoed loudly.

She had seen Tyler in action. He had been amazing, actually. He was definitely calm in dangerous situations. He was smart too. She would have never thought of hiding like they did. Knowing Emma was safe would allow him to work even more to find out who was trying to hurt her. She owed him that much.

Mallory shifted slightly in the chair and let her mind wander around the room. It was decorated for a man. She could smell the unique scent of Tyler's aftershave and old books. He was a reader. She had forgotten that about him. When they were in school, he was always reading something—mysteries and legal action novels had been his favorite. She hadn't missed the irony in that.

Out of the corner of her eye, she saw movement. Sami had nudged her hand for attention. She had never had a dog before. Maybe she should have. The thought occurred to her that maybe getting a puppy would help Emma after things settled down.

She bent low and gave Sami a quick kiss on the head.

"Thank you for being good for Emma."

She rewarded the dog with a soft scratch behind the ears. Sami trotted off, taking all the attention for what it was worth, and returned quickly with her favorite toy, the oversized tennis ball. She nudged Mallory with the ball and whined.

Chuckling, Mallory stood and walked toward the back door. Sami immediately dashed out into the yard and waited for Mallory to toss the ball. Rearing back for the longest throw she could muster, she tossed the ball, and immediately, Sami took off at full speed to retrieve it.

"Careful now, you'll spoil her."

Mallory didn't turn to acknowledge Tyler's presence. He probably knew she was headed out the back door before she ever opened it. She simply replied, "She's earned it."

She could hear him coming off the deck steps. The grass muffled his footsteps as he approached her. He took her by the shoulders and turned her around to face him.

"You're upset." His voice was soft, and his words seemed to cover her like a blanket.

Instead of looking him in the eye, she turned and scanned the yard for Sami, who had taken a detour on her game of fetch. "I... no. Yes." She turned back to Tyler. "Of course, I am. Since Damian died, things have been happening that I truly only thought I'd experience in a movie theater."

"Yeah, I get that." He lifted his hand and tucked a strand of her hair behind her ear. "Not that it will make things better, but I just received a message that they reached the cabin safely."

"Thank you." She let out a throaty laugh and shook her head. A single tear fell down her cheek. She swiped it away quickly and took a deep breath, trying to hold back the flood of tears that threatened to spill over.

Damn. Tears again.

"Don't." He took her into his arms. "Don't cry."

She couldn't help herself. The tears just seemed to start spilling over like a broken dam. They stood there, unmoving. They were a perfect fit. Being in each other's arms seemed like the most natural thing.

Afterward, she leaned back and wiped her eyes. "I'm sorry. I should be stronger about all of this."

"By whose rules? I think you're entitled to a little breakdown. A lot has happened in a short time." His hand rubbed her back, and his voice kept a soothing tone.

"Yeah, I guess that's the understatement of the year."

"I know what I'm doing, Mallory. Trust me when I say I won't let anything happen to you or to Emma."

"The detectives have several questions about a lot of things. Things that made me look guilty even to you."

"Maybe we can't answer them right this minute, but we will."

Mallory moved away from him. "If Kendall's not the killer, then who?"

Tyler rubbed the back of his neck. "I don't know. If he was involved with something ... there's no evidence of it. Yet."

Lifting her hands up in defeat, Mallory shook her head in disbelief.

"I can't believe you don't think Kendall is capable of this entire thing. You don't know her; you haven't lived through her crap." She pointed a finger at her own chest. "I have. Emma has. Damian did. The people she interacts with vary from rich to shady. She's a chameleon, Tyler, but still, I don't know any of them personally. As far as I know, she doesn't have any close friends. Anytime Damian would talk about rehab or counseling, she would go off on a tangent."

"What about work?" Tyler asked, wanting to keep her talking as he moved closer to her. He could now see her mind working. This was much better than emotionally beaten Mallory. "There must have been people she interacted with through working."

She rubbed her arms as she thought about that. "I really don't know what I can tell you. I had never even heard of this Nick Hanson guy. I don't know where she picked him up along the way. Anytime we dealt with her, she was trying to make our lives miserable. Like I said, it was never about wanting to see Emma; it was about making Damian and me pay and, jeez, doing who knows what else."

She shifted her weight back and forth and stared at the ground with intense concentration.

"Don't you think it's possible that those two, Kendall and this Nick guy, planned this out themselves, without any help? Her levels of aggression have increased."

"Maybe the kidnapping was a mindfuck," he said. "Maybe there isn't anyone else involved and they are just damn good at covering their tracks. Maybe Damian really was the victim of a drive-by shooting. Maybe there's something deeper here with the insurance—a scam, maybe—that we haven't realized. All theories are possible at this point."

"I just can't for the life of me figure out why he would fall for any of her crap a second time. Why meet her? Why pay her off?"

"We have a drive-by shooting of a businessman about to break a new company into vast financial success. From what I can tell at the precinct, the 9-1-1 calls came in within minutes of the shooting, one from the convenience clerk and another by an unknown female. By the time the police did their investigation, there was nothing but a generic description of a black Escalade."

Mallory raised her head with her eyes squinted. "Wait. What did you just say?"

"The black Escalade was nothing more—"

"No." She shook her head. "The other part, about a female."

"Son of a bitch." Tyler had his phone out, dialing Detective Johnson. They finally might have struck a lead.

～ ～ ～

Tyler sat across the street as the scorching heat beat down on his car. In order to get more leads, it was time for desperate measures, and working with Johnson and Clark seemed like a good idea— even if they were actively trying to put Mallory behind bars.

After Tyler had begged Johnson to get the script of the un-identified caller, he tried not to dwell on the fact that this wasn't done earlier. It showed the call had been made from a motel lobby. Nowhere near the crime scene.

"You need to let me be the one to talk to him," Detective Johnson said.

"He will clam up in seconds. Do you know how many business-men have walked in and out of that motel in the last hour?" Tyler raised an eyebrow at Johnson. "It's pretty clear Mr. Kingston, the manager of this seedy place, is running more than a motel. And I bet my year's salary that Kendall Jenkins is employed here."

Beads of sweat were starting to trickle down their necks. They watched as Edmond Kingston pulled into the parking lot and en-tered the motel. A quick surveillance of the area revealed another gentleman leaving the motel while adjusting his tie.

Tyler made Detective Johnson give him his suit jacket. He fin-ger-combed his hair and tucked in his button-down shirt. "This better work."

"Remember: I'm the nice guy. You're the one with the no-non-sense police attitude." Tyler joked and then slapped Johnson on the back with one hand and headed toward the hotel. He looked over and gave Detective Clark a wave. Then snickered because that man could not contain his anger at having to play nice.

"You guys hear me okay?" Tyler asked as he adjusted his jacket, pulling firmly on each sleeve.

"Coming through clear," Johnson said.

"Here we go," Tyler said, sucking in a breath as he waltzed into the motel carrying an overnight duffle bag and went through the same routine as any other customer.

"I need a room, please."

"Smoking or nonsmoking?" the clerk asked.

"Smoking." Tyler tapped a credit card on the counter. "I sure have been busy. I hope to relax a little while I'm here. You know?"

The clerk looked up, slightly grinned, and kept typing. Politely she asked, "How long will you be staying with us, sir?"

"Just one night."

The clerk kept entering the information. Tyler then asked, "Are there any amenities? Hot tub? Sauna? Lounge?"

"There is an indoor pool with a hot tub. A nightclub is just down the street."

"A friend told me to talk to an Edwin Kingston. He is the manager, right?"

"Yes, sir." The clerk picked up the phone and buzzed for Mr. Kingston.

Tyler glanced at his phone, and it wasn't more than ten seconds before their target, Mr. Kingston, was behind the counter. He was a round man with salt-and-pepper hair, dressed in a cheap, tailored suit. His gaze was magnified behind his glasses, but there was also a spark of interest.

"McCormack." Tyler reached his hand out.

Mr. Kingston motioned for Tyler to walk toward the other end of the counter.

"How can I assist you, Mr. McCormack?"

"A friend thoroughly enjoyed his stay here last week," Tyler said with an undertone that surely Mr. Kingston didn't miss.

"I'm glad to hear that. Was there anything in particular he enjoyed?"

"Well, he didn't expand on specifics, but he does like dark-haired women. He mentioned that he received an excellent massage."

Mr. Kingston was silent for a moment. Tyler barely breathed as he forced himself to remain calm. There wasn't any way to force the man to openly offer up the unspoken services of the motel, so instead, he remained patient. It paid off, because the manager did not hesitate when he said, "I believe we may have something for you."

The clerk walked down and handed Tyler a room key. "You will be staying on the second floor, room 212."

"Thanks." He turned back to Mr. Kingston. "I'll be looking forward to that massage."

Tyler shook the manager's hand and walked toward the elevator. A short minute later, he was walking down to the hallway to room 212.

Within fifteen minutes, a knock sounded at the door. After checking the peephole, Tyler opened the door to Mr. Kingston.

"I assume you are happy with your accommodations?" His smile this time seemed genuine.

"Yes, sir."

"We have several businessmen who enjoy what our motel has to offer. However, there are some amenities we do not advertise to the public."

"Bingo." Tyler heard the whisper confirmation crackle in his ear.

Tyler forced a grin. "Yes. Don't ask; don't tell. I'm familiar with the concept."

Heart pounding, he shifted slightly, forcing the manager to turn his back to the window, ensuring he would not be able to take off running when confronted.

Mr. Kingston placed a white piece of paper on the small table by the window.

"This is a number you may call and receive the entertainment you were looking for within the hour. The rate is also included. Cash only, please."

Tyler chose that moment to reach into his pocket and pull out his badge. "And this is where you tell me what I want to know."

"I beg your pardon." Mr. Kingston immediately became skittish and began to sweat.

"I'm not here to bust your operation. However, I will let you know that this entire motel is under surveillance at this time. One word from me and we will shut this thing down, and you won't see the light of day for a very long time."

The man stood still as a statue.

"Or you can look at one photo and tell me what I want to know."
He nodded once.

Tyler showed him a photo of Kendall. "Has this woman done work for you?"

Oh, yeah. He knew Kendall. The flash of recognition was in his eyes.

"Don't lie to me. It's not worth it."

"Yes. Ms. Kramer has done several jobs here."

Tyler flipped the photo of Kendall back into his pocket. Kendall changed last names more often than he bathed his dog.

"When is she scheduled to be back here?"

"That's just it. She has missed three of her last appointments. She hasn't answered her phone either. Kendall has several regulars, and they have not been pleased with her absence."

Tyler kept a whole string of expletives from escaping his mouth.

After explaining to Mr. Kingston that working with the police would be beneficial, he also explained the intelligence of keeping this motel running legally.

There was no doubt in his mind that Kendall made that call that occurred a full three minutes before the clerk had called in the shooting, which could only mean that she knew about the shooting before it had happened.

CHAPTER 20

~ ~ ~

It took an hour and a half to complete the chores she had ordered herself to do. First, she had vacuumed the downstairs. Sami was a beautiful dog, but she sure did shed. Then she wiped down the bathrooms and tidied up the kitchen. It was the least she could do.

Tyler had instructed her to stay off the phone and Internet. Both could be traced, and he didn't want to take any chances with her being alone. He had set the alarms and closed all of the windows. She felt barricaded in. Literally.

Without Emma and her parents, she suddenly felt very alone—and somewhat stir-crazy.

She looked at the clock for the hundredth time. The day seemed to stand still as she waited for Tyler to come back. She knew he was fine. This was his job. But still, so much had happened in such a short time. She worried every moment of the day.

She sat on the couch trying to read a book she had taken off one of his shelves—well, her eyes were tracking the page, anyway. If someone asked, she probably couldn't explain one thing about the plot. Her left hand absently petted Sami while her mind wandered.

The shadows began to crawl across the room as the sun began to set. Mallory tossed the book aside and pulled her legs up to her chest. She wrapped her arms around them and rested her chin on her hands.

So many things had happened in so little time. It was hard to deal with it all. She was somewhat disturbed at the way her feelings were beginning to resurface for Tyler. To say the least, it was confusing. In some bizarre way, it felt completely right having him back in her life. Would she even have a life if the police arrested her? She knew Emma would be taken care of, but it tore her heart knowing she wouldn't have her mommy or her daddy.

The now familiar sound of the security system beeped, indicating that Tyler was back. As he walked into the living room, he looked around.

"Wow. Did you clean up in here today? Thanks, but you didn't have to." He touched her shoulder and settled next to her.

"There wasn't much else to do. How did it go?" she asked, immediately wanting to know.

"The detectives went back to the station. I filled Alexander in on the way. The manager confirmed that Kendall worked the day the 9-1-1 call came in. It has also been confirmed that that particular call came in three minutes before the clerk's. That gives us enough probable cause that she had prior information of the shooting."

"But it doesn't clear me. It just shows she's involved." Mallory's tone sounded defeated. "Are they going to think I set that up too?"

"We'll keep digging. I also have the guest list of the motel that day. We'll start making connections." He put his hand under her chin and brought her eyes up to meet his. "You okay?"

"Just exhausted," she said. "And thinking about everything that's happened."

"Hey, evidence turned up today. That's a good thing. Let's get you some rest. We've taken every precaution to secure this house. Nothing will happen tonight. Emma and your parents are just as safe and secure."

"Do you ever wonder what might have happened if things turned out differently? I mean, if you had actually talked to me at the college that day?"

The question took Tyler off guard. "Um … yeah. I used to a lot."

"We've both had good lives. I mean, well, I have Emma, and you have had two very good careers."

Tyler smiled at her and wondered where she was going with this. "But—"

"I think you know what I'm trying to say." She pulled her lip between her teeth and looked him directly in the eye. "Things happen for a reason, but I never forgot about you."

"Maybe it does, but here we are, Mallory, and it's pretty clear we never got that closure stuff people always talk about," he said with a side grin.

"No, we didn't." Her eyes went to Tyler's mouth.

Mallory held her breath, thinking maybe this wasn't the right time. Maybe she had said too much. They had shared a few kisses and moments, but maybe that's all it was.

"Honey," he said, his eyes searching hers. "I don't know what's happening here. But I know I've wished for it for years." He took a strand of her hair and played with it between his fingers. "I can't make any promises. I don't know what's going to happen tomorrow or if we will win this thing. I only know that right here, right now, I want you."

When she looked up at him again, he could tell she wanted him every bit as much. It was as if time had faded away and it was the two of them again.

"I want you too," she whispered, the words rushing out of her competing with a heavy sigh.

He framed her face with his hands and then pulled her to him. He placed his lips gently on hers, almost like a feather. With a little moan, she opened her lips for him, and the passion ignited between them. Their tongues danced with each other. She threaded her fingers in his hair and moved up on her knees. Her touch was driving him insane. His hand moved toward the center of her back, caressing her as she pushed him back against the couch and straddled her legs across his lap.

Reaching for the hem of her T-shirt, he pulled it up and stroked his hand up the side of her stomach. There was so much tension and need between them. The connection between her skin and his hand sizzled with need. This woman righted his world again.

He wanted, needed, to save her, to protect her, to make her his own again.

Ding-dong.

"You gotta be kidding me," Tyler growled as he stilled.

Mallory sighed. "I don't want you to answer it." She began to make a trail with her lips down the side of his neck. His nerves sizzled in every place her lips touched.

Tyler responded to her by moving his hands up and down her back, pressing them together.

Ding-dong.

"Son of a bitch. They're not going away." He willed himself to put space between them. They both straightened their clothes. He kissed her quickly on the mouth.

With a deep growl, he said, "We're not finished here. Not by a long shot."

He turned and walked toward the door. Fear nearly paralyzed him when he checked the peephole. He prepared himself for the possible arrest they feared was coming as he opened the door to the detectives.

Detective Johnson spoke first. "Good afternoon, and no, we are not here to arrest her."

An equivalent weight of a ton of bricks felt like it was lifted off Tyler's chest.

"Do you have time for a visit?"

Tyler looked at Detective Clark, who remained silent and emotionless. Yeah, he was about as excited to be here as Tyler was to see him standing there. He stepped to the side and motioned with his arm for the men to enter his home. He turned to see Mallory standing in the entryway, silent as a mouse but emanating concern. Immediately, he went to her and placed a supportive arm around her waist.

"Why don't you go upstairs and turn the television on? This shouldn't take long."

Mallory's first reaction was to refuse to leave, but she also was intelligent enough to realize the detectives were not going to speak freely with a suspect sitting in the same room. She turned to the detectives and nodded.

When Tyler heard the door to his den close and the television turn on, he motioned for the men to enter the living room. "What have you got?"

It was Detective Clark who actually began. "This information just came to our attention when we got back to the station."

Detective Johnson held up a hand to thwart his partner from continuing. "We initially held off on sharing this piece of evidence until it had been processed through the lab. No fingerprints or other DNA had been found on it. It's clean. After much deliberation and debate, we have decided to share with you."

Johnson reached into his suit pocket and pulled out a tri-folded document.

"It's a copy of the original document that is registered as evidence, of course."

Tyler reached over and took the papers. Upon examining it, he discovered it was the paternity results. He quickly scanned the document and realized it was confirmation of what Mallory had told him. Damian was not Emma's father.

Son of a bitch, Tyler thought. Damian had known. Then he flipped the page over and read the return address on the copy of the envelope. The blood seemed to rush from Tyler's head. It sounded like an ocean flowing through his ears, and he felt certain that every cell of his DNA had frozen into ice cubes. If Mallory knew that Damian had this information, it would be the motive they needed to charge her with murder. If Mallory knew who had sent it and never told him, then … words failed him.

He cleared his throat once, then again. Finally, he found his voice. "You're certain this is what I think it is?"

"Yes." Both detectives responded at the same time. As he glanced at both of them, he had to give Detective Clark credit. There was an actual look of concern on the man's face.

All Tyler could do was nod his head over and over. Every muscle began to twitch. His jaw could easily snap as tightly as his teeth were clenched. He looked at the document again and read the section one more time just to make it real.

His reaction surprised him. It wasn't to find the truth. It wasn't to rush out and find a way to finally convict a murderous criminal—the same criminal who had ruined his life. He honestly didn't care at this moment if Mallory was guilty or innocent either. The urge to run upstairs, grab Mallory, throw her in a vehicle and drive as far away as possible was engulfing his mind, his thoughts, and his instincts.

He forced out the words, "This does not prove anything."

"Not necessarily," Detective Johnson replied. "Look at the return address. It's local. He's here."

"You have no proof that Mallory knows about this. We just found strong evidence that Kendall knew about the shooting before it happened. There's more hard evidence of motive against Kendall than all the circumstantial evidence you keep trying to pile on Mallory."

"We are following all possible leads here. We have also put an APB out," Detective Johnson stressed, with a hint of frustration. "You came to us wanting to collaborate. Here we are."

"Kendall was blackmailing Damian—and this could prove she was—and I sure as hell will make a case against her. Now you're trying to tell me Lonnie Jaxon is somehow involved with Mallory. You're both nuts. I'm not going to let Mallory take the rap for this. This … this only proves that her life is in danger, and so is her daughter's."

God help me if I'm wrong. No, Tyler immediately pushed that thought from his mind. He had to protect her. Lonnie Jackson was the most evil bastard walking the earth. There was no way Mallory was involved with him.

"Look, we also cannot ignore the fact that this document could have obviously motivated Ms. Jones to take matters into her own hands. Desperate mothers do desperate things. We need to show this to her; we need to find out if she has had contact with Jaxon."

"Get out."

Neither detective moved. Instead, Detective Johnson continued.

"Be careful, Tyler. You know more than any of us exactly what folks are capable of. This man is a known killer. You of all people know he stays one step ahead of the law. Don't ignore your gut instinct."

Fury snaked up his spine. With his teeth gritted and his voice at a growl, he distinctly repeated, "Get. Out."

This time the detectives rose from their seats. It was Detective Clark who had the last words. "Look, you and I may not see eye-to-eye. Hell, it's safe to say we don't even like each other. But what happened to that girl out there in West Texas was not your fault. You did the best you could. Probably better than any of us could. Just don't lose your objectivity here. Keep yourself alive."

There was nothing Tyler could say. Nothing he wanted to say.

CHAPTER 21

～ ～ ～

A good while later, Tyler sat on his back deck, his thoughts rioting. Knowing he should have gone upstairs to interrogate Mallory about her possible knowledge of Lonnie Jaxon and the paternity papers, he couldn't bring himself to do it. He needed time to absorb the magnitude of the situation.

Mallory could be working with his worst nightmare.

Mallory could be unknowing and innocent.

Either way, Lonnie Jaxon's wrath had wormed its way back into his life. This couldn't be happening. Not again. This time it had come full circle. Despite the fact that he had uprooted his life, started a new career, and left everything behind, it might have well been just yesterday.

This time was different, though. He wasn't sitting in a courtroom with his hands tied. Whether Mallory was guilty or not, he didn't want to see her murdered, and unless he stopped Jaxon, that's exactly what would happen.

There was no avoiding it. The conversation had to happen. She had to know about the case and how he had gotten an innocent woman killed. She had to know how much danger she was in. He leaned his head back against the lounge chair and made himself concentrate on breathing. In. Out.

～ ～ ～

The sky was glowing bright, even though it was the middle of the night. The lights from the police cars and ambulance danced in the darkness like strobe lights. Tyler killed the engine of his car and stepped out. Everyone stopped and stared at him as he walked closer to the edge of the glistening water. With his own voice echoing across the silent listeners, he tried to ask the detective if the body lying by the edge was still alive. No one would answer him.

With an unsteady breath, he walked closer to the blonde, lifeless body.

"No!" His voice shook with sadness. "Is she …?"

Again, no one would answer him. The looks on the faces of the law enforcement officers working the scene were condemning him to hell. It was his fault. He let her die. He didn't save the innocent. He'd set the guilty free. Accusatory eyes sentenced him to hell.

His stomach threatened to revolt. As he bent down to get a closer look at her face, it was as if she stared directly into his soul. It was a long time before he had the courage to look away. Finally, Tyler scanned her body and witnessed the evidence of the torture she had endured in her final moments. Every cut. Every gash. Every rope burn. His heart beat so loudly that it echoed in his head. He gave attention to each careful step that the evil monster had taken to ensure there would be no evidence found on her person.

He felt as ice cold as the body of the lifeless innocent lying before him. The guilt threatened to lurch him into the water and drown him in guilt. He opened his mouth, but no words could express the depths of his sorrow. Despite the medical examiner's warning look, he stroked her hair and touched the cold flesh of her hand.

"Why didn't you help me?"

Tyler's head jerked up to stare at her incredulously. Again, he tried to speak, but words would not form. Her blue eyes began to shimmer in the light, and her gaze reflected his own thoughts. It was almost impossible to break the connection. He had failed her. He hadn't believed her. She held his gaze with eyes that implored him, *You could have saved me.*

It was then that he screamed her name. "Mallory!"

"Tyler."

"God, I'm so sorry. Mallory!" He reached to hold her. To comfort her. She kept floating out of his reach.

"Tyler, it's me. Wake up."

He was floating backward, away from her. A voice from a distance was pulling at him.

"Tyler, please wake up!"

And then he was awake once again, with an unbending truth that he was responsible for an innocent woman's death. He hadn't been able to beat Lonnie Jaxon then, and he feared with all of his life that he wouldn't be able to save the blue eyes watching him now. Somehow, they had become one in his worst nightmare. He couldn't save Jennie. He *had* to save Mallory. Still hazy from the nightmare, he fought against the emotions flooding through him.

"Are you okay?" Mallory spoke to him with a voice of concern. "You were having a bad dream."

He looked around, blinking his eyes to regain focus, and he realized he had fallen asleep on the back deck. He had fought the idea of going into the house and, instead, had hidden while trying to make sense of his next move. The events of the day had brought back horrendous nightmares again.

Realizing he still had a grip on her arm, he released her. "I'm … um … sorry. I hope I didn't hurt you."

She rubbed her arm where his grip had been but shook her head in denial.

"No, I'm fine." She placed her hand on his thigh and began to pet him like she would have touched her daughter. "It must have been pretty bad. You were calling out."

"Look, I'm sorry. I usually never have people staying with me, so when the nightmares happen, there's no one around to hear it."

The look on Mallory's face indicated that she wasn't about to let it drop.

"It's okay. Really."

Except that it really wasn't. There was no way Tyler could

continue to avoid this conversation. It may not change the past, but it could definitely impact the future.

She searched his face for answers, but he just stared out into the yard deciding how to begin. Finally, she spoke. "Do you want to talk about it?"

"Honestly, I'm surprised you've waited this long." Once he started, the words just seemed to fall out. "You know about the case."

"Yes, I know about it. I wondered if there would come a day that you decided to tell me your story. Oh, Tyler, I can't imagine what you went through." Her voice was sympathetic when she spoke.

"I spend every day trying to put it behind me. To move on. To start over."

"Something that significant and life-altering never truly goes away, though, does it?"

"Never before had I ever wanted to lose a case. Jaxon deserved the death penalty, and I wanted to be there when they put the needle in his arm."

"You did your job. What happened to that girl was not your fault," Mallory said, reaching over to brush his hair out of his face; the gesture was a familiar comfort he remembered.

She simply was there. Silent and supportive. He realized she wasn't going to drill him with questions about the case, as most people did. He knew he needed to ask her about Jaxon, but sitting there with her, he realized he didn't want to lose her. He didn't care what the connection was anymore. Because he loved her.

And that was just one hell of a situation.

"Jennie was an innocent girl who had been raped and tortured by Lonnie Jaxon. I had evidence that could have proved him guilty of that crime as well as being a serial rapist. I was on the wrong side of the law. It wasn't my burden of proof. Had I done the moral thing and made sure that information and evidence got into the right hands, I would have been dead within twenty-four hours or disbarred—at the minimum. Or worse, he would have killed my father to punish me. So … I won, because that's what I did best.

My life solely consisted of freeing the guilty, and I actually slept at night. I hid my conscience behind the notion that all men deserved a fair trial."

Disgusted with himself, he turned his back on her and swung his legs to the other side of the lounge chair. With his head in his hands, he breathed a heavy sigh. "But not this time."

She placed her hand on his back and asked, "So what happened then?"

"The press had a field day. The sadistic bastard had the audacity to smile for the cameras. He tortured poor Jennie and then smiled for the damn press. My God, he even ended up getting television interviews. I can't imagine what it was like for her. I won't ever forget the look she gave me when the verdict was in. She knew she was dead, and I didn't do a thing."

"You can't think like that. I know it's hard, but she wouldn't have wanted you to blame yourself. If nothing else, know that."

"I should have found a way. If I had done something differently, maybe she would be alive."

"Then you would have been dead, or your father, like you said. You know as well as anyone that you have no control over clients—no matter how well you work the case. Besides, you haven't changed that much over the years. I'm certain you did everything in your power to get the prosecution to pay attention. You can't do your job *and* theirs. And you can't control fate."

"I put my profession above someone's life. Where's the justice in that?"

"Jennie died because an evil, sick bastard hurt her. Bottom line, he's responsible." She squeezed his shoulder. "You have to stop blaming yourself."

"It's not that easy." He looked over at her. "That's my story. That's why I'm not a lawyer anymore. I lost my edge. I handed over the rest of my cases to my partner, packed a bag, and left for six months. My father had a heart attack, and Alexander found me. He dragged me back here, and the next thing I knew, I was doing a little work for him here and there. Honestly, if it weren't for him, I don't know where I would be today. He kept me moving forward."

He forced himself to look at Mallory—to make eye contact with her and to ask the question that had the potential to change both their lives.

"Tell me, then, if you knew about how dangerous he was, why didn't you tell me you were contacted by him?"

~ ~ ~

She couldn't have been more stunned. As Mallory searched for words, she turned her head so he couldn't see the hurt in her eyes. She opened her mouth to speak and then shut it again. She shook her head back and forth to gain her wits.

"What on earth are you talking about?"

"The detectives showed me this earlier." Tyler reached into his back pocket and took out the copies of the paternity test and the envelope addressed to her from Lonnie Jaxon.

Mallory read it and then leaped to her feet and stumbled backward, as if the paper she held burned her skin.

"Oh, my God! How did they get this?" Her face turned accusatory toward Tyler. She pointed a finger at him and became outraged. "You kept this from me! You sat out here and didn't come to me with this information? How could you? I need to get to Emma."

There was no avoiding that accusation. Despite the fact that he wavered in his trust for her, she had a daughter that needed protection.

"It is what it is, Mallory. I needed time to think things through."

"Why? Because you don't trust me? Is that it? You think I know this … this person Lonnie Jaxon?" She trailed off, shoving her hands in her hair, and she turned away from him. He hated himself for being so indecisive, but right now, more than anything, he needed to maintain professionalism.

"I know you're worried about Emma," he said, "but she's safe. No one can get to her."

"That's why you wouldn't tell me where the safe house is." She spoke quietly. Her back remained turned away from him. "It wasn't to protect me from making a mistake. You think I'm guilty of these terrible things. You think I killed Damian because he found out about the paternity. You think I am capable of all these horrible acts."

She turned to go into the house, but not before she slapped him right across the face.

CHAPTER 22

～ ～ ～

Kendall stepped out of the front door to her apartment building holding a small duffle bag. She was so totally freaked about how everything was unraveling that she decided the best thing for her to do was to think about herself, and that meant it was time to get the hell out of town.

She was barely evading the police, and she sure as hell was not up for another meeting with the hot-looking detective. There was no way on earth she was going down for kidnapping and murder. How the hell had things gotten so far out of hand?

It seriously concerned her that she hadn't heard from Nick. How was she supposed to keep him under control if she couldn't find him? She held her left hand to steady her tremors so she could glance at her watch. She had just enough time to make it to the bus station.

The sun was just viable over the horizon; orange and pink lines were shooting out into a cloudless sky. If she hadn't been in such a rush, she would have stopped to snap a picture of it on her phone. Instead, she hurried down the steps to get herself farther away from the trouble in town and the danger she knew she couldn't avoid any longer. Had she known how deep things were going to spiral, she would have never started messing with Damian and Mallory. All she had wanted was a little revenge. Emma was her child, dammit; she should have control of what happened in her life. Isn't that why they called it the Law of Nature?

It was no surprise that she wasn't cut out for the traditional life of the domesticated mother—it was dreadfully boring, with too many do's and don'ts, but she did want a relationship with her own child. Kendall knew she had always reacted first by jumping in way over her head without any consideration to consequences. It made life interesting, at least. Just because she liked a little spice in her life didn't necessarily mean she was a project for head doctors. She simply liked getting her way. But this time, she had somehow found herself without her child and in way over her head. Shit happens, some people would say. Others would say, know when to cut your losses. In this situation, she agreed with the latter.

Just as she was about to turn the corner and head toward the bus station, someone grabbed her from behind with a strong grip covering her mouth. She slammed an elbow backward into his solar plexus, but he was anticipating the move and dodged the brunt of the blow. Instincts kicking in, she attempted to head-butt the attacker; motivated that she heard a grunt of pain, she tried to jerk free for a moment. Her attacker was slightly taller and a lot stronger. She realized he was wearing a mask when she was trying to jerk herself free. He held onto her arm and wrenched it backward, causing her to shriek with pain.

She lost her balance and fell to the ground. His arm circled her waist, pulling her back into his grasp, but she wasn't giving up easily. Fighting against him, the momentum sent them both falling hard onto the concrete. He body slammed himself on top of her. She still tried to scramble, but her efforts became useless. He outweighed her and outmuscled her. Before she could get free of him, his fist closed around her hair, pulling her neck painfully back and making her gasp for breath.

This time she frantically tried to shake her head back and forth in an attempt to evade the white handkerchief that covered her mouth and nose. The sweet stench of the cloth overwhelmed her senses and made her feel like she was headed for a bad high. Her legs began to buckle and her arms felt like concrete. Finally, her world began to fade to black.

~ ~ ~

Mallory stood over the bed folding her clothes into her suitcase, trying to calm her nerves. She was mad at herself because she shouldn't care if Tyler believed in her or not. She and Tyler had never been meant to be. She had gotten over him years ago, so she was sure she could do it again.

Except that lately, since he had popped back into her life, what he thought about her had somehow begun to matter. His distrust hurt her. The fact that he pretended to care, pretended to believe her, caused an acute sense of betrayal deep in her heart.

So she had to leave.

She was a successful, professional woman. She would march in there with her head held high and demand to be told the where-abouts of her daughter and her parents. She would go to them, and together, they would figure out how to prove her innocence. If not, she would hug her daughter with all of her soul and beg her father to take her safely out of the country. And he would do that for her. The idea of it already broke her cracked heart into pieces, but she had sworn to protect Emma, and that's exactly what she would do—even if it meant prison.

That thought brought fresh tears that Mallory frantically swept away with the back of her hand, and she walked into the guest bathroom to gather her toiletries. She paused at the sink and gripped the edge for support. Her head bent, she took in a few deep breaths. How had her life become so unraveled? She looked at herself in the mirror. She almost didn't recognize herself. Her features were tense and her skin looked tight. She battled to find her resolve with the urge to hide under a rock.

How in the hell had Lonnie Jaxon gotten his hands on the pa-ternity results? How had Damian intercepted the letter addressed to her? Had he known for long? Had he planned on confronting her? Did Damian lose his life somehow because of Lonnie Jaxon? Why did he really meet with Kendall all those months? Was he paying her off? Questions swarmed in her head.

Mallory knew one thing for sure. She would be damned if any of this harmed her daughter. She would not go down for anyone. Even if it killed her. Squaring her shoulders, she dug deep down into her soul for the courage and strength to face this situation—without Tyler.

When she returned to the bedroom, he was standing in the doorway. He was on his cell phone, and his eyes were staring at her suitcase. She could see the red imprint of her hand on his cheek. She didn't feel one ounce of guilt over that.

Upon seeing Mallory, he disconnected the phone, and with a quick nod toward the luggage, he asked her the obvious question, "Going somewhere?"

"None of your damned business." Her words were tightly clipped as she walked over to her suitcase and dumped her toiletries in without care to organization.

"I beg to differ," Tyler responded.

"You're fired, Mr. McCormack. I'm not your client anymore; therefore, I don't have to answer to you." She never looked at him. She just kept packing her things.

It didn't take an idiot to realize she was more than furious.

"I wasn't accusing you earlier. I was just trying to learn about any possible connections you may have had with a very dangerous man. The truth is, you've never talked to me about anything except your relationship with Damian and Emma. I don't know anything of the years of your life or the people in your life in between us and your marriage."

"And now you're suddenly curious? Why? Is it professional interest or personal? Are you now working with those other detectives to put me behind bars, or do you just want to sleep with me again? Which is it, Tyler?"

Her eyes threw daggers at him, but they shimmered with unfallen tears.

"Because, guess what? You can't have it both ways. I should

have stuck with my original instincts and stayed the hell away from you. I see now what a grave mistake I made asking you for help. I haven't been myself since Damian died, but now I'm going to make smarter decisions. I am leaving. Tell me right now where to find my daughter."

"I have to ask questions, Mallory. It's how I do my job."

He chose not to argue her points but to explain his.

"Your *job*? Which job? The one with the department, or your freelancing games? How can you sit there and lecture me when you can't even make sense of your own life? You stand there and push everyone away. Your career, your job, your friends. How can you effectively determine if others are guilty when you can't even see how buried you are in your own?"

"Ouch." For a moment, he was at a loss for how to respond. She had a point there. Instead of pulling the pin on that grenade, he tried to focus on the issue at hand. She didn't need to leave. He bravely, yet cautiously, took a few steps to close the distance between them. Mallory visibly stiffened, so he stopped a few feet away from her.

"Look, Mallory, I'm sorry. I know I did everything wrong with you years ago, and it looks like I'm not doing much better now. It isn't that I don't care. It isn't that I don't want to prove your innocence and protect you. Because, God knows I do. That's what I want more than anything—to keep you and Emma safe. And, hell yes, I want to sleep with you. But right now, you are in danger. I have to ask questions and look at things from all angles in order to keep you safe."

Tears swam in her eyes, creating a blurry vision for her, but she never wavered in her stance against him. She fought those tears with fervor, but she knew if she spoke, she would fall apart. So she said nothing and stared pointedly at him.

"And now I've made things even more messed up because I don't know how to channel what I'm feeling for you." He paused, not even breathing, and waited for what he'd just declared to make its way past her anger.

Mallory creased her eyebrows together and slowly took a

breath. He chose that moment to take her by the shoulders and bend down to look into her eyes.

"Mallory."

"I don't know what to say. One minute, you're my knight in shining armor battling the bad guys for me, and the next, you're judge and jury declaring me guilty. I need you on my side, Tyler, one hundred percent, but only if you truly believe in me."

It's now or never, she thought. She needed him to know everything.

"I have to know I can count on you. There's no one else. Not just because my future is at stake but because I'm starting to feel a whole lot for you too. And I sure as hell don't like how vulnerable that makes me."

For a guy who had declared his adult life as relationship and commitment free, he sure did seem to find himself in one hell of a complicated mess. At that moment, he hated himself for causing her any more grief and anguish. He regretted the fact that he had done so when all he wanted was to make her his.

"Sweetheart, the last thing I want to do is hurt you," he said softly. "I don't want you to go. Please. I don't have the words to tell you how much you walking out that door scares me."

He had lost her once because his feelings were too intense. Not this time. He was not going to lose her. He *couldn't* lose her.

"Do you trust me, Tyler? Do you believe in me?"

He blinked. She stared at him with conviction. "Yes. Yes, I do."

"So where do we go from here?" She asked herself as well as him.

"I'm not sure … knowing Lonnie Jaxon is somehow involved in this ups the threat level immensely. I do know that leaving here is the worst thing you can do."

Their gazes locked and held, and Mallory's heart clenched at the flood of emotions she was feeling.

"I'm still angry with you."

He gave her a side grin. "Yeah, well, that probably won't be the last time."

"I'm scared, Tyler. I can't face all of this alone. I need you. And

I need you to believe me when I tell you I never received that envelope."

Tyler didn't hesitate when he said, "I believe you."

Then he was crushing his mouth to hers, their tongues taking possession of each other's. She tilted her head back, giving all of herself to him. Heat exploded between them. He backed her to the bed as he yanked her suitcase to the floor. They both tumbled onto the mattress. He framed her head between his hands and looked down at her.

"Damn, what you do to me."

How could she be so angry with him one minute and want him so desperately the next? Moments ago, she was furious with him, and now she couldn't get close enough to him. Her brain was resenting him and his wavering trust. But her body—wow. Her body was begging for him. With a small smile, she wrapped her arms around his neck and brought him back to her lips.

For that moment, nothing mattered but the two of them. They made quick work of shedding barriers of clothing. The skin-on-skin connection seemed to make their desire even more desperate. This was so different than when they were younger. It felt new, but it was also familiar.

Mallory shifted until she was on top, straddling him and kissing him. A groan escaped him, and she glanced up to find his jaw tight and his head thrown back. His pelvis lifted into her demandingly. The friction they stirred could have started a fire. His skin felt warm and strong as she moved her hands up his chest. Under her touch, she could trace the outlines of his muscles. Her lips followed the path of her hands.

His fingers tangled in her hair and pulled her closer, and his tongue began to do erotic things to hers. Her head arched back as he traced a path to her ear. A hiss mingled with her breath as she reveled in sensations of each nip and caress on her skin. He remembered all of her sensitive places. He hadn't forgotten how to make her feel hot and alive.

Tyler slid lower, leaving a trail while his fingers curved around her hips. Nothing she had ever done before matched the way her body came alive at his touch. It was too much. Mallory shuddered, and for a moment, she hesitated to catch her breath. He chose then to move his concentration to her breasts. Her entire body erupted with chills when his mouth found her breast. His other hand covered the other as he molded it to his hands. Her nipples puckered with excitement as his tongue danced across them, giving each equal attention. She held him and pressed her hips to his.

Without a second's warning, he flipped them. As she lay there, his gaze perused her body with absolute desire. The hunger in his eyes almost undid her. The way he touched her, she swore she could feel it in the depths of her soul. Then his hands were there, in the center of her thighs. Her heart threatened to beat out of her chest. She teetered along the edge between pleasure and excitement. His invasion made her squirm, and before her world exploded into a fury of spasms, he wedged his body between her thighs. He held himself up by his arms as he kissed her in a way that thoroughly claimed every part of her. His thigh nudged between her legs with a rhythm that kept her swollen and ready.

Her fingers greedily wandered to his erection. He was engorged and straining beneath her grip. She stroked him with a firm but sensual grip. Her thumb pressed against the vein underneath him, and when she trailed the length of him, he flexed beneath her touch. At that moment, Tyler could have died a happy man. He had her in his arms. With her cocooned beneath him, his world was right.

"Now, Tyler." Anticipation seared his brain as her words literally rocked his world.

Without a word, he took her hips in both of his hands and thrust into her in one claiming motion. They both froze as the tumultuous sensations overcame them. He placed a gentle kiss to her brow. That's when she realized he was shaking. She cradled his face in her hands and locked her legs around him. She brushed her fingers through his hair and brought their lips together again. She rocked her hips against him, desperate for relief and wanting, needing him to move inside her. Tenderness warred with lust as together they began to move. Their bodies undulated in a synchronized rhythm. With each touch, each kiss, their need consumed the other. One of his hands slid down and cupped her behind to adjust his angle deeper. At that moment, nothing else existed but the two of them. Their bodies touched everywhere. Every muscle, every nerve was set on fire as they chased each other's relief.

CHAPTER 23

~ ~ ~

Mallory lay in bed listening to the water from the shower run. What they had done had been amazing. She couldn't remember it ever being like that with Damian. Never in a million years did she think Tyler would be a part of her life again. He made her feel protected from all danger that lurked around her, and it filled her with hope that together, they could prevail. But her head was afraid to let those emotions take root when it could all so easily be crushed. She wouldn't regret any of it. She would savor what time she had left with him. Besides, he made no mention of a relationship or future. Sleeping together was probably some sort of reunion for him, because memories of feelings resurfaced.

But he'd meant what he said. He wanted her to stay, even if it was only because Lonnie Jaxon was somehow involved. She wouldn't let herself think of anything other than the fact that she needed him and his ability to prove her innocence. She couldn't afford to; her heart couldn't take the disappointment when he walked away again. And he would. That's what Tyler did.

"We need to talk," Tyler said, walking back into the bedroom with a towel hung around his shoulders. He had put on his jeans. He had just spent the last twenty minutes distancing himself from the one woman he wanted to lose himself in. He had to regain his objectivity. He couldn't afford to compromise her safety just because he had lust in overdrive.

"Not exactly the words a girl wants to hear right after mind-blowing sex."

She shifted herself up to a sitting position and quickly tossed Tyler's T-shirt on to grasp some sort of protective barrier. She had a hard time keeping her attention on his face, though. His bare chest made her want to repeat the last hour. She trailed her eyes up to his face, and with his hair messy and damp, she immediately wanted him again.

Because he couldn't help himself, he leaned over and kissed her still-swollen lips. One kiss turned to two. He leaned back and gazed at her. Her hair was still mussed from their lovemaking, and she smelled like him. Memories of what they had done still hovered over them. He forced himself to get up off the side of the bed and put a little space between them.

"Mind-blowing is right, but the clock is ticking. I know my timing sucks after … well. I just know there is something we are missing."

"Okay, we can talk to the *n*th degree, but I still don't have any answers. I have no idea how Jaxon even knows me, much less had any knowledge of the paternity."

"Look at it from this perspective: Damian knew about the paternity and never said anything to you. There's no date stamp on the envelope, so we have no idea how long he knew about the paternity. But if you think about it, it all fits. He was meeting Kendall monthly to pay her off for keeping quiet that he wasn't the father. It's the only thing that makes sense. So the question remains: How the hell is Jaxon involved—and why?"

"Way to ruin my temporary make-believe world."

"Honey, trust me: what we just did was not make-believe. It was definitely real, and I want to do it again," he said, caging her between his arms. The action was so intimate that she felt warm all over.

"In order to do that, we have to put trouble behind us."

He kissed the top of her head so gently that it made her stomach flutter.

"And that Nick Hanson. How does he fit into this? Could I just be the victim of parallel hells?" Mallory ventured. "Maybe there's a chance Kendall is messed up with both."

"Neither of them fit the profile of anyone who has worked with Jaxon. He is picky of who he chooses to let in his organization. He holds his refined appearance in high regard; he wouldn't waste his time with thugs and whores."

Tyler sat on the edge of the bed and placed his hand on her thigh. Touching her was like a lifeline.

"The kidnapping attempt was sloppy at best. With the paternity exposed, it would make sense that Kendall got him to do it. She would have felt justified in taking back something that was hers. Maybe she had Damian shot out of anger."

"We still don't have our hands on Damian's personal computer. If we're lucky, he may have something on there that will shed some light. Do you think he upped his insurance because he was worried someone might be after him?"

"Maybe. In the meantime, you have to do everything I say. I don't want you hurt in any way."

Tyler waited for her to respond. He was in this for the long haul, no matter what. He had committed as much as he stood under the hot shower. No more back and forth. There was no doubt in his mind that Mallory was not in cahoots with Jaxon. Somehow, some way, he was going to nail that son of a bitch to the wall and shove his testicles down his throat. Or die trying.

He was careful not to make any declarations to Mallory when they made love. And yeah, that's what they did. It was more than sex. He would keep his emotions in check for now. So much more easier said than done, but when this was over, they owed each other a chance at happiness together.

She nodded in agreement that she would follow his lead.

"Okay, then," he said as he dipped his head down and slanted his mouth over hers possessively. As much as he would have liked to linger there for another hour or so, he pushed himself up and off the bed. "Let's get you dressed; we have a computer to find."

"What? Now?" Her voice sounded slightly confused. "It's almost dark outside."

"It's easier to maneuver the back roads in the dark." His eyes were taking in her body beneath his T-shirt. He liked her that way—nothing but his clothes barely covering her.

"I'm coming with you?" she asked as she headed to the bathroom.

"Yeah, actually." He was still watching her intently. He knew he was making her self-conscious because her cheeks filled with color.

"But if you don't hurry and get dressed, I can't be responsible for causing a serious delay."

With a mischievous grin, she closed the bathroom door.

～ ～ ～

Tyler poured himself a second cup of coffee and stifled a yawn. The three of them huddled around his office as he worked his magic on Damian's personal computer. The second attempt to retrieve it from his office had occurred without incident. Tyler had taken extra precautions navigating the back roads and doubling back twice before he felt confident they had not been followed.

Alexander had shown up with pizza and was currently concentrating on his own laptop. Mallory sat between them and took notes as they shared ideas and strategies. Tyler felt like his world had righted again—except for the fact that his future happiness revolved around catching a killer and keeping his woman alive.

"The flowers."

"What flowers?" Alexander asked.

"Ohmigod. He's the one that sent me the flowers," Mallory said incredulously.

"Who? When?"

Tyler watched the exchange between the two and tried to follow where her thoughts were going.

Before clarifying the questions, Mallory asked, "May I ask a question?"

Both men waited.

"What is it about me that makes me such an easy target to pin all of this on?"

Alexander shifted his glasses and cleared his throat. "Nothing."

"That's not true."

"Just walk me through it and tell us what's on your mind, honey." Tyler redirected her because he was afraid she was about to lose her train of thought.

He kept his eyes on her as she rose from the table and began to pace around the room with her hands on her hips.

"The day we buried Damian, I received a huge, almost inappropriate, bouquet of red roses. I was so repulsed by the card, I thought maybe I had received them by mistake. Damian and I had an agreement that he would not waste money on expensive flowers, so I knew he hadn't sent them before the accident. Anyway, the card said, 'One door closes; the other one opens. Your heart is destined to be mine.'"

She turned and looked at both men. Neither of their expressions changed until she added, "The card was signed 'L. J.'"

Tyler's jaw clenched. "That's it. It's not about money. It's not even about Emma. Mallory, it's about you."

"No, that's crazy! Like I told you before, I've never even met the man."

He rose so quickly from his chair that it scraped the hardwood floor and nearly knocked over. He came around and pulled her from the window. Alexander's eyebrows rose as he stopped typing and jerked his head toward Tyler's actions.

Gripping her arms in both of his hands, he spoke to her in a grave tone.

"Lonnie is a lot of things, but *crazy* isn't a word I would use to describe him. He will do whatever it takes to get what he wants. He wants you."

"Oh, wait. Oh, no." Suddenly, she was very concerned. "The

police will think that card proves I have had contact with him. There's enough incriminating evidence that this will just be icing on their damned cake!"

At that moment, Tyler was more concerned with keeping her alive than with what the police thought. He turned from her because he knew fury emanated from his pores. He felt lethal. In that moment, Tyler knew they had figured it out. This web of danger was spun at the hands of one evil, sick fuck.

"Where's the card?" Alexander asked.

"I almost threw it away, but it was weird enough that something made me hang onto it. Especially looking back now at the timing of it. It's in the kitchen drawer."

Tyler walked across the room to the whiteboard and picked up his dry-erase marker. He added to the timeline with distinct, quick marks. Mallory and Alexander turned their attention to him.

Commanding himself to speak in a calm voice, he said, "Kendall and Damian began monthly meetings about six months ago after the adoption was final. We believe he was paying her off with 5k each meeting. Damian is killed in what can only be classified for sure at this time as a drive-by shooting. There is still no lead on the Escalade or anyone in it. Two 9-1-1 calls are made. We can now place Kendall as the caller of the one made three minutes earlier."

He made a new tag on the line.

"Mallory receives flowers from 'L. J.' the day of the funeral, which we can assume is Jaxon. Bogus divorce papers and an anonymous tip, which I might theorize as coming from Kendall, ignites the investigation onto Mallory for murder-for-hire." He paused and then continued speaking, more to himself than to anyone else. "Now, where does Lonnie boy fit into all of this? We need to see if we can tie the Escalade to him. It's probably a wild goose chase; he covers his tracks quite well."

He kept scribbling his timeline as he walked his way through the events. "After that, a shooting at the Jones residence, a kidnapping attempt on the dead man's daughter." Drawing two arrows from Emma's name, he wrote as he spoke. "Is it because Kendall felt justified in taking back what was hers, or was it a sick game by Jaxon?"

Alexander walked to the board, picked up another marker, and added another arrow. "Somewhere in here, Damian became aware of the paternity results." He drew another tag, and under it, he wrote "Nick Hanson." "And I would bet good money that Jaxon had Nick doing some dirty work that Kendall just might not know about."

"Even though it goes against his style, you might be right."

Mallory added, "I don't see how this makes the entire thing about me. I seem to be the scapegoat. Everything is pointing at putting me in prison."

"Not exactly. His game is to make you desperate. To need his help. I bet my life, if you turned to him for help, all of this would go away."

It was Alexander who spoke. "But there was one thing he wasn't counting on and that's—"

Tyler finished his sentence for him. "Me."

CHAPTER 24

~ ~ ~

The next day, Tyler approached the table where Lonnie Jaxon was having lunch. "Hey, asshole, fancy meeting you here."

Lonnie's hand halted midway over the breadbasket. He looked up and glared at Tyler as he uninvitingly took a seat at the table. If he was surprised to see Tyler, he hid it with practiced restraint.

"Greetings, Mr. McCormack. What have you been doing with yourself since you gave up such a lucrative career?" He made a *tsk-tsk* sound and shook his head with feigned disappointment.

Tyler reached for the remaining roll and took his time buttering the bread. He didn't care if Lonnie had been about to eat it. His sole purpose in doing so was to irritate him. The squint in his left eye confirmed his success.

"Mmm … this bread is so fresh and tasty." He licked his fingers when he finished. "I just love honey butter, don't you?"

"What, may I ask, has motivate you to interrupt my lunch?"

"It seems I've interrupted more than your lunch, Lonnie."

"Do tell." A sleek black tablet sitting on the table gave a notification ping, but Lonnie ignored it.

Tyler didn't. "Does your tablet have the new Identify Smart features?"

"Yes, it does, but I'm sure that's not the purpose of your visit."

"Yeah, well with the president of the company dead and all, I wonder who will take over the company, Lonnie?"

"I'm sure there was a contingency plan in place, as with any lucrative company."

"Oh, I agree. I bet his widow knows the plan, don't you, Lonnie?"

The man said nothing to that, but he failed to hide his impatience with the questioning.

"Guess what else, Lonnie?"

Again, the man remained silent.

"She's a friend of mine. A. Very. Special. Friend."

With barely a glimmer of reaction, Lonnie spoke without emotion. "From what I hear, your friend has had a lot of trouble since her husband's untimely death."

"Interesting that you know about that, since none of it has been made public."

"People talk, Mr. McCormack. You of all people should know that."

"If I had my way back in West Texas, you'd be rotting in prison right now, waiting on the needle."

Lonnie's jaw tensed slightly, just enough so that Tyler knew he was poking the tiger.

"Then lucky for me, you didn't get your way. Or should I say, lucky for you."

Tyler didn't miss the unspoken reminder of how close to death he had been.

"Don't get overconfident. One day soon, you are going to run out of luck. I'll be right there when it happens. You're not untouchable." Tyler flashed his most confident grin, and the two men wordlessly warned each other.

Before getting up to leave, Tyler leaned forward and lowered his voice. "Raped and murdered any more young women lately? You don't have me by the balls this time, and don't forget, I know more about you than you do, you sick bastard. Lawyers need to know about their clients and all that. Maybe you've lost interest in dark-headed girls that remind you of Mexico. You've moved on to blondes. But know this: if you come even remotely close to Mallory or her little girl, I will kill you with my bare hands."

A waitress approached the table carrying a tray of food.

"My dinner is about to be served. I think it's time for you to leave, Mr. McCormack."

Tyler stood and shoved the chair back into place. He leaned and spoke directly into Lonnie's ear.

"Enjoy your lunch. Pretty soon, the only dinners you'll be having will be served in a maximum-security prison, you evil son of a bitch."

~ ~ ~

It was twilight and Tyler stood by his kitchen window looking out at the sunset as Sami sniffed the yard during her evening routine. Mallory lingered in the doorway watching him. The light from the window cast a soft glow that mixed with the LED lights from the computer screensaver.

She felt at a loss. He hadn't said more than a few sentences all afternoon. And he'd hardly touched his dinner. A small part of her couldn't help but wonder if he was second-guessing her again, which made her angry and hurt. Knowing she had to get a grip and have a little faith in him was easier said than done. Besides, he hadn't betrayed her, so she tamped down on those emotions.

What was plaguing him went very deep. His jaw was clenched, and the muscle in his cheek flexed. She deduced that he was probably reliving the past and stressing about the present. She knew all too well that his meeting with Jaxon had upped the ante. They were all concerned about an increased level of aggression.

She had read about the court case, the sensational media coverage, and the accusations that Tyler was a dirty defense attorney when it was all going down. She hadn't wanted him to know that. But since he had shared his story with her, she was even more confident that her assumptions were correct. Because she knew Tyler. He was a good man that found himself in a no-win situation.

Mallory's heart squeezed as she continued to watch him. She

had experienced fear and hell in the past few weeks—but nothing like what Tyler had been through. He had absolutely no one to turn to. There was nothing he could do. And now, because of her, his worst nightmare was back. She truly regretted that she had brought this back into his life.

When he confronted Lonnie, it was like throwing fuel on a burning fire. They all knew it. The frustrating thing was that they could do nothing but wait and see how he reacted. The best they could hope for was to be alert and ready for when he did. She trusted him to keep her parents and daughter safe. She trusted him with her life. The rest would have to wait on Jaxon's next move. Her skin chilled at the thought of what that might be.

"Can I get you anything?" she asked, knowing she should keep her distance but walking over to him anyway.

He shook his head, his eyes remaining on Sami outside.

"She looks so normal out there, running around without a care in the world," he said, his voice so low it was almost inaudible. "I'm too nervous to let her go out alone without supervision. What if he comes and hurts her just to get back at me? It sucks feeling this useless."

"That's the way he wants you to feel," Mallory answered. "He wants you to worry and keep looking over your shoulder. It's part of his game. It's how he manipulates people into acting out of fear. You showed him today you aren't afraid of him. I'm sure no one has ever approached him like that. You were very brave."

"Since when did you get so good at reading criminals?" He attempted a smile but failed. He then turned to open the door and whistled for his dog. Sami came running into the house and trampled toward her water bowl.

"So what can I do to help? I'm not useless."

He looked at her and joined their hands. "Lock yourself in a room and stay safe?" He gave her a hint of a smile. "I honestly don't know if I would survive if something happened to you."

"You won't let that happen," she replied.

With a shake of his head, he pulled her into his arms, his eyes never leaving hers as he bent his head to kiss her. She responded to his lips, answering his kisses with hers. The way their bodies responded to each other was like a powerful drug.

Tyler began trailing his tongue from her ear down the side of her neck that sent shivers racing through her. His fingers began to trace the edge of skin that separated her tank top from her cotton pants. Slowly, his right hand began to move up her side and continue to explore until he found her breasts. He molded them and kneaded each in his palm. The sensation was burning a fire deep inside her.

Pressing against him, she tilted her head back and he began to nip and lick his way down to the space between her breasts. He eagerly pushed her top up to bare her completely. He bent to take one of her nipples in his mouth, his hands hard against her backside now pressing them closer together. His tongue danced and teased her until she was panting with anticipation. Mallory threaded her fingers through his hair keeping him close to her. Nerves that she hadn't even known existed had sizzled to life. Everywhere he touched her made her skin sizzle to life.

She suddenly felt cold. She couldn't catch her breath. Every cell in her body wanted to scream in protest. It took her a moment to register that he was yanking the blinds closed, locking the door, and resetting the alarm.

When he came back to her, the look in his eyes was a mixture of heat and trouble. She wanted to comfort him and take his concerns away, but her desire for him was too selfish. With each touch, however, it felt as if it was him who was comforting her. With gentle hands, he guided her backward until she was against the wall. He began to tug on her pants, taking her panties with them, but with each inch he lowered them, he began to kiss the exposed skin. He lifted one leg over his shoulder and kissed her in her most private place. She gasped at the first feel of his tongue.

Her legs threatened to crumble, and she would have fallen without the strength of his hands holding her up. She looked down at him and their eyes connected. Keeping her gaze, he lifted her leg, kissed the inside of her thigh, and placed it over his shoulder. The sensual things he was doing to her with his mouth had her mindlessly heading toward oblivion. Not once when she was married did she do this. The position should have made her self-conscious, but with Tyler, she felt bold and daring. With her body trembling, she threaded her fingers through his hair and held him to her.

Her eyes shuddered closed as her head fell back against the wall. She no longer had control over her own body. Her hips naturally began to move against him in a sexual dance. The rhythm between them began to increase as the pressure threatened to burst. When it almost became unbearable, she groaned with pleasure knowing she was at the edge ready to fall. Her stomach tightened as the climax flooded through her. He stayed with her, holding her rigid against him through the last shudder. Then he left her.

"No!" She reached for him out of the most exquisite frustration she had ever experienced. Her chest was rising and falling with excited gasps.

"Shh. I'm not going anywhere." He took her into his arms and kissed her with such passion she thought she might pass out.

He leaned back long enough to make haste with removing his own clothes. Within seconds, she was back in his arms. Her body was demanding more of his touch, more of his mesmerizing kisses. His hot breath on her skin made her tremble with desire. When he claimed her mouth again, it was a deep, searing kiss that revved all of her senses into overdrive.

With both of her hands, she grabbed his ass and rocked herself into him. He let out a deep growl of approval. Their bodies spoke to each other. Each knew where to touch, where to kiss.

He took both her legs and wrapped them around his waist. Taking himself in his hands, he rubbed her swollen and sensitive entrance. Then he pushed inside her slick walls until he was fully sheathed. She could feel him everywhere this way. With one arm wrapped around her waist and the other under her thigh, he began to slowly move. The connection was so deep that she felt him in all the places she kept hidden.

She held onto him and kissed his shoulders. The movement and sensations between them felt like they were the only two people on Earth. As their bodies spoke to each other, she could feel him tensing and contracting with need. She gave just as much back to him. They climbed higher and higher, riding the waves of pleasure with each other. Tyler began to move faster and stronger. She met him with every thrust, making the friction between them even hotter.

He groaned at the same time he said her name. The blended sound did something to her soul and she let go, shuddering around him. He pulled her closer to him and found his own release. She could feel his chest rise and fall against her, feel his hot breath against her ear; both were incongruous with his gentle lips on her shoulder.

Neither of them had the strength to move. They stayed together for a long moment, just existing.

When he finally pulled back, her body still tingled. He carried her to the bathroom and sat her next to the shower. As he ran the water, the steam began to swirl around them. Mallory sat speechless and watched the water spray. She had no words to express how he made her feel. She loved this man with all of her heart. She always had. She also knew that if she told him how much she loved him, he would leave. Just like last time.

And just like that, her heart sank. He had the power to destroy her if he did. She had no choice but to keep the depths of her feelings hidden. The only thing she knew for sure was that when this thing was over, she would never regret a moment they had together. Tyler wanted her to trust him, and she did. She also believed that he trusted her and believed her innocent. It might not be enough to overcome what lay ahead, but maybe it was enough just to be in the present. She would remain strong and accept the fact that he'd come into her life, not once, but twice, which was a gift to treasure deep in her heart.

With a smile, he pulled her to her feet, and after a tender, soft kiss that spoke to her more than any words, he led them both under the water. She leaned back against him and relaxed under the warm stream.

~ ~ ~

Tyler woke to the sound of his cell phone. Reading the screen, he silenced it as quickly as he could. Mallory's body was tangled in the sheets next to him, her head on his chest and one leg draped over his. For a moment, he wanted to ignore the outside world and devour her again. They had made love several more times that night. In the tub, on the bathroom counter, and finally making it to the bed. A few years of this and he might finally tame his need for her. Maybe.

He had always known she was the one who got away. What he didn't realize was that she stirred desires in him that he didn't know he had. He felt both elated and panicked that she matched him so perfectly. It would take time for those feelings to settle. But time wasn't something they had. With that sobering thought, he tightened his hold on her. She shifted and he thought he had awakened her, but her breathing took on a steady flow again.

The thought of losing her a second time was scarier than any fear of love and commitment he may possess. He wasn't naïve enough to believe love conquered all. The reality of their situation was too alarming. She could easily be arrested at any time—or worse, Jaxon could get his hands on her.

Just the thought of Jaxon harming someone he loved made his mind reel and his body tense. It could push him to kill without hesitation. Because, yes, dammit, he loved her.

He thought about waking her and showing her just how much he did love her, and when he was done showing her, he was going to tell her. They had to talk and decide together what to do about it. He felt confident enough that she felt something for him too. He would not run from it this time. Just the opposite. He wanted to spend the rest of his life showing her just how much.

The phone vibrated a second time. Reaching for it, he read the caller ID and then swore silently. He might as well get it over with. He moved stealthily away from Mallory, disentangling their limbs as carefully as he could without waking her. Trying to not even disturb the air, he moved through to the living room and into the kitchen, where he could speak without waking her. He finally clicked on the missed call and prepared to have the conversation he had avoided so many times. "Good morning, Chief."

"Why the hell have you not returned my calls?"

"No greetings or salutations?"

"All pleasantries are bypassed for insubordinate employees."

"Okay, look." He sighed heavily. "Let's cut the bullshit. You'll have my resignation on your desk by noon. You know as well as I do that I'm not cut out to take time off for the emotional healing crap that the department ordered me to do."

After a significant stretch of silence, Chief Watson said, "You needed it. You were strung tighter than a drum."

No shit. And even tighter now. "And it's obviously not working for me. Inactivity obviously isn't the remedy. Catching a known killer that I put back on the streets is the only thing that will ever cure me."

"Even if you did, McCormack, it won't bring that girl back."

"I need to keep working." He would *not* discuss Jennie.

"Is that what you call it? Working? I didn't know going rogue was within the guidelines of police work."

"How about believing a suspect is innocent until proven guilty?"

"I'm waiting for an explanation, McCormack."

"It's not that easy. The evidence Johnson and Clark have against her is circumstantial at best. I've already had the opportunity to prove some of it wrong. There's no way she could have planned the kidnapping attempt on her daughter. She was with me the whole time. Ask Johnson; we've even collaborated some."

"Can you give me another suspect?"

"I'm getting there."

"That's a no."

"No, it means I'm getting there."

"You've gotten yourself too involved."

"Not that I feel the need to defend myself, but I'm a big boy."

Chief Watson swore under a heavy sigh. "You've crossed too many lines."

"Just accept the resignation, Chief. It will keep you and the department out of potential lawsuits." Suddenly, Tyler felt very weary. "Enough said."

"Not so fast. I'm not done yet."

"I can't wait."

"I'm pleased to see you're finding a reason to live life again."

"You getting mushy on me, Chief?"

"Be careful."

Knowing that any further talk would be futile, Tyler bid his farewell and disconnected the call.

CHAPTER 25

~ ~ ~

Detectives Johnson and Clark stood behind the medical examiner while she assessed the body lying in the bushes of the Greenway.

"She's been dead for at least forty-eight hours, but I will have to confirm that through the autopsy. This heat could potentially alter the findings."

Yellow crime-scene tape marked off the scene as policemen searched the area to gather evidence. The young woman's body was lying on the ground, naked, with her hands bound and bent across her chest, and her feet were tied at the ankles. Her skin had red scratches and smelled of bleach. Her body had been scrubbed clean. The medical examiner lifted her fingers with gloved hands to assess how each fingernail had been clipped to the quick. Not a trace of hair had been left on the victim's body.

The examiner had made her initial assessment that the body had been moved. "There's no way she was raped and tortured here. There's no sign of struggle and no signs of chemicals he used on the ground. The bruises and cuts seem superficial, and there is no trace of blood around the scene. Unfortunately, the signs of rape are pretty brutal. It will take more examination to give more concrete answers as to what happened to her."

"I don't think I'm jumping the gun here by stating the obvious. Lonnie Jaxon has taken up residence in this town, and now we have a dead girl with similar signs to his calling card," Detective Clark shared.

"Let's not make that public yet. We'll spur on a media frenzy and put the city in a panic. We can't rule out the possibility of a copycat," Detective Johnson added.

"No, but if it looks like a duck and all that ..."

Turning his head with a feeble attempt to get the gruesome images out of his mind, Detective Clark took a deep breath.

"You going to clue in McCormack? I may not care for the guy, but I think he has a right to know about this."

~ ~ ~

When Lonnie heard the headline news that a body had been found, he had been beyond elated. He was sure they would interview McCormack. He scanned each station, waiting for it, but it never showed. He wanted to see the grief and the panic he knew his nemesis would exhibit. Not getting the opportunity irritated him on so many levels. He stared at his plasma screen and pondered his next move.

There was no way he would be able to keep Mallory from him. They were meant to be. As the news segment began, he was sure there would be recalls of the public scandal he'd endured in West Texas. This would be a perfect reminder that Tyler had no chance of beating him. Mallory would also realize that Tyler was not good enough. She deserved a more eloquent and sophisticated man. She deserved someone who knew how to pleasure her.

His mother had always said, "If you want something done right, do it yourself." That was when she taught him how to pleasure her. She wasn't happy with the man she had been seeing—he didn't do it for her. So she taught Lonnie how to do it right.

One thing he was sure of was that his next move had to be calculated perfectly. It was time that he and Mallory become more acquainted. He looked down at the photos on his desk. With his finger, he traced the lines of her face. She was such a woman he admired. He marveled at her strength to fight for a young child. She loved the little girl as her own. He knew; he had heard the story from her late husband. He had chosen not to leave when he'd presented him with Mallory's secret. A little more urging and Lonnie was sure the marriage would have dissolved. Instead, he died. What a tragedy. At least he was no longer in the way of his and Mallory's happiness.

He picked up a photo of Mallory hugging the little girl. It took a special heart to be able to love another so unconditionally. Her maternal instincts were so unlike his own mother's. A woman who loved a child so intently would have the ability to love the man as well. Yes, Mallory Jones would be the perfect mate. She would be strong enough to learn the ways in which he wanted to be loved.

He was reminded of his special love, and he wanted to feel that way again. She looked nothing like his brown-haired, brown-eyed Lena. Mallory had blonde hair and blue eyes. But she stirred something in him deeply. It was important for her to appreciate the things he had done for her. It wouldn't be long until he was able to share those things with her. It had taken time, but he was eliminating all of her worries and clearing the way toward their happiness.

In the meantime, he would just have to make due. He glanced at the woman bound and gagged as she lay waiting in the center of the room. The terror in her eyes did not come close to matching the pain she was about to endure before taking her final breath.

～ ～ ～

"The truth is, my gut tells me he's been fixated on Mallory from the beginning. I think there's a possibility that every bit of what has happened, all of it, has been a smoke screen. He wants everyone scrambling and for Mallory to feel her world is coming to an end, so he can swoop in heroically and sweep her off her feet."

Tyler spoke to Alexander in a hushed voice. Mallory had gone to make them lunch, and he didn't want her to overhear.

"That's a pretty extravagant plan to pull off."

"Believe me, I've thought of that, but nothing else really makes sense."

"That's one hell of a warped crush." Alexander puffed his cheeks. "There's one thing you've not taken in to consideration, and hear me out before you explode." Alexander leaned forward and rested his arms on his legs. "Like you said before, he's probably been fixated on her for a while. Tyler, she's blonde-haired and blue-eyed. Jennie was the first victim of his that wasn't dark-haired and dark-eyed."

Tyler sat motionless. He stared straight ahead and didn't even blink. He hadn't thought of that connection, and it made fear snake up his spine. Before Tyler had a chance to respond to that revelation, Mallory walked in, her expression so grim that he was instantly alert and on his feet.

"What happened?"

"A body of a young woman was found. She was raped and murdered. It was just on the news." She dropped down into the chair Tyler had vacated.

He opened his mouth to speak and then shut it. Nothing he could say would help the poor woman or make Mallory feel any better. Instead, he picked her up, sat down, and placed her on his lap. He held her for a long moment, not caring if it made Alexander uncomfortable.

Tyler and Alexander exchanged looks that spoke volumes.

Lonnie Jaxon was at it again.

~ ~ ~

Kendall Jenkins jerked awake with fear, blinking and trying to focus her eyes. Her head felt like it could explode. She couldn't move her hands. She twisted and pulled against the ties that bound her wrists above her head. The more she jerked, the tighter they felt. Giving up the struggle, she stilled herself to gain control of her breathing. She was taking in air hard through her mouth, and her heart was pounding out of her chest. For someone who didn't scare easy, she was petrified.

Looking around the room, she could hardly make out anything because it was so dark. She had no idea how long she had been there. There were no windows for her to be able to judge time. She tried her best to calm her nerves and to think.

Her memory began to return. Things had gotten way out of control. She was leaving town. She remembered that much. Someone had grabbed her and drugged her. She tried to remember past that, but it was blank. Until now. She jerked her head toward the sound of a click and saw a lighter flame glow bright in the darkened corner of the room.

She wasn't alone.

She could hear someone puffing on a cigarette. She could only make out the shape of a body, but she couldn't see a face. She recognized the smell of the tobacco smoke. Pall Malls.

"This is insane, right?" At the sound of his voice, she recognized him immediately. Nick. He scooted his chair closer, leaning back to prop his feet up on the corner of the cot she was tied to.

"We start out thinking we've got the perfect plan. Things were finally looking up, and we were going to hit payday. Then the fucker up and dies. I tried to go with a plan B, but hell if that got fucked up too."

Still confused and foggy from whatever she had been drugged with, she couldn't make sense of what he was talking about. "This isn't funny, Nick."

He took a long drag on his cigarette before he answered. "No, it's not."

Because he scared her, she became angry. "Let me go, asshole. Get these ropes off me. Now."

"You see, now, that's not possible." He bent his head to the right and looked at her. "I gotta do what my new boss says, and he wouldn't look too kindly at me letting you go."

She knew then that her life was in mortal danger. Nick wouldn't hesitate to kill if the price was right. Kendall tried for the familiar.

"Come on, Nick. It's you and me, remember? We're a team."

"Then why didn't you tell me the kid was mine?"

Right then, she understood it all. The memory of walking into her bedroom and finding Emma's picture tossed on her bed. It's why he had come back. Emma had been plan B.

"You never cared. She had a better life with Damian. Besides, you always said kids were a pain in the ass."

She couldn't help herself; she tried to fight against the rope. Blood began to trickle down her left wrist. Her heart beat louder in her chest. She had never wanted to be a mother, but bile rose in her throat as fear for her child threatened to consume her. It was an unfamiliar emotion.

"You leave her alone!"

The door opened behind them, and a man in a dark suit walked in. "Now, now. This does not sound like a pleasant reunion."

Nick immediately rose to stand. He took a few steps back and seemed to have lost his gusto.

"No, sir. She just woke up. I was just—"

He never finished his sentence. The man wordlessly reached up and fired a bullet between the eyes of the employee who was no longer of any use to him. Witnessing the blood that exploded through the back of his head, Kendall let out a scream as she watched Nick fall lifelessly to the ground.

Every cell in her body vibrated in a panic-stricken frenzy. She began to kick and thrash about, trying to free herself. But the man stepped over Nick's body and stood by her bed. In a calm tone, he informed her, "You can either stop fighting or I can put a bullet in your head too."

Instant fear froze her.

"You will do what I tell you to do. Or I kill the little girl. Understood?"

Afraid to speak, she nodded her head in agreement.

"Good. What I want right now are answers. And you will give them to me."

CHAPTER 26

～ ～ ～

Austin rain was a rarity. Today's weather would more than likely set almanac records for the month of July. Mallory couldn't remember the last time it had poured this much. The clouds had settled in and had provided a welcomed relief from the blistering heat. The steady, heavy rain had lasted for a few hours and showed no signs of letting up soon.

Mallory sat on the floor in the doorway and watched the rain off the back deck. The gutters were overflowing, and the water was beginning to form trenches in the landscaping. She figured Sami would end up rolling in the mud once she was allowed to go outside. In the meantime, the Labrador stayed obediently at her side with her head resting on Mallory's thigh. Occasionally she would look up and whimper, hoping for permission to play in the rain.

"Not quite yet, Sami."

She missed Emma terribly. Tears filled her eyes as she sat and wondered what her little girl was doing at the moment. Her head understood the safety of not having contact with her, but her heart couldn't stand it. She longed to hear the sound of her sweet voice and the noise of her play. Tyler continued to assure her that her parents and Emma were completely secure, but she had reached a point of exhaustion with the entire situation. There was no doubt that she was taken care of and her parents were keeping her preoccupied with fun activities. It just didn't dissuade the emptiness she felt without her.

When she closed her eyes, a few tears escaped down her cheeks. Wiping them away, she let her mind drift to happier times. She could hear her feet pattering across the hardwood floor in their home while she was chattering a mile a minute. She could envision her propped on her knees on a stool at the kitchen bar explaining her day at school with such detail and fervor that it made Mallory chuckle.

"So where's wonder boy?" Alexander had approached her from behind. He didn't startle her, like Tyler always did. His steps were heavier and not near as stealth.

She looked up at him and saw signs of fatigue. He rubbed his eyes and stretched. He had spent hours doing research and trying to piece leads together.

"He's sleeping," she said with an attempt to sound cheerful.

"Is he okay?"

"I guess that would depend on your definition of okay." Mallory leaned her head against the doorframe.

"He's had a rough few years," he said as he pulled up a chair to sit next to her. "Jaxon did one hell of a number on him. The media showed no mercy. Sad thing is, he's been his own worst critic, and he won't let up. As painful as it had been to witness that entire trag-edy, there's nothing anyone has been able to say to make things better."

"What was done to Jennie was beyond human, but it wasn't Tyler's fault."

"What's happening here isn't a cakewalk either."

Mallory appreciated Alexander's sympathy.

"I am beyond grateful for the help you have both provided. I honestly don't know if I would have survived this far. I'm so sorry Tyler is having to relive this."

She became overwhelmed with the rush of emotions and she couldn't hold back the tears that streamed down her face.

"We're going to fight him. God willing, justice will prevail this time." Alexander placed a hand over hers and gently squeezed. "We all have to believe that."

Mallory thought that the conversation had come to a natural end, so she was a little surprised that he hung around instead of going back to the investigation. She kept her gaze toward the outdoors and continued to watch the rainfall.

With a theatrical sigh, Alexander said, "So I'm going to go out on a limb here and just ask."

"Ask me what?"

"Not that it's any of my business, but ... um, are you two ...?"

Mallory ranked her bottom lip between her teeth and looked down at her clasped hands. "I guess you might say the jury is still out on that one."

"Not for him, it isn't. You'd have to be blind not to see that."

She looked at him, surprised.

"Darling, he is totally, unconditionally, in love with you. Take a look at the guy; the evidence is written all over his sappy face."

Mallory's heart did a flip, and she couldn't hide her desire to hear more about it. "And what evidence have you seen?"

Alexander looked over his shoulder just to make sure he wasn't about to be bopped over the head for gossiping about his friend's romantic notions. Lowering his voice just a bit, he shared his insight.

"For one, there's not been another woman since he's moved here. You're looking at the total sum of his social life. Me. Personally, I thought he might be trying to become a monk. Number two, pay a little attention to the way the man looks at you; there's no denying it."

Really? They had reconnected physically, and it was beyond incredible. She still shivered when remembering what he had done to her, several times. She knew he still had a thing for her—he had all but said as much. But in love with her? She hoped like hell Alexander was right.

"Thanks, counselor," Mallory said and gave in to the smile that she couldn't hide.

"No problem. I bill by the hour."

"Ha-ha."

"You're billing what by the hours?" Tyler asked.

Mallory's head whipped around, and Alexander's face couldn't hide his guilt. Tyler shuffled his bare feet into the kitchen, yawning and scratching his hand over his head, trying to wake himself up. Tyler had slept, but he didn't look rested. His hair was a sexy mess, though. He had changed into a pair of low-hanging gym pants and a T-shirt. Mallory thought he looked yummy. It could have been the conversation she'd just had, but she would have sworn his eyes warmed when he looked at her.

"Nothing, just idle chitchat," she said as she tracked his movements to the refrigerator and pulled out a cold sports drink.

"Anybody hungry?" Tyler asked as he moved sideways toward the pantry and stood there examining its contents.

Mallory stood and closed the back door. "I can make us dinner."

Tyler turned to look at her over his shoulder. "Are you taking orders?"

"Well, our supplies are slightly limited, but if it's for spaghetti, then yeah."

"Works for me," Alexander chimed in. "I'm never one to turn down home-cooked anything."

The guys gathered around the bar as Mallory made her way around the kitchen. Listening to them carry on a conversation that had nothing to do with kidnappings and murder helped her to create a domestic little fantasy while keeping reality at bay, even temporarily.

Thirty minutes later, Mallory served the spaghetti and buttered garlic bread. The three of them gathered around the table. She watched Tyler as discreetly as she could as he brought a forkful of pasta to his mouth. Everything about him seemed to intrigue her. The way he chewed. The way his throat muscles flexed as he swallowed.

He glanced at her and winked. Busted. She could feel her skin heat with embarrassment at being caught. She had to get herself in check. This might not last. For all she knew, he was simply reminiscing about their youth and closing a chapter in his life. Even if not, she could still end up in prison for a crime she didn't commit. She looked down at her plate and focused intently on her meal.

Alexander finished his meal with a very loud burp. Without an "excuse me" or "pardon me," he left and trotted quickly back to the office. While he was gone, Tyler leaned over and kissed her sweetly on her cheek.

"You okay?" he asked.

"I'm fine," she replied.

Alexander reentered the kitchen carrying a sheet of paper. "Read what I found while you were getting your beauty sleep, which didn't work, by the way."

"What's this?" Tyler asked as he scanned a list of names on the paper.

"Recognize any of the names?" he said, nodding at the paper.

Mallory's eyes darted back and forth as if he were watching a tennis match.

"All of them. Gilmore is a Fifth Circuit Court judge in West Texas. Armond is a corporate attorney for Hughes and Mancini here in Austin. Maxwell ..." He pondered for a moment. "I recognize the name, but can't place him."

"He had a fatal car accident," Alexander confirmed and then unveiled his findings. "Gilmore and Armond are dead too."

With a fork full of pasta halfway to his mouth, Tyler froze. The tension in his body was palpable.

"What did you say?"

"Here's the kicker. Maxwell is a family court judge here in the city. He died around seven months ago from a head injury sustained during a mugging."

"Ohmigod. Judge Carter Maxwell?" Mallory's voice was breathless.

"The one and the same," Alexander replied.

"He was the judge that awarded Damian sole custody and approved my adoption of Emma. And the attorney that handled Emma's adoption was Mr. Armond, but he was a family-law attorney."

"He ventured into corporate law about a year ago," Alexander confirmed.

Tyler narrowed his eyes and glanced at the names on the list again. "Lonnie has been busy," he said darkly.

The temperature in the kitchen seemed to drop to a sudden chill as Mallory watched both men calculate the severity of the accusations they were making. She crossed her arms and tried to rub the goose bumps away.

"He has escalated. He's gone so far off the books now that I don't know how to follow his thoughts."

"He's covering her tracks. He thinks he's protecting Mallory. There's enough reasonable evidence for an investigation. We need to turn over what we've discovered, Tyler, to the chief."

"I don't get it. Mallory doesn't fit his victim profile. Her age, her previous marital status—and she's a mother, for Christ's sake. It just doesn't fit his preference. Neither did Jennie. All of his previous victims were late teens, early twenties, single, and brunette. What changed for him?"

"You know what changed." Alexander looked at him gravely. "His fixation altered. It happens."

Pushing his plate back, Tyler stood and paced the room. He cradled his hands at the back of his head. Both Mallory and Alexander remained quiet as he thought. His tone serious, his eyes piercing Alexander with unspoken concern, he said, "It's time you knew something."

"Tell me what it is."

Tyler began to speak, but Mallory halted him with her hand. She stood with her back straight and her head held high.

"I withheld a document that proved Emma was not Damian's daughter. I kept it hidden through the court proceedings. I never even told Damian. The adoption process went through without a hitch. I thought no one knew. I didn't think it would ever surface."

Alexander blew a low whistle and pondered her admission. "What do you mean, you thought no one knew?"

Tyler left the room and returned with the documents that the detectives had shared. Alexander examined the papers.

"He had to have been following me for a long time, then. The adoption process took nearly a year."

"Definitely a possibility. All of these deaths are centripetal around a common point: you," Alexander said.

It was clear to Mallory that they'd all reached the same conclusion at the same time.

"Kendall's life is in danger."

"Get on the phone and alert Detective Johnson," Alexander said to Tyler.

"One by one, he's taking them all out," Mallory concluded. "Do you think he had Damian killed?"

"I don't know. But in his sick way, this is how Lonnie plans to win you over. By making all of your problems disappear." Tyler walked over to her and put an arm around her in support.

"So you think that in some sick, twisted way that by him killing everyone, I would be indebted to him and see him as my hero?"

"I don't think that," Tyler answered, "but Lonnie Jaxon does."

Tyler's cell phone rang. He looked at the caller ID and frowned. "McCormack."

Tyler felt the hairs on his neck rise as he listened. "I'll get back to you. There's something I need to share with you."

He snapped his phone closed, and his expression turned grim.

"That was Johnson. The victim found today fits Jaxon's MO."

CHAPTER 27

~ ~ ~

They had no idea it was him, but he knew who they were.

Did those wannabe undercover cops think he couldn't make them? They would be just as discreet wearing neon signs. The she-man in woman's clothing and her fat, hairy friend were sitting across the street on a park bench reading. Seriously? About half a block up, they had a third dressed in running gear listening to an iPod. Not a drip of sweat fell off of him, and his shoes were brand-new. They were all way too obvious.

Lonnie had spotted them within minutes of driving to his residence in the passenger's seat of a realtor's company vehicle. He had spent the afternoon with the real estate agent. She was classy, friendly, and well into her forties. She had spent the day doing her best to reel him in—and not just for the sale of property. He made sure he flirted and kept her interested and busy.

His disguise was so life-like that the woman had no idea who she was really dealing with. Today, he wore a salt-and-peppered goatee mustache and green contact lenses that were framed in studious, gold-rimmed glasses, and he was wearing a perfect dark-haired wig. His hands were free from his usual jewelry, save the gold watch on his left hand. So when they rode down the street to his residence, no one was the wiser.

He was pleased with his time spent surveying property, because now he knew the exact location of Tyler's home. Although he had used Google Earth to view the land from his computer, he desired to see it in real time. He had mentioned the general location as an area where he was interested in purchasing property on which to build a semi reclusive homestead. He had requested an appointment time long enough for them to see several properties. She had offered to pick him up, and he'd politely accepted. It was a naturally perfect disguise.

The highlight of this game of cat and mouse happened when they were slowly driving by Tyler's residence. Two cars had swiftly left the driveway, obviously in a hurry. Immediately, he had recognized Mallory in the passenger seat of Tyler's SUV. Her hand was intimately placed on his shoulder. He glanced in the side rearview mirror to confirm that neither vehicle had hesitated.

He became angered with Mallory. How could she lean so close to Tyler over the console of the front seat? Had they become romantically involved during her stay? Was she throwing herself at him, like the slutty realtor was doing to him?

Just within the few seconds he saw them, he knew she was like a bitch in heat. He was sure she was fucking him. She would feel regret once she knew all of the many things Lonnie had done for her. She would beg him for forgiveness. It would be up to him to reprimand her for her wrongdoings.

Her first punishment would be for him to eliminate Tyler McCormack. Although they had history together and he'd had high hopes of them resuming their professional relations, he had crossed the line by violating his woman. He was becoming a nuisance. He might even let Mallory watch Tyler take his last breath. It had become difficult to concentrate on the remainder of the properties with visions of torture running through his mind, so he feigned a headache and requested an early return.

The realtor had offered to drop him off in the parking garage to avoid the heat of the short walk. It was the perfect plan. None of Austin's finest had a clue that he had returned home anyway, but it was better to play on the side of caution.

"Mr. Stephens?"

"I beg your pardon?"

"I asked if you would like for me to join you in your home to continue to discuss your property choices."

The woman was relentless. She had made several hints and gestures that she would be more than happy to spread her legs for him. He turned his head to her and seriously considered taking his anger and frustrations out on her. He would have enjoyed hammering her so hard he made her bleed.

Tapping down on his irritation, he let her down as politely as he could. He simply didn't have time to deal with the body. Rash decisions made for mistakes.

She drove off, not being able to hide her disappointment.

He would have to be careful leaving the building again, but it was necessary. He had work to do.

~ ~ ~

Tyler stared at the young woman's body. So many wounds. Some small. Others were deep. Intended to do harm. To make her suffer. The scouring marks of the scrub brush he'd used were telling signs. He didn't need to examine the body any further. This was the work of a very sick, very twisted man.

He had seen hell. But these girls had experienced it. Each time he closed his eyes, he remembered Jennie's body. Now he would have this memory too. He took shallow breaths; the odor in the room was not natural. Nothing could really mask the smell of decay and blood that permeated the room.

He did his best to not feel. Not to think. Fate had brought this evil into his life once. He'd failed then. Now fate had brought him back again. He would not fail twice. He couldn't fail twice—even if it killed him.

The other detectives only cared about solving the mystery, and yes, they were good at their jobs. Tyler knew they would be looking for every possible thread of evidence. The people in this city, this state—hell, even this country—would be demanding answers. Tyler knew, without a doubt, that all of this was because of one man.

The door behind him opened with a swishing sound, but he didn't care about propriety. He refused to greet whoever it was. The sound of heavy footsteps echoed in the silent room.

"You up for this?" Detective Johnson asked as his dark hand clasped him on the shoulder.

It figured he would be cautious of Tyler's state of mind— post-traumatic stress, severe emotional trauma, and all that other mumbo jumbo. It baffled him how anyone could ever think a person could be "up for this."

"I thought you should know," Detective Johnson said quietly, "but I'm sorry you are going through this again. We need your help. You know this man better than anyone."

His eyes never left the young girl's face. "Her family?"

"Detective Clark told them about an hour ago. They are on their way here to identify the body. Her name is Selena Martinez. She worked at Habanero's Mexican Restaurant. She had been missing just under three days."

"Yep, that's about how long he keeps them. Does what he wants. Takes what he wants. Throws away what he doesn't need."

"We're going to run a full autopsy and see what matches up with prior reports."

"Good." Tyler's jaw tightened.

Jesus, what a tragedy. A sick, sick tragedy. In the world of good versus evil, evil won too many damned times.

"It appears the killer used bleach to scrub her body clean of evidence."

Tyler didn't have to look underneath the sterile sheet that covered Selena's body. He knew her nails were cut to the quick. He knew her body was free from hair follicles. Tyler drew in a long breath. "They won't find a single trace of evidence to link him to the crime."

"The press is going to be all over this." Which meant Tyler would be all over the news again too.

"I know."

"If there is anything I can do, don't hesitate to ask."

Tyler stiffened at the familiar, yet often empty, spiel. It was the same that everyone used to show support, but rarely meant.

"There's not a damned thing anyone can do."

~ ~ ~

"Tyler McCormack to see you, Chief."

Chief Watson jerked his head up in shock. His hands stilled over his keyboard, and he leaned over to push the button on his intercom. "Send him in immediately."

As the leader of the department, Chief Watson had several reasons to be pissed as hell at the detective and several more reasons to fire him. Bets were being made all over at how long it would take McCormack to show up. He'd had reservations about him from the very beginning. He had the talent, the instincts, and the intellect to be a damn good investigator. He sure as hell was overqualified for the position. It's not every day an attorney gives up the courtroom and chooses a lesser-paying position in the legal field. Instead, he gave the man the benefit of the doubt. The man had demons to battle—the type that some people never overcome. Now his cause for concern had amplified with the return of Lonnie Jaxon and the dead bodies beginning to surface. His curiosity was surely piqued. During their earlier conversation, McCormack had basically quit.

The door opened and Tyler walked in. There was no sign of atrocity on the man's face. There was, however, a hell of a lot of determination in his expression and demeanor.

"Hey, Chief."

"Have a seat." The chief looked at him over the top of his computer. The icy stare he provided was intended to intimidate. They both knew it was wasted energy.

"You've been busy."

Tyler had the audacity to throw his head back and laugh. "You must have had a better opening statement than that."

"Exactly why are you here? You were quite clear with your intent to resign. Did you want to hand deliver the written one?"

Tyler leaned back in his chair and rubbed his hand under his chin in thought.

"Wow. The mayor, senators, and probably even the governor breathing down your back? You that worried I've gone over the edge?"

"This case has begun to attract attention. Yes. The fact that you have snubbed your nose at direct orders and legal protocol provides issues of its own."

The chief tapped a pencil on his desk.

"Detectives Johnson and Clark have issued reports that provide enough probable cause to issue an arrest warrant on Ms. Jones. They have yet to do so. It's clear you have been working other angles to counter that."

He kept his face expressionless. The department was filled with people who questioned his credibility, and at the moment, it felt as if Chief Watson was leading the pack. Tyler couldn't help but still hold the man in high regard.

"Sir, if you would please hear me out."

Over the next thirty minutes, Tyler explained how the common thread of the murders and other criminal activity circumvented into one evil plot at the hands of Lonnie Jaxon. He concluded his summary with, "I just want to make sure we explore every option before you move forward with the arrest warrant. I may not be able to tie the gentlemen's deaths or the kidnapping to him, but it does fit the pattern of his obsession with Mallory. The body in the morgue clearly exhibits that Jaxon's sexual activities have resumed. She died the same way as the others. That girl died at the hands of Lonnie Jaxon. There is no doubt in my mind, sir."

The chief nodded as he took off his glasses and tossed them on his desk.

"Then explain to me," he stated, "exactly how you plan to get hard evidence to prove this theory."

Something deep inside Tyler snapped. "I've gotten the goods on this sick son of a bitch several times over. Anyone who watches *Law and Order* on Tuesday nights can see he's guilty of heinous crimes. The problem is, if you're looking for cold, hard evidence, you'll be waiting one hell of a long time. He won't go down that way. I'm going to have to catch the evil prick in the act."

He gripped the arms of the chair and started to rise.

"Sit down," Chief Watson ordered. "I know you've been through hell and back."

"No shit," Tyler said, but he eased back into his chair.

"No one could have predicted that he would show up again."

The computer pinged an e-mail notification, but the chief ignored it as well as the alerts on his phone.

"Who's watching Ms. Jones at this time?"

"She's downstairs, sir, with her attorney, Alexander Blakely."

With a frustrated sigh, the chief silently pondered his next move. Everyone in the APD Criminal Investigation Unit knew that Tyler McCormack was a ticking time bomb. He couldn't ignore the psychological reports. It stated quite clearly that he had not recovered from the stress induced during the trial. Further evidence to prove that was documented with the beating he had given the attempted rapist. However, if McCormack was right, he was the one that knew Jaxon well enough to bring him to justice—this time for good. The chief dragged both his hands down his face.

"Keep your damn resignation between us for the time being. But if this goes bad, you'll need to submit it. Stay on the right side of the law. And for heaven's sake, keep Johnson and Clark in the loop. You're going to need backup."

"Thank you, sir."

"If anyone asks, I chewed your ass out for the continued and repeated insubordination and failure to comply with medical advice."

"Yes, sir."

"You have my permission to use whatever resources you need.

Detective Johnson is a good man; use him. As far as I'm concerned, you have the green light to follow all leads. You're an intelligent man, so don't forget to look at this with a critical eye. We don't need mistakes."

"Chief, we need to put an APB out on Kendall Jenkins. If this theory pans out, her life is in danger."

"Consider it done." The chief looked at him with raised eyebrows. "What's your plan?"

"Simple. He's coming after me."

CHAPTER 28

~ ~ ~

Mallory woke to the smell of pancakes and sausage. She reached across the bed to snuggle with Tyler, but her muffled mind registered that she was alone. The night they'd spent together came back with a rush. Rolling over and propping her head on the pillow, she couldn't suppress her smile. Tyler had held nothing back.

After a quick shower, she pulled her hair into a ponytail. As she reached for jeans and a shirt, her cell phone vibrated on the nightstand. During the conversation last night, he had told her about his talk with Chief Watson and that he wanted them to limit their cell usage, but it was probably the office. Or about Emma.

She looked at the screen, but she didn't recognize the number. Before she could decide whether to answer it, it had stopped buzzing. She hesitated with her finger hovering over the icon.

"Good morning," Tyler called as he carefully balanced the breakfast tray. "I wanted to bring you breakfast in bed, but it looks like you're already up."

Mallory scooped a strawberry off the plate and replied, "I can fix that."

She jumped right back into bed.

"After last night, I've worked up an appetite."

Scooting to the head of the bed, she made herself comfortable as Tyler settled the tray between them and sat down facing her.

"I hope you still like pancakes. I worked hard on these."

"Mmm. They smell scrumptious." She kissed him affectionately. "Thank you."

Tyler picked up another strawberry and held it to her mouth. As she took a bite, their eyes held, and he tensed.

"Thinking about last night?"

"Mmm. Hmmm." She grinned at him. "How could I not?"

He picked up a sausage link and dipped it into the syrup.

Mallory scrunched her nose and couldn't help but giggle.

"You always used to do that."

"What?"

"The sausage-and-syrup thing. You would eat most of your syrup before you ever touched the pancake," she said, poking fun at his quirky eating habit.

"Hey, don't knock it until you've tried it."

He picked up another sausage, dipped it, and held it out for her.

"Oh, no, you can't make me try that." She turned her face away. "Pancakes are for syrup. Not pork."

She popped a bite of pancake in her mouth, and he reached over with his fingertip and swiped a lingering drop of syrup off the corner of her mouth. The contact made her body shiver, and goose bumps washed over her.

Reading her thoughts, he leaned forward and replaced his fingertips with his lips. He answered her unspoken words with a whisper.

"Yeah, me too."

He kissed her again; this time, the draw between them began to sizzle.

Mallory's cell phone vibrated again. She moaned with disappointment.

"It has to be work-related." Reaching over, she grabbed her phone and read the screen. "I don't recognize the number, though."

After taking a huge bite of pancakes and strawberries, Tyler mumbled over his food.

"Go ahead, answer it; talk quickly, though."

"Mallory Jones." The sound of Mallory's professional tone was an aphrodisiac for Tyler. It was a side of her he was unfamiliar with, but it intrigued him all the same. The woman in his bed was a tigress, but this woman was cool, confident, and shrewd. The woman she was with Emma was warm, loving, and supportive. She was complex with so many layers that it was no wonder he had never been able to fully let go. She was the one woman against which he measured all others.

As she moved away from the bed to pace, she glanced back at him and took note that Tyler was intently eating her portion of the breakfast.

"Yes. I understand. I've done that. What do you need?"

Mallory hesitated, listened again, and then, with the best of her ability, tried to regain a professional tone. Again, she spoke.

"Yes, of course, I'll make it happen."

Mallory stood still and held the phone for a long moment before closing the call.

"Everything okay?" He could tell she was suddenly stressed.

The sound of Tyler's voice made her jump. She looked over at him and quickly regained composure.

"Yeah, it's nothing. Um … I'll just be a minute."

She closed the bathroom door and sat on the edge of the tub and covered her face with her shaking hands.

Mallory's world had just collapsed. Again.

Mallory pushed back her hair. Her hands clenched into fists. Looking around the bathroom, she saw a wrought-iron towel display. She walked over to it and slowly removed the bar from the wall anchors.

She had no choice.

She closed her eyes and wiped away the tears that spilled over her cheeks. What she was about to do would seal her fate. She would lose the one man she had always truly loved with her whole heart.

"I'm sorry, Tyler," she whispered. "Please forgive me."

Quietly, she opened the bathroom door, holding the bar down and behind her thigh. Tyler had his head bent and was devouring the remains of the breakfast. Mallory's heart broke a little more at how adorable he looked.

It was now or never. For a moment, she hesitated. For a split second, she doubted. She wondered. She pushed the doubt away just as quickly, not willing to gamble any chances.

Swiftly and quietly, Mallory raised the bar over her head and brought it down across the back of Tyler's head.

～　～　～

Alexander walked slowly through the house. It was neat and tidy. The only brightness came from the golden sunlight streaming through the windows. There was something wrong.

He could feel it.

They were scheduled to meet at nine o'clock this morning. When he noticed Tyler's SUV missing, he didn't immediately jump to conclusions. But when Sami came running up the steps muddy from wandering outside, he began to wonder. Then, when Tyler didn't answer his phone, his concern began to crescendo.

Full-out worry and apprehension evolved when he tried to open the front door. And could. The alarm did not go off; for as long as Tyler had lived here, he had been a fanatic about the alarm system. It was the only way he slept at night.

Alexander carefully made his way through the house. He had his phone out and ready to dial 9-1-1. Carefully making his way down the hall, he paused in each doorway and looked. Again, nothing was out of place.

He approached the master bedroom, taking notice that the door was ajar. He heard no noise. Something niggled his curiosity and made him proceed in further. He stopped, stunned to see Tyler sitting at the base of the bed. A gun pointed straight at him.

"Shit, Alex, I almost blew your fucking head off."

"Hello to you too."

Tyler withdrew his weapon and clicked on the safety. He placed the gun on the floor beside him and lowered his head into his hands.

"What the hell happened here?" Alexander's voice was a mixture of relief and concern.

Tyler didn't look up. He couldn't tell which hurt worse, his head or his heart. The second he had opened his eyes, he knew she was gone. Everything felt empty: the bed, the house—his gut.

"The best I can figure is that Mallory clocked me over the head with this and took off." He held up the towel rod. "I haven't been able to stand enough to find out much more."

"She didn't like the pancakes?" Alexander's joke fell flat.

He shook his head and then immediately wished he hadn't. They'd spent the night making love, and he'd let his guard down. Dammit. Was it always this? Had he been played like a fiddle?

No; his mind rejected all of those faults. Something went down. He just needed to get a clear head and piece it together. His instincts were not this far off base. No fucking way. Where was she? What had happened?

"Well, your vehicle is gone. The alarm was off. Nothing else seems out of whack, except for you, of course."

"I'm concussed."

"Ya think?" Alexander took a look at the back of his head. "I need to get you to a doctor. Then we have to report this."

"No and no."

Alexander raised both eyebrows at his friend's response.

"Something happened, Alex. She got a business call, or so she said. Next thing I knew, I was waking up with a bump the size of Texas, and she was gone."

Understanding Tyler's frustrations and determination not to waste time in finding Mallory was one thing. Ignoring medical help was another. He began to argue, but Tyler continued before he could speak.

"Besides, there has been no message from her. It's Jaxon. He knows I'm getting close. He's got her running scared."

"We can get a trace on that last number. It's doubtful that it will do any good. Probably a burner cell, but it's worth a try."

He began to dial Detective Johnson and fill him in, but Tyler put a hand up to stop him.

"Problem is, they may not believe us. They are going to see this as Mallory being guilty as hell."

"Well, shit."

Tyler tried to stand, but he stumbled. Alexander rushed to his side and urged him to the edge of the bed.

"This is a cluster fuck," he said.

"I would agree with that, yes," Alexander replied.

"He's going to kill her if we don't find her."

"Take a breath, there, wonder boy." Alexander gave him a crooked smile. "Let your instincts work. Where do we start?"

CHAPTER 29

~ ~ ~

Detective Johnson answered on the first ring. "Whatcha got?" Tyler bypassed any pleasantries and filled the man in on the situation.

"We can get an APB out and a chopper looking for the SUV now," Johnson said.

Tyler looked at Alexander and gave him a thumbs-up. He disconnected the call and picked up the frozen peas and placed it to the back of his neck. Hell, he didn't even know he owned a bag of frozen peas.

"This plan has a lot of room for error," Alexander shared.

Tyler used his free hand to tick off answers.

"Number one: neither of us could come up with a better plan. Number two: if they arrest her, she's safer, at this point, behind bars. Number three: the chances of the chief arming me with a small arsenal to blow Jaxon to pieces is slim to none."

"If the stars were aligned, and all that jazz," Alexander replied.

"Up until now, he's been operating in the background. My gut tells me that he's losing patience. He's ready to claim her. Whatever he's about to do, it's ugly."

"It could also mean more bodies."

Neither of them acknowledged that that meant Mallory's.

Tyler walked to the bathroom and dropped the peas into the sink.

"Don't underestimate the danger we are facing, Alexander. I wouldn't put it past him to have policemen on his payroll."

"I, for one, am glad you finally decided to cooperate with the men in blue."

"I didn't," Tyler replied. "I need backup, and Johnson is the least asshole on the force."

"Well, it is what it is."

"We're wasting time."

~ ~ ~

Mallory drove the speed limit to the edge of downtown. Rush hour traffic nearly caused her to have a heart attack. The sun, blazing red-and-orange streaks, pierced the sky and reflected off the pavement. The waves of heat steaming off the ground after the rain made her feel like she was on the highway to hell. Maybe she was.

What if she had killed Tyler?

That one phone call had changed everything. She was on her own now. As she drove towards her destination, the conversation replayed itself in her mind over and over.

"If you want to see Emma alive again, you'll do exactly as I say."

Mallory had frozen as she heard the words through her cell phone. Before she could register a response, Kendall continued. "I know you're there with Tyler McCormack. Move away from him now and act natural, or she's dead, Mallory."

It took less than a millimeter of a second for her maternal instincts to kick in. She cleared her throat and moved away from the bed.

"Yes, I understand. I've done that. What do you need?"

Mallory had tried to speak in the best professional voice that she could muster, but she was hyper-afraid that Tyler would sense her panic.

The man she needed to help her had been less than a few feet away, but she was drowning alone in a sea of fear. She felt double-edged emotions rip her heart in two: relief that he sat there, focusing on his breakfast, battled with panic that he wasn't going to be able to help her. She wanted to tell him, beg him to help her, but she feared if she didn't follow their orders, she would lose her daughter forever. *No! No! She can't have Emma!*

The entire event felt like Mallory was watching it from a distance. Her body threatened to shake apart in pieces. She prayed vehemently that Tyler wouldn't pick up on the fear that poured over her. She had to do this to save her daughter.

How did they get her? This can't be happening! she had thought.

Kendall spoke again. "You will get away from McCormack and meet me alone. You have two hours to show up at the secluded park where Emma had her fifth birthday."

"Yes, of course; I'll make that happen." Mallory's mind spun frantically as she thought of an excuse that Tyler would believe.

"We will know if you make any calls. You tell McCormack or you go the cops, and Emma dies." Kendall gave her warnings and disconnected.

What could she do? Tyler's protection of her had been impenetrable. He had sworn that Emma was completely protected too. Every part of her wanted to scream at him for lying to her, but she was afraid that as soon as she did, that her daughter would be killed. What had happened to her parents? Were they even alive?

Tears flowed down Mallory's face as she continued down the highway. Having to choose between two people she loved was unfathomable. Mallory had no choice. She had to choose her daughter. She had sworn to protect her, and she would. Tyler would never forgive her.

Too many fears threatened to hinder her ability to drive. She had to focus. She had to get there.

Just another two miles and she would be at her exit. She would be arriving early, so she slowed down. She was afraid to be early and afraid to be late. She kept looking in her rearview mirror for any possible signs that she was being followed.

To the right of her vehicle, she noticed a black SUV. The other traffic had moved on, but this car paced her. Mallory realized the vehicle wasn't just another mindless passerby. This person was watching her. When their eyes met, he nodded at her.

She kept driving. Should she try to outrun them? She sped up slightly. The black vehicle did the same. She looked at the passenger again, and he shook his head as if to scold her.

"Oh, no. Ohmigod. Oh, please God, let me get to my daughter."

Mallory felt like she was suspended in a moment of doubt. Maybe Kendall had had a buddy follow her. Maybe Tyler had an undercover cop watching the house.

Or maybe it was someone entirely different. It's not like she was experienced at this sort of thing.

She exited the highway and executed a right turn at the intersection. Suddenly, she felt very foolish. And very scared. Why hadn't she thought about taking one of Tyler's guns?

After rubbing her hand over her face, Mallory pushed the hair back from her eyes. She folded her arms around her middle with her shoulders hunched. Her heart felt like it was going to beat out of her chest as she sat and waited for the eternal red light.

When—*if*—Tyler started looking for her, would he understand why she'd left the way she did? He had finally trusted her fully, and now she looked guilty as hell. There was no doubt; she was guilty. She had harmed another human being.

Mallory froze at the sight of the man sitting in the vehicle behind her. Hot waves of heat seared through the window and burned her skin. As she stared, wide-eyed, at him through her rearview mirror, she knew she would never know freedom again.

And she would never see Emma again.

◦ ◦ ◦

"Screw this up and I'll kill the kid."

Kendall tamped down on her defiant nature in favor of a slight chance of staying alive. Not for a split moment did she doubt this man would do just that and kill her too. She'd been around bad men before, but nothing compared to this devil.

He was pure, unadulterated evil.

"She will be here. She wouldn't do anything to jeopardize the kid's safety."

"She better be."

Kendall couldn't help herself. She licked her lips and tried to speak with a calm voice. "Why did you kill Nick?"

As soon as the words were out of her mouth, she quickly wished she had kept her mouth shut. The look on his face was void of all emotion. It instantly made her fear for her life.

"He no longer was useful."

Oh, dear God. I won't make it out of this alive. Kendall swallowed her fear and redirected her eyes toward the road.

"You shouldn't worry yourself about your dead boyfriend."

That statement jolted Kendall. How did he know Nick had been her boyfriend?

"I'm not."

He smiled, and the smile turned to an eerie laugh that echoed in Kendall's mind. From one second to the next, Kendall's life choices replayed in her mind. Her lies were exposed with truths. Her vindictiveness replaced with regret. She pressed a fist to her stomach and prayed for the safety of the child she had wronged.

Sounds of gravel crunching under tires alerted her to the vehicle that appeared at the end of the road. Mallory.

She felt the acid in her gut begin to churn. She wondered if there really was a hell. She would soon find out.

Kendall couldn't stop thinking about Emma. She hadn't thought twice about letting someone else raise her—but now? Now it could be possible that both her mothers were going to die. Kendall owned the choices she had made in her life. She had never considered how they affected others. Not even her daughter. She had been wrong—very wrong.

She watched Mallory's vehicle slowly approach. The woman had never really done anything to deserve the pain Kendall had caused her. She loved Emma and had raised her well. Kendall had never even wanted to acknowledge that.

As Kendall watched the "real" mother of her child get out of the car, she could sense her fear, even from a distance. Her eyes were huge as silver dollars and her hands trembled. Her back was stiff and her movements were jerky.

Mallory's head swung around as she looked in every direction. After a few seconds, she continued to walk toward them.

Kendall's mind flashed to Nick. She had watched the man put a bullet right in his head. She had seen his brains and blood splatter everywhere. She heard his head crack as he hit the floor.

I don't want to die.

She couldn't stop picturing Nick dead on the floor. Then Emma, scared, crying for her mother. Crying for Mallory. A sharp pain pierced her heart that she had never felt before. Emma would never cry for her that way.

"Do what I tell you. Or they all die."

The man moved out of sight. Kendall waited until Mallory was twenty feet from the bench where she was to meet her. The urge to run away was intense, but she knew she wouldn't make it three strides before he killed her.

There was no way out.

He may have been watching her every move, but he could no longer see her face. That gave Kendall an opportunity to maybe give her nonverbal cues. He might kill them anyway, but at least she would have tried. More than the weight of the world was on her shoulders.

"Hold it."

Mallory froze in her tracks. "I'm here. No cops. Just like you said."

"I don't want to hurt you. Open your shirt. Let me see that there's no wires."

Suddenly self-conscious, Mallory took a deep breath. She bunched up the bottom her shirt and pulled it to her chest.

"Turn around."

Mallory slowly turned a full circle. "No wires."

When Kendall nodded her head, Mallory lowered her shirt. "Where's Emma?"

"Don't." Kendall looked her in the eye, adrenaline making her appear jumpy. "I've had a real shitty couple of days, and frankly, I couldn't care less about your inquiries. I do the talking. Got it?"

Mallory jerked her head in submission.

"Do you realize how much you owe him?"

Confused by the question, Mallory asked, "Who?"

"Just answer yes or no."

Trying her best to follow along, she went with her instincts. "Yes."

"You're lying. You have no idea."

"I'm sorry."

"Yes, you are. You're ungrateful. You're selfish. Things are so much better for you now, and you need to appreciate that."

"I ... I do. I'm grateful for all that I have."

"He's protected you. He's fixed everything for you."

"Kendall. I don't know who you're talking about. Where's Emma?"

"Shut up! Don't ask questions. Just listen to me."

Her movements were skittish. Kendall took a few steps closer to Mallory. Her eyes darted toward the bushes and then back to Mallory.

"I've been cruel. I am no good. I've wronged you."

Mallory was becoming more and more hyperaware that Emma was not there. She was afraid to move. Confused about how Kendall was acting, she wondered what she had gotten herself into. She did her best to answer the questions correctly and not anger her.

Emma. Oh, my sweet child. I'm so sorry, Tyler.

"It's okay, Kendall. We can move forward from here."

"No, we won't."

"Yes, we can. We can make this right."

"I blackmailed Damian. He came to me to let me know that Emma wasn't his. I blackmailed him because I wanted money. I knew he would pay for taking what was mine."

Mallory kept her best poker face in place. She didn't budge an inch. There was a shift in the atmosphere.

The look on Kendall's face did not match the words coming out of her mouth. Mallory's instincts were now humming and in full throttle. Something was very wrong. She didn't know how to respond. She couldn't imagine Kendall would escalate like this. She would never admit fault. Not unless she was backed into a corner.

"Did you kill Damian?" Mallory had remembered how Kendall had avoided eye contact during all of their confrontations before. Now she was staring her down, dead-on.

"I'm trying to explain!"

"Okay. Okay."

"I've wronged you. I will never be a burden to you or Emma again. Because of him, all your troubles are over."

Before Mallory could answer, Kendall opened her jacket. Mallory could see a contraption belted around her waist. Their eyes connected, and suddenly, Kendall yelled, "Run!"

～ ～ ～

Tyler did his best to ignore the throbbing pain in his head. The pulsing was constant, and every so often, he thought he might puke. The heat searing through him from the muggy air made his lungs feel weighted. Sitting on the top of the building didn't help.

He peered through the binoculars and could see how tense Mallory was standing. Kendall was a little more than six feet in front of her, but the sniper couldn't get a clean shot. She would pay dearly if she harmed one hair on his woman's head.

Tyler willed himself to gain an icy, detached control. That's what was needed right now, not his overwhelming desire to storm in and blow the crazy bitch's head off.

But the moment he had Mallory safe again, he was going to tan ʳ hide. His head still hurt like son of a bitch.

254

"How many?" Detective Johnson whispered to the SWAT team member.

"Two that I can see. Mallory and Kendall."

To Tyler, he said, "We could storm in."

"No, she could get hurt. Something's off." Tyler snarled something under his breath and continued to watch intensely.

"Wait." Tyler zoomed in for a closer view of Kendall's face.

"She keeps darting her eyes toward the bushes at her left."

"Could be someone else." Detective Johnson asked the other officers. "No one can get a visual there without being exposed."

They both fell silent as they assessed the situation. Tyler's gut told him that Jaxon was close. Was he behind the bushes? Nick Hanson, maybe? He had to assume that whoever it was would be armed and dangerous.

He focused on Kendall once more. The bitch. Lowering his binoculars, he asked again, "Clear shot?"

The sniper responded, "Negative." Continuing to peer through the scope, he said, "Thing is ... you're not going to like this, McCormack."

Tyler's blood ran cold at the sound of the sniper's tone. He put the binoculars to his eyes again and said, "What?"

Tension crackled in the air.

Suddenly, Kendall opened her jacket, and Mallory turned and took off in a full-out sprint. Tyler yelled, "Take the shot!"

CHAPTER 30

～ ～ ～

Tyler was there. He was really, really there. Slowly, Mallory stood up from the back of the ambulance. She felt … well, awkward. She looked at him, and his brown eyes darkened as they gazed back at her. She feared his rejection. She felt empty as the implications of her actions bombarded her.

"I had to do it. I'm so sorry. She said she would kill Emma." She sobbed, and tears she could no longer control streamed down her face.

"You didn't deserve what I did to you. Please forgive me. You are the only one I have that believes in me, and I betrayed that."

"I figured it was something like that."

Wait. What? Was he serious?

Tyler gathered her to him and held her as tightly as he could without crushing her. He buried his face in her hair and inhaled her scent. He couldn't voice the relief he felt. If he tried, he would simply lose it. He gave her the gentlest kiss, hoping it told her everything he couldn't at that moment.

She leaned her forehead on his chest. He could sense the adrenaline letdown as she continued to shake. She was near a breaking point.

Without lifting her head, she whispered, "Emma?"

"Is safe. I made contact where she is. Nothing has been breached. Mallory, she's safe. And so are your parents."

Detective Johnson walked up, holding his pistol. He shook

his head, indicating that no one else was found on the scene. He looked over his shoulder as the other ambulance commenced to transport Kendall to the hospital.

"She won't be going anywhere for a while."

"Good riddance," Tyler murmured. "Anything else to report?"

"Nothing." The detective continued, "We will continue to process the scene. There were several tire tracks, but one set was fresh. If those match up to one of Jaxon's vehicles, we've got him. We'll get photos ready. Hopefully, Kendall can ID him."

"I'm ready for the son of a bitch to show himself. This dancing around is making me nuts. It looks like we botched his plan; he's going to be furious."

"Take her home. Get some rest. Get that hard head looked at. We'll take care of the reports on this end."

The detective held out his hand to shake Tyler's.

Giving him a firm grip, he said, "Thanks."

It was a communication between men, between colleagues who had found common ground.

"Ma'am." Detective Johnson nodded his head toward Mallory and walked over to the other policemen working the scene.

~ ~ ~

Later that evening, Mallory came up on one elbow on the couch. Tyler had been standing at the back door watching Sami. Motionless, he stood with his shoulder against the doorframe. His hand hung loosely from the belt loop of his jeans. He wasn't wearing a shirt, and the muscles in his back made her mouth water. He held a beer in his other hand.

He hadn't spoken many words to her since they had returned. The experience had taken a toll on her, and she had fallen asleep after Tyler allowed her to talk with Emma on the private line. He didn't seem to want to talk now either. A small pang in her heart made her wonder if Tyler would ever really forgive her. He claimed to understand that she was acting out of fear for her daughter. After all the grief she had given him about trust, the irony hadn't escaped her that she hadn't trust him when it had really counted.

"How did you find me?" she finally had the courage to ask.

He glanced back at her over his shoulder. "My vehicle is linked to the security system."

Oh. She hadn't thought of that. "What time is it?"

"About six. You should eat."

"I might in a bit." She rose from the couch and walked over to him.

"When did you decide to become a web designer?" The question came out of nowhere.

"Actually, I stumbled upon it. In my second year at college, I took a computer-design class as an elective. I was really good at it. It became a passion almost overnight. I changed my major that semester."

"It was a smart choice. I've looked at some of your work. You're good."

"Thank you." Mallory was wondering why he was chatting about her profession, but at the moment, she was just grateful he was talking.

"You've been very successful. You'll be able to continue to take care of Emma comfortably."

That comment made her heart stop. So that was it. When this was over, they were over.

She didn't respond. She didn't have the heart to.

Tyler took a long draw on his beer and then said, "Nick's body was found. Bullet to the head."

She absorbed that for a moment. Then she finally addressed the elephant in the room.

"I never wanted to hurt you."

"I know. I've already said you don't have to justify it to me." He continued to stare out at Sami.

"What's the statute of limitations on broken trust for repeat offenders?"

"What?" He tilted his head and looked at her questioningly.

"Since this thing has started, you've had to repeatedly question my trust. Today, when I hurt you, I figured I shattered what was left because I didn't ask you for help."

He propped his hands on his hips and looked down at his feet.

"It was dangerous as hell what you did. You could have been killed. I'm mad as hell at you for taking such a risk; I'll admit that."

He sighed and raked his fingers through his hair. He whistled for the dog and waited while she came running.

"I'm so relieved I didn't hurt you too badly."

"I've got a hard head." The joke went without laughter.

"What happened to you after you left Texas?" Mallory figured he wouldn't answer. Especially since she was pretty confident that whatever had grown between them was firmly over after this thing ended.

After releasing a long, slow breath, he told her. "Once they found Jennie dead, I knew I could never wash my hands of her blood. It was my fault he was a free man. It seemed ..." he spread his hands in a gesture that indicated he had no words to describe it, "just."

He scratched his chest and gathered his thoughts. "After they buried her, I couldn't make myself return to the office. I packed up and headed out. I had no idea where I was going. I just left. Word in the media and on the street: I was a dirty lawyer. I didn't really care. I was done with it. For the longest time, I kept tabs on him, waiting for him to slip up. Then he disappeared and I couldn't track him. I ended up here in Austin, and you know the rest.

"I originally thought the bastard ended up here because he found me." Tyler's eyes were black with emotion. "I guess I was wrong."

Ping. Mallory's phone indicated she had an incoming e-mail. She turned her head to glance at the incoming message. She creased her brow and clicked the message.

259

From: L. Jaxon

Date: July 15, 2015

To: Mallory Jones

Subject: With Sincere Sympathy

Ms. Jones:

I would like to extend my sincere sympathy. You have been through quite a tragic series of events. Your strength and resilience is superior to others'. It is an admirable quality that you possess. Your daughter has an exemplary model of worthiness and honor.

I'm sure our paths will cross again soon.

Give Mr. McCormack my best regards,

L. J.

"Um, Tyler? Read this."

As soon as Tyler read the e-mail, he moved quickly to retrieve his pistol and cell phone. His lips were in a thin line; his commands were clip and direct.

"Let's go, Mallory. Now. Grab your bag. We're leaving."

Tyler moved swiftly. He began stuffing weapons and gadgets, as well as his laptop, into a huge black duffle. He stomped into the utility room next to the garage and grabbed a go-bag for Sami and her leash. He whistled and clicked his tongue once and Sami came trotting behind him.

"Tyler! Tell me. Where are we going? What did Lonnie mean by that e-mail?"

"It means he's done hiding. Game on."

Tyler chose not to elaborate on the hidden meanings of the e-mail because he hadn't truly figured them out himself. But he knew without a doubt that it was a fatal warning. Jaxon never gave warnings.

Tyler ignored her wide eyes staring at him from the passenger's seat. He clicked his speed dial and waited for it to connect. When it did, he spoke with determination.

"Move to the second location. Now ... no, I have good reason to believe it is necessary ... it might be best if you switch to the burner cell ... good ... let me get a secure handle on the situation, and I will get back to you ... be smart."

"You're moving my parents and Emma."

"Just to be on the safe side."

"Where are we going?"

He didn't answer her, which made her glare at him even more intently. He clicked another button on his cell and put the phone to his ear.

"Enter into Mallory Jones's e-mail account and trace the e-mail from Jaxon. Let me know as soon as you get an IP location."

"Who was that?" Mallory asked as soon as he hung up.

This time she was awarded with an answer. "ICD. Internet Crimes Division."

"Oh."

She didn't ask him to elaborate because he was already on the phone again.

"Johnson, it's him."

As soon as Tyler finished explaining the e-mail and actions that he had executed, he added, "For the next few hours, it might be best if we disappear and regroup."

"I'll sit on ICD," he replied. "McCormack, hang on ... interesting. I was just informed that the e-mails originated from Nick Hanson's residence. I'm dispatching a team there now."

Tyler pounded a fist on the driver's door. "Dammit! He's playing with us now. Be careful, but you won't find him there."

"I'll be in touch."

Jaxon needed to be ready, because Tyler was going to bring Armageddon.

He suddenly questioned the intelligence of commuting to his safe place in a vehicle Jaxon would undoubtedly recognize. It was possible they were being followed this very moment. It was also quite probable that he had just reacted as Jaxon wanted.

Erring on the side of caution, Tyler took the next exit and drove west on Highway 180, heading toward the small town of Bastrop. Once he settled into the flow of traffic, he glanced over at Mallory.

She sat with her head facing forward and her hands clasped tightly in her lap. If she bit her lip any harder, she was going to draw blood. Maybe it wasn't so smart for them to stay together. The APB that was issued on her was nullified once Kendall was arrested, and the chances of her willingly walking into a jail cell were slim to none. He considered delivering her to the safe house and going after Jaxon alone. The problem was, he didn't have enough confidence in the APD to assign someone to her that wasn't on Jaxon's payroll. He certainly wouldn't entrust her to Detective Clark, even though Johnson thought highly of him—which brought him back to the original plan of keeping her with him.

~ ~ ~

The phone was ringing when they entered the house. Tyler let it go to voice mail. He immediately checked the locks and engaged the alarm system. Then he went around and ensured that all the windows and shades were drawn. When Mallory walked to turn on the living room lights, he told her to keep the house dark.

"Why did we come back here? I thought we were going to another location after you traded in your vehicle."

"Jaxon won't come back here."

"How can you be sure?"

Tyler guided her to the kitchen. He motioned for her to take a seat at the bar and then took out items needed to make sandwiches. "Hungry?"

"No."

"Eat anyway. It's important to keep your strength up."

After she commenced to make a ham and turkey sandwich, he answered her previous question.

"Jaxon knew I wouldn't keep you here once we received the e-mail. It's highly probable that he either followed us himself or had us followed. That's why we made the switch with the vehicles. Once I was confident we weren't followed from the airport car rental, I figured it would throw him off our trail. So we backtracked. He won't be expecting me to do that. Besides, no other place has this level of security. If I had the slightest thought that he would think I would come back here, we wouldn't be here."

After they finished eating, they made their way toward the bedroom. Guilt washed over Mallory was she saw the remnants of their breakfast in bed that morning.

"Don't."

Tyler closed the distance between them and kissed the curve of her neck. His actions surprised Mallory.

"I'm so glad you're still with me," he said.

The shadows in the room cast a dark glow on her face, enhancing the blue in her eyes.

Without asking, he pulled her into the bathroom and started the shower. He began to undress her with care. She began to quiver, and tears threatened to fall. He made haste with his own clothes and he led them into the shower.

They spent time kissing and touching. They washed each other with slick, soapy hands, exploring every inch of each other. The act of cleansing became heated foreplay as Tyler knelt in front of her and made love to her with his mouth. She had renewed energy and moved restlessly beneath him as she grasped his hair between her hands and moved him up to her. He kissed a path from between her thighs up her stomach and paused to give him uninhibited attention to each breast. By the time he returned to her lips, she was aching with the need to have him inside her.

She wrapped both her arms around him as he lifted her legs and hooked them around his waist. Bracing her against the shower wall, he nestled himself deep inside her. With each sensational stroke, the pressure inside her began to build and finally exploded in an ultimate release. His piercing eyes bore into hers as he tightened and let himself go.

"Thank you, Tyler."

He chuckled. "You're very welcome, but I think it should be me thanking you."

He squeezed her bottom and pressed himself into her as they stood, breathing heavy.

"No, I mean thank you for not giving up on me." She took his face in both her hands and gently kissed him.

Tyler's heart swelled. He was speechless. He nuzzled her neck and held her tightly as the water continued to coat them.

CHAPTER 31

~ ~ ~

Alexander swallowed. He had thought nothing of it when he decided to take the meeting request. He saw an opportunity to add a client and he had seized it. It wasn't until he had entered the building that he realized he had walked into a trap.

"I have been interested in meeting you for quite some time. You've known Mr. McCormack and Ms. Jones for some time now. They're two of my favorite people."

"Yes, but as you know, I cannot discuss another client's matters." His voice shook, but he scrambled for professionalism.

"I have just one question. I'm sure you can handle that, Mr. Blakely." Jaxon twisted the diamond ring on his pinky with his thumb. "I do come bearing gifts and all."

Alexander's eyes darted to the vial of cocaine that sat with the accompanying materials within arm's reach.

"And what question is that?"

"I want to know where I can find my friends."

Alexander knew his options were limited. He could give Jaxon their location and be killed, or he could remain loyal and not betray his friends—and be killed. Either way, he was a dead man. His hands began to shake uncontrollably.

Jaxon picked at imaginary lint on his suit.

"If you don't answer my simple question, I will be very disappointed."

"I ... I really do not know where they are."

Jaxon's eyes narrowed in glaring disgust.

"He never called me. I truly did not know he changed locations. I swear."

"Now, Mr. Blakely. I came here to see you because you are an honest man."

"I swear to God. I don't know where they are."

"Then snort the powder and see if it helps your memory."

At that moment, Alexander knew. Karma had come back to bite him in the ass. He had enjoyed the guilty pleasure and had partied outside the law many times. And now it would be his final act.

"I don't think I should." Alexander gave a feeble attempt to politely decline. "I have a court hearing tomorrow."

Both men remained unbending. Both men also knew that Alexander was full of shit. There would be no tomorrow for him.

Jaxon slowly opened his jacket, retrieved a pistol that had a silencer, and pointed it at Alexander's heart.

"I do hate repeating myself."

With unsteady hands, Alexander reached for the vial containing the white powder. He could see his reflection as he began the act of preparation. His eyes held fear, and his jaw shook as if he were freezing. He picked up the small straw. It took him less than a few seconds to snort both lines.

Lonnie Jaxon was leaning against the wall, arms and ankles crossed, looking perfectly relaxed as he watched Alexander's nose begin to gush blood.

~ ~ ~

As soon as they left the shower, Mallory fell into a deep sleep. Tyler kept vigil watching over her. He knew she thought he had pulled back after what had happened earlier. Quite the opposite had happened, actually. The terror he had experienced watching her with Kendall scared him to depths he hadn't known he possessed. Those emotions, mixed with the love he felt for her, almost undid him. He had no idea how he was going to ever live without her again.

She must have sensed him watching her. She blinked a few times, stretched, and then smiled up at him. "Hey."

"Hey, yourself."

He tucked a loose hair that had fallen into her face behind her ear. Mallory nuzzled his hand with her cheek. And just like that, he wanted her again. He leaned closer and took her mouth with his.

Bleep, bleep. His phone indicated an incoming text message.

Now was not the time to ignore any communications. He leaned over and picked the cell up from the nightstand.

"Alexander needs to meet."

Tyler returned the message, indicating he wasn't comfortable leaving Mallory alone.

Another message came in.

"He says it's urgent. That he's received intel that might nail Jaxon for good."

"It's okay. Go. I'll be safe with all of these alarms and codes. Sami and I will hide out here until you get back."

"Promise me. No lights. Stay away from windows. Stay right here. I won't be long."

She sealed her agreement with a kiss. "I promise."

"I shouldn't be more than an hour, tops."

Tyler quickly threw on jeans, a shirt, and shoes. In lieu of brushing his hair, he tossed a cap on his head. After double-checking all security, he headed out.

Just when he had entered the freeway, he received a security notification on his phone. Tyler looked down and muttered, "What the hell?"

As Mallory flipped around in the bed trying to get comfortable, her stomach began to growl. "I don't think he'd mind if we ventured to the kitchen and found some cookies."

Sami readily agreed with her and jumped off the bed.

The house was dark as she passed through the living room, taking caution to stay away from windows and doors. When she entered the kitchen, she poured herself a glass of milk and scrounged for the chocolate chip cookies she knew he kept in the pantry.

Sami did her best to sit and wait patiently, but she whined when Mallory didn't move quickly enough.

"Okay, you can have one. Just don't tell on me. Chocolate is not good for doggies."

Carrying both the glass of milk and the package of cookies, Mallory began to make her way back to the bedroom to wait for Tyler's return. She had just situated her pillows when Sami let out a low warning growl.

Before she could blink, two shots were slammed into Sami.

"No!"

She scurried across the floor to the now-bleeding dog.

When she turned, she realized she had moved away from the gun that Tyler had told her was in the nightstand.

"Remembering this, Mallory?"

Yes, the gun that she needed was in Lonnie Jaxon's hand.

Hearing him say her name, seeing the emotionless smile across his face, made her stomach churn. Something inside her was done. A newfound sense of strength empowered her. What kind of sick bastard put bullets into an innocent animal?

"What did you do to Tyler?"

Because she knew. She may not have all the details, but she knew deep in her heart that this man was the reason Tyler had left.

"Your fuck buddy can't protect you now. He's been such a distraction for you and me. I've been waiting for too long to have you to myself." He shrugged. "Besides, you need to choose better company."

"What did you do?" Mallory's heart sank.

Lonnie reached out and tucked the same strand of hair behind her ear, as Tyler had done earlier. His touch made her recoil. She tried to hide it, but the smirk on his face turned into an evil grin.

"I have been looking forward to spending quality time with you. I'm fascinated with your golden hair and your sea-blue eyes. It's such a different attraction for me."

"Why did you kill my husband?" If she was going to die after all, she deserved answers.

"Now, Mallory, I have done several things for you. Killing Damian Jones was not one of them."

"But you have killed for me." She chose her words carefully. She prayed with all her might that Tyler was alive and would be back to save her.

"Oh, yes, sweet dear, I have cleaned up all of your messes. You can spend your days showing me how much you appreciate my efforts. We will be a family, the three of us."

Mallory felt her palm connect with a loud crack across his face before she had even registered her actions. "Don't you even mention my daughter."

The look on his face frightened her to her core. She had made him angry. He gripped her wrist so hard, she thought he would crush her bones. He whipped around and grabbed her hard between her thighs. His breath was hot against her ear.

"I could end your life right now for that."

"I'm dead anyway, right? That's what you do to all your women once you're done with them."

He reached up and grabbed her hair by the base of neck and squeezed so hard, her scalp burned.

"I always knew you would be a challenge to tame. You have such a strong inner strength. It's what attracts me to you, but my sweet Mallory, there is such a thing as respect. I demand you to respect me."

He pushed her to her knees.

"You've been a bad girl, doing bad things with McCormack. I have to punish you for that. You only have yourself to blame."

Mallory's hands had instinctively grabbed the sides of his wrists. Every cell in her body was vibrating with fear.

"I'm sorry. I didn't know. I will do better."

Keeping his gun pointed at her, he walked around so that she was kneeling before him. "You ruined things between us. I wanted to cherish you the way you deserved. I cleaned up your messes. I made you free. Instead, you have chosen to ignore all of the things I did to make your life better. I can forgive those things. Fucking McCormack is something you must be punished for. You will know pain for that."

She forced herself to breathe in. Breathe out. "Forgive me for not knowing the things you did for me. Please. Tell me so I can thank you properly."

He rubbed the end of the pistol from her temple to jaw. Then he traced her lips with it. "I eliminated anyone who knew of your dirty little secret. I saved Emma from any future threats by the man who tried to take her. And I have done away with any distractions between us. But you must be punished still."

No, Tyler, no. Mallory lifted her chin. "I'm not afraid of you."

"You should be." His tone was deadly. He moved the pistol down and traced the mounds of her breasts. "I can be very demanding."

She was petrified. A sob escaped her throat before she could stop it. She didn't want to die at the hands of this monster, but she refused to back down.

"Such courage and strength. I hate that we will only have one night before our time together is over. I truly have little desire to kill you, but I must. What you have done is unforgivable."

"Kill me now, then. I won't let you terrorize me to get your rocks off."

He slapped her hard. Pain exploded on the side of her head. She fell on her side. He yanked her up and ground his crotch into her. Bile rose in her throat as he licked the side of her face. But she remained stiff and unbending.

"I don't think she's interested."

It took all his strength not to burst in, charge his nemesis, and shoot the bastard on sight. Instead, he braced himself in the doorframe and took a calculated assessment of the situation. Terror slowly intensified as his brain assimilated what was occurring.

At the sound of Tyler's voice, Jaxon had twisted Mallory around in a choke hold and put the gun to her head. Her eye was nearly swollen shut, and her lip was bleeding.

"Don't fucking move. If you so much as twitch a muscle, I'll blow her head off."

The sound of another gun clicking and ready to fire came from the other doorway.

"Let me put a bullet in him, McCormack; my finger's itching to pull this trigger," Detective Johnson said.

Tyler wouldn't let himself look at his dog lying and bleeding on the floor. He would not let himself dwell on the fact that he had brought her home, trained her, and cared for her since she was a six-week-old puppy. He could barely resist the urge to put a bullet in Jaxon's head for that alone. The punishment would be too quick, too easy. He wanted this man to rot in hell for a minimum of one hundred years.

"Drop the gun, Jaxon. It's over," Tyler ordered. He could see the unmitigated fear in Mallory. He could not let his emotions control him. He had to stay focused.

Jaxon spread his lips in a grin as he held the gun at Mallory's temple.

"Please, Mr. McCormack, do pull your trigger. It would be so romantic for Ms. Jones and myself to end this life together. We could continue our affair in the afterlife."

Mallory watched Tyler mentally assess their predicament. He made eye contact with her for a split second. Then tightened his stance. In that split second, he hoped she understood everything he hadn't told her. That he trusted her. That he loved her. She was and always would be it for him.

"Not this time. You're not escaping justice again."

Tyler didn't budge. He kept his gun aimed and silently prayed that Jaxon would remove the gun from his woman's head. Yes, *his* woman.

"You see, you're out numbered this time. There are two guns aimed at your head. If we both shoot at the same time, and yeah, we've got a signal to do just that, your body won't have time to react." He prayed to God he was right.

"Oh, I'm disappointed in you, McCormack. For such a good lawyer, you've shown yourself less than efficient in weaponry discharge and the human body. My hand will instinctively flinch, and she will be dead before I hit the ground."

"Then let her go, Jaxon. There's no reason for both of you to die today. You've lost this time."

"No way." He shifted to a tighter hold on Mallory. The standoff seemed to go on forever.

Before he could calculate his next move, Mallory said, "Tyler," and before she had finished saying his name, she dropped to her knees. Jaxon flinched, losing his balance just enough that it gave him the opening he needed. *Pop!* He fired his weapon point-blank into Jaxon's head. *Pop! Pop!* Two more shots sounded from the doorway sending him tumbling back onto the bed.

Mallory crawled over to Tyler, and he knelt down and cradled her to his chest. "Sami."

"I know, honey. I know."

Detective Johnson entered the room and checked for a pulse. He shook his head.

It was over.

EPILOGUE

~ ~ ~

Three weeks later.

The entire Austin area was blissfully enjoying the fall weather. The past few weeks had steadily been in the low 80s.

Tyler sat on his deck and patiently waited for his oversized, hyperactive, red-haired bundle of fur to sniff every single bush on the premises. Odds were not looking good that the pup would choose one to finally pee on. The puppy had big brown eyes that could sucker anyone into thinking he was purely innocent. Tyler had learned otherwise.

Seeing the ten-week-old puppy's attention dart to a bird as he raced across the yard for a game of chase made Tyler throw his head back and guffaw. There would be no boring days in the near future with this ball of energy.

"Cody, come!" The puppy paused and looked at Tyler but took off after the bird again.

Yeah, they had a lot of work to do.

Alexander had shown up with the furry rascal the day he was released from the hospital. It had been a life-changing event for his friend. His heart had actually stopped beating after he snorted the cocaine. With his knee, Alexander had been able to hit the Panic button that Tyler had insisted be installed under his desk in the event of a hostile client entering his office. It had saved his life. The paramedics had arrived within minutes after Jaxon had exited the building. When Detective Johnson had been informed by dispatch, he had immediately called Tyler.

He thanked God for that day, because good had finally prevailed.

Tyler and Detective Johnson spent the next three weeks diligently filing reports and participating in extensive debriefings. Upon further investigation and search of Jaxon's penthouse, enough evidence revealed that the murders of the two judges, Gilmore and Maxwell, and Mr. Armond were indeed a result of the deranged plot by Lonnie Jaxon to win Mallory's heart. Consequently, other arrests were pending when a payroll list of names had been discovered. Detective Clark was one of them.

Unfortunately, the one murder that could not be pinned on Jaxon was Damian Jones's. It currently remains unsolved.

Kendall was presently serving time in jail awaiting trial due to bail being denied. She was singing like a canary and providing information about Nick Hanson in hopes of receiving a lighter sentence. Mallory had been cleared of all suspicion when copies of the divorce papers and other evidence were found in Kendall's home.

The chief of police had officially lifted Tyler's sabbatical and had reassigned him as Detective Johnson's partner. Alexander still badgered him incessantly to return to practicing law. It was a decision he quietly grappled with, but for now he was content.

Tyler's father had returned from the beach house with Emma and her grandparents the following week. That was the last time he had seen Mallory. Tyler wanted badly to reach out to her, but he knew she needed time to get her business dealings in order and give her daughter the support and attention she so desperately needed.

Damn, he missed her. Several times, he'd picked up the phone to call her, only to stop himself. Too much had happened in a very short time.

It was a toss-up of who heard the vehicle turn into the driveway first. Tyler hurried down the deck and rounded the corner in haste to make sure Cody didn't charge under a tire as he ecstatically danced in circles with anticipation of visitors.

Tyler opened the door as soon as the vehicle stopped, kissed Mallory senseless, and whisked her out of the seat for a hug. Within seconds, his right arm was cradling Emma as she wrapped both arms around his leg, but just as quickly, he was released as she took off to play with the frisky puppy.

"You have a puppy?" Mallory smiled, which made her eyes light up.

Tyler smiled and leaned in to place his lips on her forehead and inhaled the scent of her hair. God, he'd missed her.

"Yes. An unruly one at that. Meet Cody. He has no boundaries. I think he might have a learning disability," he told her. "He sniffs around outside, gets distracted with everything except doing his business—only to go back inside and pee on the hardwood floor."

She laughed. "He'll catch on," she assured him, reaching up to give him a quick kiss. "I've missed you."

"Damn, woman, I've missed you too." He held her tight and breathed in the smell of her hair again. He loved the way she fit perfectly in his arms.

"Not that I'm complaining, but what brought you out?"

"I put the house on the market."

Tyler was shocked. "You did what? You're moving? Where are you going?"

His mind began to panic. She was leaving. She must feel she needed to get away from all the bad memories. He had blown it. Dammit, why couldn't he get this right? Her words instilled an ache in his heart that threatened to swallow him whole and made him rub his chest to relieve the pain.

If she walked away this time, it would permanently and unbearably destroy his life. His world meant nothing without her. He figured she needed a new start, something that he couldn't give her. He knew her life had been upended, and he couldn't stand for her to be unhappy. It would kill him if she left, but he would let her go, if that was what she needed to be happy.

She said he had saved her life. That was so wrong. It was her who brought him to life again. She had saved *his* life. This woman, who he measured all others against, had made him want to put the pieces of his life back together. To become a better man. He wanted to live every day proving that he was better. For her. For Emma.

He had hoped to give her a home. Not just another place to live but a place where love and happiness grew every day. He had hoped that Emma would become his daughter. They would maybe have more children together.

He stood there watching the single most important person in his life tell him she was leaving, and he was powerless to make her stay.

Mallory took his face in both of her hands. "Breathe," she told him. "Listen to me. I'm not letting you slip away from me this time."

"But moving? How is that going to help? How am I going to protect you if you're not here? How am I going to get to know Emma? I can't do anything to make you change your mind?" This sliced his heart in two. He was seriously teetering on the edge of losing what little grip on his emotions was left.

"Tyler, you've already done that." Her smile was so tenderly sweet, and her eyes were shimmering so that they had a look of cut blue glass. She simply said, "Besides, I'm taking the advice of my counsel."

"Remind me to punch Alexander." Reaching up, he took both her hands in his and laced their fingers. "Don't go."

"I'm not."

His blood literally froze in his veins. He stared at her in utter bewilderment. He was starting to get confused.

"I don't want to waste another day living my life for someone else. And, well, since my attorney informed me that you still love me, he advised me to sell the house. I want to move in with you."

"You do?"

"Yeah, but I need some hard evidence to back up that advice."

He pulled her tightly in his arms and let his hands drop to grab her hips. He backed her against the side of her vehicle. He pressed himself into her so that their bodies were perfectly molded together. He placed a love bite on her neck. As he nibbled his way down the side of her throat, he whispered, "Is that hard enough?"

Savoring the private, stolen moment between them, she leaned her head back and bit her bottom lip. "Mmm. Yeah, but I need verbal evidence."

He looked in her eyes. "He's right."

"About what?"

"I love you." He couldn't help it; he framed her face with his hands and searched deep in her eyes. "There has never been another woman for me. It was always you. You own me heart and soul."

Mallory's eyes flooded with tears. "I love you too."

Tyler smiled. He had everything he needed right there: the woman he loved, a little girl he would soon call his own, and a future that could only get better.

CPSIA information can be obtained at www.ICGtesting.com
Printed in the USA
LVOW11s0804260216

476764LV00004B/78/P

9 781483 438856